JUSTICE

Michelle LeFort

ISBN: 0-9701823-9-2
ISBN-13: 978-0-9701823-9-5

DEDICATION

My life and my love surround my family. Many of them are missed. Thank you to everyone who puts up with me and my insanity. Best friend forever bracelets make life worth living. (KLR) The best things in life are free and last infinity.

CONTENTS

Michelle LeFort

ACKNOWLEDGMENTS

Thank you to Jai, Kris, Lila, Devan, Layla and Madden.   Loving them is
the sustenance of life.

Chapter One

"We, the people, find the defendant ..." the pause amidst the crowded room lingered intentionally longer than normal. "... not guilty on the count of murder in the second degree."

When first entering the courtroom three weeks prior, Elaine focused immediately upon the judge's leather chair. For some reason the large gold medallion above it held her interest through most of the happenings in the courtroom daily. If she focused closely enough, she could nearly sit without attempting to flee from the room and being placed in the restricting handcuffs and leg shackles that she wore when returning to Jail. The medallion had a sunburst with thirteen rays extending to the edges. A shock of wheat, a tractor moving through a field and words she couldn't quite make out ... except for 'freedom' and this was as close to it as she might ever get.

In the beginning, she focused on the immediate nature of the word and fantasized about what it would be like to see daylight again from a perspective she chose, rather than the deputy transport that brought her to court each day. Elaine had no real thought process during the trial. She just fantasized about lying on a beach or curling up with a good book next to a fire place in New England, situations she could control. This one she could not. She did not hear the verdict.

When the courtroom went from complete silence to a buzz, her attorney's rose, nudging her to do the same as the judge retired the jury and closed the case. It was all a fuzzy blur. Elaine Justice, static with an anxious energy, shook her head, looking from her two lawyers to the judge who was smacking the gavel on the piece of wood. Had she heard right? If she had prayed, would they have been answered?

Room 316 had to be cleared for Honorable Judge George Mastiff to gain control. The case had drawn on twenty-one days and had more publicity than it could handle. It took twenty minutes to finish up and for the judge to retire the bench and leave the room, leaving the crowd to return to the buzz.

On Tuesday, May 2, at 7:12 PM the Grant County Sheriff's Department responded to a 911 call of a man found unresponsive by his wife. They found Tyler Santana dead at the scene. The call had been made by Elaine Justice, his wife of seven years. Deputies responded, EMS responded, ambulance personnel responded. He was deceased. The investigation began immediately and was tagged a homicide.

Elaine was taken in for questioning by 8 PM and released around 5 AM. Returning home to the devastation of the crime scene was not an option and so she headed for a hotel, fell into bed and slept the weariest sleep she had ever had. She was awakened at 2 PM to the sound of fists pounding on the door by the Grant County Sheriff's Department and was arrested, not seeing daylight, ending up here today.

Within the first 72 hours of the investigation, Tyler's

murder turned into charges filed against Elaine. Using the catch-all second-degree murder charge, she was left to rot in a county jail cell the last seven months. She didn't do it. She pled with her attorney, who, often, urged her to plead out on the case. But, in all of it, she knew she did not do the dastardly crime they accused her of and in the end, she was free.

Hugging her, the attorneys jabbered about how lucky she was and how she could now enjoy her freedom. However, the thought of walking out into the cold, dark world outside was an unpleasant thought. Wealthy and socially accepted in the community when this all began, Elaine knew that her plight would never succeed in this town after the trial. She had not let herself plan too far ahead and for the most part, her plans were how to kill herself in prison. Did she have a will to live?

As the buzzing drew to a mild chatter, she stood watching everyone leave the courtroom except for the reporters. Trevor Santana, Tyler's brother, rose and looked at Elaine before leaving. He was a kind man, a man who had always been supportive to Elaine, and, in the end, had been the most rewarding testimony given for Elaine. He knew, and Elaine knew he knew. By the grace of God, he was strong enough to state his beliefs on the witness stand.

Jason McKutchens touched Elaine on the shoulder again and repeated, "Do you need a ride somewhere, Ellie?"

Back to reality, Elaine shook her head.

Jason was a great lawyer and instrumental in releasing her from this situation. Whether he believed her or not, he provided a grand defense and won the case. "Do you have anywhere to go?"

Elaine's financial situation was in shambles. The cost of twenty-one days of trial was astronomical alone, not to factor in the fact that in digging for defense evidence, Jason had found millions of dollars in outstanding debt that Tyler had acquired behind Elaine's back. She literally had no money left and had signed over the house she had inherited to the firm as a retainer.

"I do, yes. Thank you." Elaine realized that this man had given her life back and accepted the hug he offered. "Thank you,

Jason." She whispered in his ear. He escorted her out the back of the building to a car waiting in the rear. Sneaking through a small crowd, Elaine escaped without having to face the press.

Chapter Two

The drone at the front of the room spoke of unimportant aspects of sales and marketing. It was a huge letdown to anticipate something new and to sit through hours of this conference wasting time. College professors spoke of more paramount possibilities than these so-called professionals and Casey Waters knew why. As he partially paid attention, he used his phone to research his boss.

Finding two accounts that linked him to international sources, it was all making sense. Casey's boss was stalling this out, because it was Casey's job to fix the mess they were in. The company was losing millions to destructive financial behavior, or so it looked. Blaming it on managers of the production facilities and faulty budgetary guidelines, it seemed that the bigger picture might look a little different.

Casey stirred in his seat, the suit and tie strangling him as he desperately searched for a reason to stay. If he left the conference early were the ramifications worth it? The lights went out and a new Power Point was presented, as boring as the last three. Casey fell into thought. The holiday was grossly approaching and he hadn't one plan made other than spending it with his family. There were gifts to buy and holiday cheer to spread. With just a few days left, he would need to act quickly. Out came the phone and a note application. He made a list of all the things he wanted as gifts and sent the note to his assistant back in Charlotte. She could buy the gifts, wrap them and make him out a hero and this year, he would let her.

Looking around the room at the three hundred other attendees, Casey wondered if they were learning anything new or were they just taking advantage of the time away from their wives and families, hooking up with the other attendees for a week of indiscriminate sexual encounters. It seemed to be what he saw from the bar stool in the hotel lobby each night as he sipped a glass of wine, bored out of his mind. Several of the women had hit on him, for him to kindly decline. Some of the men tried to be friendly, but Casey stuck to his loner attitude. Being around people only complicated his life. He liked it like it was. Too much work and too much family made for an honest existence and he was fine.

With only an hour to lunch, Casey decided he was done. He contacted his assistant again and told her to send him files. At least he could use his time here to look at the documents and see if his hunch paid off.

Over lunch, putrid as the rest of the food they had served at this joke of a conference, he looked over the financial reports again, highlighting the hurdles he faced. The lines spoke of the infraction, but he had to prove where it came from when it hit him. If someone were to pilfer funds from the marketing area, which checks and balances in place would not catch, they could be placed in the accounts of whom? He began to make a list of all marketing firms he knew the company paid. It had always struck him oddly that there were multiple firms rather than one handling the atrocity of the poor marketing attempt. Once the list was finished and the remains of his lunch were tossed in the trash, Casey headed to the next presentation.

About thirty-minutes into the presentation, Casey felt as though he had been hit by a truck. His stomach began to rumble so loudly the guy beside him asked if he was okay. Every time it rumbled, Casey thought of the roast beef he had attempted to eat on the lunch plate. Was it bad?

With that thought, it hit him and he jumped up and headed for the restroom. An hour later, sweating, pale and nauseous his body was empty. Or so he thought. He began throwing up. Heaving up remnants of the meal. His head hanging over the cold porcelain in the abandoned restroom.

Unable to move, he muttered to himself. It sounded good to just hear his voice as badly as he felt.

He heaved again. Retching every muscle in his upper body, he threw up another three times.

Reaching for his phone, he dialed the hotel number. Glad he had dialed down on his cell that morning, he heard the person on the other line answer. "Good afternoon, thank you for calling Manchester Winds Hotel and Conference Center. This is Rachel. How may I help you today?"

"Rachel … This is Casey Waters. I'm in the restroom just outside the conference meeting room four and I am very ill. Will you send a steward to help me to my room please?"

"Immediately, Sir." She spoke into the phone, rapid heart rate causing her even more anxiety. She continued, "Are you possibly a victim of food poisoning?"

At that moment, the restroom door was slammed open by the sound of it and another stall was occupied by a fellow conference-goer.

"Oh, God ..." someone next to Casey began heaving up his lunch too.

"Could be, Rachel. I've now got company. Someone in a

stall beside ..." He threw up again, his phone falling into the toilet bowl. "Oh, Crap!"

There was no way he was reaching in to save it. He began heaving again, this time nothing came up. Empty from the top as well.

Chapter Three

Ellie, as her family referred to her, had Jason's car drop her off at the jail, this time, the front entrance. Collecting her valuables took about an hour and she was on her own. The wait was painful. She sat in the lobby on a cold chair, never seeming to warm up. Finally, the clerk handed her a manila envelope, she signed her name and walked from the situation forever.

A stop at her favorite jewelry store revealed a shameless side of her personality. Immediately she was pleased by the smell of Scentsy Candles and the smile of the sales associate. Perhaps she could enjoy this freedom?

"Is Miles available?" Ellie asked. She felt for the

moment she had re-entered her life.

"Sure, let me get him from the back, Mrs. Justice." The sales associate walked into the back set of offices leaving Ellie alone.

Her name rang out, echoing in her head. At least she wouldn't have to change that. The huge fight that ensued when she told Tyler that she was not taking his name in the marriage was well worth the battle. It was the only thing she had at this point, other than the two-karat diamond ring and the platinum Prada watch she was going to sell to Miles Murphy, the eight hundred dollar bills and pocket change she had in her purse the night she was arrested. The clothes on her back and this little treasure chest of a manila envelope were all she had. Thirty-two years of hard work, persistence, patience and education and this is what she was walking out of Duluth, Minnesota with. Her plan was to start all over.

"Ellie!" Miles walked around the display case filled with diamonds and gold to hug her sincerely. A friend of her father's,

Miles had always been a solid place in her life. "I just heard. How are you, Kitty Kat?"

"Oh, Miles …" It was good to see him. She felt herself coming to life in some way. She hugged him again, lingering in his warmth. "I'm going to be okay."

He steered her by the elbow into his office as he spoke. "I worried so about you. I couldn't come today …" He didn't have to say that he couldn't have seen her convicted. "I am so glad you came by. What can I do for you?"

She sat down in the cherry leather captain's chair opposite side of the desk chair Miles sat in and leaned forward. She carefully took the watch out and the diamond ring and laid them on his desk.

Cocking his head to one side, "Are you sure?" He waited for her answer.

Pursing her lips, taking a deep breath … one final thought in the matter. "Yes. I am. How much can you give me?"

Miles immediately took the jewelry into his soft hands and examined them. He had designed the ring for her father to give to her mother on their twentieth anniversary, so he knew the value of the ring. Next, he took out his magnifier and placed it in his eye, examining the ring in more depth. A smile lit his lips, looking up, "I do such good work. This is as impeccable as the day I took it off my work station." He dug through his desk for a manual, thumbed through, ran his finger down the page while he read and then popped his computer screen on. An internet search gave him something else to read.

Ellie watched and realized that she had no anxiety at all. What she thought would be an impossible, implausible situation was starting to look like a real option for her.

Miles found his diamond calculator and input the values into the computer. He nodded as he wrote on a small piece of paper. The next step was to calculate the weight of the platinum. He ran another set of figures. Looking up at Ellie, "If I buy it, I am melting it down so that no one else will ever be the victim of its curse ..."

This was the first time Ellie agreed. The ring her father had made for her beautiful mother was the beginning of her illness and the suffering her mother faced. Once a grand story of romantic intent; her father had purchased the ring in Tanzania, Africa. The gent that sold him the diamond had offered a story of the curse of the diamond mine, but no one believed it until Ellie's mother became ill out of the blue immediately after placing the ring on her finger. Miles had begged her father to return the diamond. The stories he had heard were verified through internet searches and the curse seemed to hold a place in Mile's heart. He always wanted the ring replaced with the original diamond, the loss nothing compared to the sight of her mother was in her illness. Shrinking to nothing eight years ago, Hannah Justice passed away and Ellie had lost life as she had known it. Ellie merely nodded.

Finished, he ran one summation and turned the paper to Ellie. "I'll do the full value of the products, but I have to call my buyer to be sure he will purchase raw today. Where are you going to go?" He asked as he reached for his phone and dialed a number.

"Away, Miles. I can't stay here." She waited patiently.

19

He shook his head and answered into the receiver, "Paul ... Miles. I have raw goods, you in the market?" He shook his head a couple of times, glancing up at Ellie and then back down to his paper scratches. "No. Okay, I have exactly one ounce of platinum and a 2.13 Karat flawless diamond." He thumped a pencil on the top of the desk waiting. "I understand, yes. I mean perfection, Paul. I designed this ring and I am going to break it down to the metal and the gem. The diamond is emerald, 2.14 karat." He waited again before continuing. "... colorless, internally flawless to perfection, and excellent in proportion. It's as good as it ever gets. I'm lucky to have it today but have no market for the expense. It's something that not everyone will want to afford. Yes. AGS lab certification 2002. I have just examined it myself. It is flawless to a fault."

Ellie knew that her life depended on whether the buyer would take her ring. Miles was afraid of it and was superstitious enough that she was surprised he even touched the damned thing. Once her father had gifted it to her mom, Ellie's life fell apart. She met Tyler right after and once married, the domestic situation turned as ugly as it could. Ellie didn't understand that someone could be so calculating. All the money her mother left to her was abused by Tyler and with the findings during the trial; he had extinguished all but what she spent fighting for today.

Miles abruptly smacked his hand on his desk nearly causing Ellie heart failure. "I know, Paul, but the value of this gem is almost Fifty-eight grand. I'm not selling it to you for that. You can steal from someone else, but this seller is a personal friend of mine. You can do better ... I'll wait for you call before I call Jansen's in fifteen minutes." He slammed the phone down on the desk.

Ellie was shocked.

"That will send him into a spin, won't it?" Miles laughed. "So, little missy ... where are you going? What are you going to do? Are you okay? We worry about you, Kitty Kat."

The strong family ties were those that bound Ellie to security and love. She knew that Miles and Mattie, his wife, would do anything they could.

"With your papa's death last year, we feel you are our own, Elliebelle. Please let me help you …" Miles sincere empathy was gestured, but not received.

"I can't stay here, Miles. I've already been the talk of the town enough and I don't want to stay. It's better that I finally start over. I want to start over … really. I do."

He tapped his fingers on the desk and said, "I think I understand and you do have the fortitude of Bella Mia …" His favorite name for her mother nearly brought tears to her eyes.

She whispered, "If only you had married her …" Ellie knew that Miles loved her mother in a way no one else did. But her father had been the romantic, suave, debonair man who swept her off her feet and then worked until he had no time for her.

"If I would have, Kitty Kat, I wouldn't have you now, would I?"

He was right.

The phone rang and he waited four rings to answer. "This will be good, I can feel it." He flipped the phone to his ear, "Yellow …Of course. Let me ask." He put his hand over the receiver and turned to Ellie, "I can get fifty for both. Take it." He whispered as she nodded and he turned his attention back to the phone. "Sold. I'll deliver in two weeks."

Ellie stood from the chair. "Can you do cash? My assets were frozen by the IRS, I'm sure. We have nothing left and the house …"

Miles stood and came to her, eye to eye, "I know, sweetie. Trevor and I talked at the club last week. I know exactly where you are. This is what I can do." He moved to the office door and closed it and went to the safe behind a vase and inside the pillar behind it, hidden well." He fumbled through a combination, taking a huge wad of cash out, three rubber bands of cash, and handed it to her."

Taking the money, Ellie stood in his presence, soaking it up for the last time. "How much is here?" She knew there was more than fifty thousand dollars.

He blew her off with a wave of the hand.

"How much, Miles?" She demanded.

"Seventy-five." He cuffed his hands over hers holding the money. "And, you will take it, keep the watch and keep me informed of what is going on in your life. Capish?"

She laughed this mob reference. "Capish, ya big fool."

"I'm no fool. You have nothing; this will not be enough." His eyes watered as he dug into his pocket and offered her a debit card. "There is more when you need it. Please let us help you?" His voice softened as a tear slipped down his cheek, wiping it away abruptly. "Please …"

"Miles … I can't. I need to do this on my own this time. Every ounce of money the family doled out came with crushing consequences. I want to do this on my own and it will be plenty. I need a car and a place to live and then I am going to get a job." She smiled at him. "I think I will finally be fine. Let me …"

He took a deep breath and scooped her up into his arms, kissing her cheek.

Leaving his office, she felt as though she had left the last part of her life, as she knew it and the necessity to move forward would include starting anew. It was a scary thought, but nothing like what life here would be like if she tried to reenter society. They shunned people for the slightest infraction. The judgment she would endure would be too much to handle. People knew that Tyler cheated on a regular basis and that their efforts to have a child were thwarted due to his inability to conceive. He made it evident at a social gathering a few years back and it had stopped all hope of her ever having a child. Moving to a new life was in motion.

Feeling as though she would be sick, physically sick, she put one foot in front of the other. Ellie walked forward, each step of freedom bringing her closer to realizing that she was free to do as she pleased.

Chapter Four

Stacy Davidson sat on the chair in her daughter's room, the third night in a row of no sleep. Her daughter, Angela, was severely asthmatic and a bout of bronchitis left her with 24-hour watch. She was tired. So, bone-aching tired that Stacy didn't know if she could take another step. Almost drifting off, she shook her head and woke herself back up. It was time to text Pascal for at least a couple hours sleep. Their schedule seemed to work and allow him to still have enough sleep to practice medicine. A generous man, she thought as she text him to relieve her.

While she waited, she thought of flowers blooming and things that made her happy. Diamonds faded, but her two children were her life. She tried to stay positive through everything, but the fact that her parents were killed when she was very young made it difficult to even imagine life without Angela or Jules. She watched Angela's little chest heave heavily as she struggled with every breath.

Pascal entered the room in a stupor, hair ruffled and messy, but as cute as a button. He was truly gorgeous. "I'm here, Sweet pea. Go get some sleep. I'll give her the breathing treatment and have her ready for you when you wake." He kissed her forehead and looked her straight in the eyes so that she knew he was serious.

Stacy trod into her bedroom and fell on top of the sheets, immediately she drifted off into the sweet slumber she so desperately desired.

Pascal administered the breathing treatment while he spoke to Angela, only four years old, like she was one of his patients. "It's going to open your airways so that it doesn't hurt to breathe, baby girl."

Angela nodded her dark curls as the mask spewed the medication into her system and Pascal could see her ease in breathing come as the minutes passed. It was hard watching his offspring so sick and he knew just how sick she was. In the end, he worried more about the fact that his wife was so worried that she would not leave the child's side. Five days until Christmas and his whole world relied on getting this child well. Passing up the option of putting her in the hospital, he chose to keep her at home. It was a call he never regretted, even though Stacy was tired. If only she would let someone else watch the child.

He would take it up with Auddie as soon as she arrived that morning. Stacy usually trusted her with the bigger household situations. Maybe Auddie would be allowed to watch over Angela while Stacy got some sleep and just took a day off. The treatment was done and he bathed his child, dressed her and prepared her for her day. Such a picture of beauty. Both of his daughters had gotten the best of each, he and Stacy. Angela had angelic dark curly hair, long and thick like his and her mother's gorgeous green eyes. She had dark skin and the Italian heritage he so relied upon for his looks. Chiseled, tiny features, aping his own good looks and delicate hands like his. This child was destined for greatness. Her maturity at four was astounding, even to his intelligence.

"Daddy," she coughed and recovered. "I would like a puppy for Christmas." Her brilliant green eyes sparkled under the long, lush lashes she batted at him, although she knew the answer.

"What has daddy said about sometimes wanting things is just that, wanting?" It broke his heart, but her asthma would not withstand animal dander of any kind. The allergist all reported the same. Her delicate respiratory system would probably outgrow this condition, but only time would tell. She was reasonably derailed with respiratory illnesses and it would not warrant an animal in the house. They had even learned that horses were not permitted and he had sold several award-winning stallions and mares to vacate the stables to protect her.

In the room bounced, Jules. "Good Morning, Daddy." She lit upon his lap and lavished him with kisses.

"Good Morning, Peaches." He kissed her back. "A thousand kisses to start your day."

She climbed down in her one-piece pink pajamas and went to her sister. "Angie, how you feeling today?" She felt little Angela's head, although Jules was only three, as if she were a bedside nurse. "Do you feel better?" She tucked Angie's curls behind her ear and smiled graciously.

"I do feel better. I think Christmas will be fine and I will be fine." She coughed a little again. It was, however, nothing like the week before. Out of the proverbial 'woods' at this point, she was still in danger of relapse. "Daddy gave me my tweetment and I feel just about fine today. I think we should go shopping."

They both turned to him for approval.

"Can we?" They chimed in unison.

The exact opposite of Pascal's coloring, Jules was blonde with short, straight blonde hair, very thin and manageable, in direct contrast to Angie's out of control curls. Jules shook her head and looked at Angie. Sizing her up and down, she added, "Daddy, she does have her color back and she seems to control the coughing. I think we could shop if she wore the mask. Don't you?"

He had to laugh. The sight of the two against him was always magnificent. He wanted his girls to be level-headed, strong women like their mother. He wanted them to make good choices and to be able to input their opinions with respect.

"I'll talk to Mommy." He grabbed them both, one in each arm, like potatoes in a bag and swung them around. "She's awfully tired and Daddy has to work today."

Jules was the first to protest. "Daddy, Mommy needs a break. She's getting grouchy."

He put them back on the floor. "I know, baby girl. I'm working on that. You two still going to honor our agreement?"

They both nodded and stuck out their pinky fingers to shake. He shook their pinkies, one in each hand and leaned down to kiss them. "You be good and do everything Mommy asks without argument. You keep your things tidy and mind your manners at all times and I'll see if Mommy can take you shopping."

Angie said, "We can't get presents for you if we don't go shopping, Daddy. And Mommy ... she needs lots of presents, because she is the best Mommy in the whole ... widest ... world."

"Right!" He needed to get dressed and ready for his day, but how he wished he could spend the day taking his daughter's shopping. Knowing the selflessness would not clear the teen years, he cherished every minute of their presence in that place. "I'll see what I can do. I have to go get ready. Angie, can you help Jules get dressed?"

Angie nodded and they bounded out of the room into Jules. They were the very best any man could ask for. He took great joy in watching them run into the other room and noticed that Angie was doing much better. The medication would wear off in a couple of hours and she might struggle again, but the medicine was working and that's the best they could hope for. The steroids would catch up and build her system to a better place, but right now she was okay.

Pascal moved quietly into the master bedroom and covered Stacy up with a quilt on the other side of the room. Gently he laid the quilt over her, tucking it around her neck. It was cold outside, but the house was always cozy and warm. Into the shower and back out, he dressed quietly and then went to wake her.

"Stacy, my love ..." he prodded her softly. "Stase, wake up. It's time for me to leave."

She stirred slowly and opened her eyes to find his smiling gaze. "Hi, baby." She kissed him as he leaned into her. "Let's make another baby ..."

Pascal was eager to please her with the idea; he wanted a son and she knew it. The three years since Jules birth had been hard on Stacy. The room was dark and quiet, only the sound of her breath in his ear as she hugged him close. "I love you, bella mia."

"I love you too, Pascal. I had a dream we had a son and I

want to try."

"Okay … maybe we can talk about it tonight? I have to get going." He slapped her playfully on the buttocks. They had not lost playful, but the last week had taken its toll on her. "Up and at 'em."

"I'm up … I'm up." She rolled over and sat up, roughing her hands through her blonde hair. "I look a mess. How could you possibly love me?" She pointed to the same mirror she saw her image projected in and laughed. "I'm a hot mess!"

"You're MY hot mess … a baby sounds wonderful." He winked at her as he exited the room and two bounding beauties entered.

"Good morning, Mommy." They chimed again.

"Good morning, my lovely girls." Stacy caught them as they jumped into her arms, knocking her back down on the bed. "We want to go shopping!!!"

The start of another day. Stacy knew that she had to take

them out and that the mask would keep all germs from violating

Angie's delicate system, but it scared her all the same. "Of course.

We must get daddy's present."

"Yeah!!!!" They bounced with delight on the bed.

Stacy couldn't help but feel a tinge of sadness that they

wouldn't be this small for long and that the holiday was upon her.

She had just lost her cook and the annual Christmas party for her

husband was three days away and she had not one thing prepared.

So much to do and so little time. She jumped up on the bed and

grabbed each girl's hand as they all three bounced on the bed.

"Don't tell Daddy we bounced."

They all giggled...

Chapter Five

Walking down the streets of Duluth, Ellie began to feel too free. What would she do? The anxiety returned and she could feel her hands shake. Once inside the bank, just three doors down, she was denied an account and left feeling the fool.

Food, she needed food. Stopping in a quaint restaurant, she sat at the table reading the menu. The smell from the kitchen gave her stomach room to growl so loudly the people next to her heard it and began whispering behind her back.

They recognized her!

The waiter approached and she ordered to go and waited until the food came, paid him with one of her original hundreds, the wad of cash stashed neatly in the waistband of her slacks, where she could feel the bulk. She knew the value of money and she needed every penny she could get to start this new life. Finally, the waiter returned and she could leave.

On foot again, she started thinking of her next step. Where would she go? She walked aimlessly, her long, dark hair blowing in what was now a cool breeze. It cut through her like the Minnesota wind was known to do in December. She had no idea if there was a threat of snow and that on the ground currently was icing over as the day's sun would melt it and the night chill would freeze it. Nearly 4 PM, Ellie had to figure something out now. She folded her wool coat around her more closely and tried to think of a place she could eat her food, now growing colder by the moment. Nothing would taste as bad as the jail's food, but there was no place to eat it.

She wandered another ten minutes before coming across a coffee shop/bookstore and entered. The clerk greeted her, "Good afternoon. Welcome to Le Café." And she went about her business.

"May I order a coffee, black and eat my lunch here? It's so cold out." Ellie didn't want to be rude.

"Sure. Let me grab that for you." Sarah, the barista, grabbed a large mug and filled it with steaming hot coffee, handing it over the counter. "That'll be a dollar seventy-five, please."

Ellie paid and took her coffee and bag of food to a small table in the corner. There wasn't another soul in the shop and she could eat in peace. As she ate the chicken picada, she thought about her options. A car. She needed transportation. A napkin and pen from her purse started a list. From there, Ellie filled the napkin: place to stay tonight; clothes; toiletries; groceries to prevent the same from happening again—no eating out in public; shoes; where to keep the cash? The list ended with that as she comfortably sat in silence and ate her meal for the first time in months.

The clerk approached Ellie, startling her. "Can I get you a

refill?"

"Oh, no. I'm fine. Thank you." Ellie smiled.

"Okay … you want some paper or something? Napkins don't keep well for lists. I know, I'm a lister myself." She laughed.

"No. I'm fine. But thank you." As the clerk started to walk off, Ellie changed her mind. "Excuse me … do you happen to have a US map somewhere I might look at?"

"I sure don't … why don't you google it on your phone?"

Ellie grabbed her list and added 'phone'.

"Oh, you don't have your phone with you? Here, you can use mine." The small girl, not more than twenty, handed Ellie a large cell phone and a rush of memories came grilling her psyche. Ellie was far removed from society and it hurt.

"Thank you …" She fumbled with the phone …

"My names' Sarah. Here, let me help you." Sarah took the

phone and looked up at Ellie. "What do you want exactly?"

Not knowing why, she blurted it, the words came flying out, "I am trying to decide a place to live ... know any nice place far away from here?"

Sarah thought for a minute. Was this woman homeless? Did she need help? A student in the humanities department at the local university, Sarah immediately took interest in this woman and so she extended her hand. "Sarah Bonilla. Nice to meet you."

Ellie shook Sarah's hand. "Elaine Justice."

Sarah's eyebrows shot up.

Ellie saw the response and started to get up to leave, scooping her list into her purse.

"NO ... I'm sorry. Elaine, please, don't go." Sarah felt empathy for this woman. The news was blurting her acquittal and Sarah now knew why she was in the bookstore. Such a quiet, out of the way place must feel safe in comparison to jail for the last few months. "I'm sorry … please. Stay." Sarah got her to sit back down.

Ellie was quiet.

"Starting over?" Sarah's intuition kicked in. She was going to help Elaine.

She shook her head.

"Okay, so a map of the US, a new place, something with sun?" Sarah got no response. "How about just like Minnesota, snow and cold?"

Ellie chilled at the thought. "NO. Sun is good."

"Okay … how about Florida, Georgia, South Carolina, Texas, Louisiana …"

Ellie laughed. "Okay … I don't need a list of all the sun states. Let's see … "She actually started thinking about it. Where would she like to go? Vacations had taken them all over the world and she knew that staying stateside was what she wanted so she could work without a visa. Her passport had been revoked during the trial and she wasn't about to step foot in a county building to do anything for quite some time. "Florida, California or, oh, well, I don't know ..."

Sarah laughed now. "Where is your favorite place on earth?"

Ellie gave it real thought in the presence of this questioning stranger. This is the first person she had a conversation with that didn't include the trial or keeping some woman off her in the jail. She had to think about it. "It used to be my home."

"You wanna talk about it?" Sarah tried to softly give her the option.

Squinting through the pain, Ellie answered honestly, "I wouldn't know where to start, Sarah."

Sarah rose and collected Ellie's coffee mug. "Let's have some more coffee and figure this out."

She returned and Ellie started in. "I didn't do it, Sarah."

Sarah shook her head. "No problem. What has it done to you, Elaine?"

"Call me Ellie, please." She thought about it. "It took everything and yet gave me everything he took from me." Looking up, she waited for a response but got none.

"What does 'gave you everything' mean?" She sipped from her mug waiting for Ellie to register the question.

"Hmmm … well, my 'former' husband was not a nice man. He never hit me or anything, we weren't that close." She laughed lightly. "However, he married me for my money." She smiled the fakest sweet smile she could muster and continued. "It was all about money for him. For that matter, for me too. I don't know any different. Ya know?"

Sarah nodded.

"So, with the murder trial, we found he spent it all and I

had to sign over the house for my defense. Lord knows, I probably owe them more. I want to start over. Earning everything myself is important to me." She did not reveal the money she had.

"So, what do you have right now?"

Ellie raised her hands, "You're looking at it."

"Wow. Fuck! Seriously?"

Ellie laughed. She was used to the cussing now, since her incarceration. "Yeah, FUCK!" She said the word and it felt great. "FUCK!!! Seriously, this is what I have. Nothing."

"You're free, Ellie … "Sarah smiled.

"I am … and it's a little scary."

"How much money do you have?" Sarah dug in her pockets and threw two twenties on the table. "Not much, but maybe it will help you out."

"I have some money. My wallet was full when I went into

jail and they forgot to take it. But, I don't have transportation. No luggage to worry about, but no shower. No home, but no expense of a home … it's all quite surreal at this point."

"Whelp, I am a great planner. Let's just start from the basic needs. We need to figure out where you can go, if you have enough money to get there and by what mode of transportation. What will you do when you get to where you wanna go?"

Ellie thought for a moment. Was it safe to let this absolute stranger into her life? If those close to her could cause this much damage, how much devastation could a stranger bring?

As if reading her thoughts, Sarah said, "Hey, you can just share what you want."

A trusted door opened for Ellie and she began, "I have two undergraduate degrees in Psychology and Astronomy and a master's in social work."

Sarah laughed. "Girl, what were you planning to do with that?"

Ellie laughed now. She was right. What was she planning to do? "I don't know. I went to school because I loved my sorority and I took classes I liked and, well, that's what they gave me. The masters had a plan in mind. I wanted to help battered women. I spent all my time waiting for a second chance. A reason to feel not good enough was my daily distraction. Spending all my days in distraction just made me a non-thinker. I was a doer, Sarah. I just did what I was supposed to do like my mother did. Social groups, fundraisers, mingling, parties, the life ... you know. We were wealthy. I shopped. If I could shop for a living, I would do great."

"People do get paid to do just about anything these days." Sarah pondered. "Okay, so we have no idea what you want to do ..."

"Not true ..."

"What? Beg pardon?" Sarah had moved to another thought and had to reel herself back in. "What would you like to do?"

"I would like to waitress."

Sarah sat dumbfounded. Minutes past and neither said a word until Ellie broke silence. "I want to waitress. Maybe a nice restaurant or a bar? Maybe I could bartend?"

"Why? Help me understand. You're educated and you want to waitress? You want to write or something?"

"No. I want to fade into a background somewhere and observe normal people in hopes that maybe I can be normal someday ..."

"I like you, Elaine Justice." Sarah smiled at her.

"Have you ever heard the song, Claire De Lune?"

Sarah nodded. "I have. Beautiful song."

"I want to fade into a background and feel like Claire of the Moon ... I want to think. I want to feel. I want to see what things are like in another world. I refuse to return to the place hence I came ... I heard that one time and it sounded good. Well, the girl in jail said it differently, "Bitch, I ain't goin' back!" They both broke in laughter. "But, I liked what she said. Bitches … I am not going back there ever again. Not that lonely, cold place I lived in. But, I'll miss my home. That is where I grew up and Tyler … my former husband, he was so greedy and needy at the same time. I'm glad he's dead." She looked up to see what reaction Sarah might have.

"Did he hurt you?" Domestic violence was something Sarah was familiar with, growing up in a home where she was beaten as a child.

"No. I didn't love him enough to let him hurt me. We fought, but I stood up to him. I was not a victim. Well, until that night."

"What happened, Ellie?" Sarah had followed the story; everyone had followed the story. A city councilman was killed brutally by his wife. The papers screamed domestic violence, abuse, how she used him for his money. The news skews things and Sarah had the opportunity to get the whole story and Ellie afforded the opportunity to tell it. "What happened?" She prodded softly.

"I came into the room and he was dead. No one believed I was in the gym with my iPod and headphones. I didn't hear anything. We had been fighting for weeks over an investment he wanted to make. It would have required my signature and I wouldn't give it to him. We yelled in front of our housekeeper, Savannah. Her testimony scared me, especially after my thoughts of him sleeping with her were proven. I thought she was going to put me away, but my attorney tore her apart. After he was done, I thought she killed him."

"Who do you think did it?"

"I don't know. I racked my brain in jail and come up empty every time. Everyone hated him. Who didn't want him dead leaves no one. I don't know and I don't care. They didn't want to kill me, so who cares?"

"Right. Yes, you are right. You are free and can never be charged again and don't have anything to gain or lose if they do or do not figure it out." Sarah was pleased with herself. She watched Law & Order. She could figure things out. "Okay, so back to you ... first things first. Where?"

"Stick a pin in that phone map of yours." Ellie didn't care where she went. But, she was thinking winter was a pain in the ass. "I want sunny and bright with no beach. I hate the water."

Sarah was already googling things. She came up with four options. "Okay, here. Four places with sun, no beach and no water, inland retreats, moderate size, not huge, not small: Tomball, Texas; Palm Springs, California; Flagstaff, Arizona; and Asheville, North Carolina. Okay, I chose these, because I know they are near tourist sights and your avail to waitress will need tipsters. Anything sound good?"

She thought for a moment. "Axe, Flagstaff, too hot. Palm Springs is in the desert too, axe that leaving what, Tomson, Texas and Asheville, North Carolina?"

Sarah corrected her, "Tomball, Texas and I just threw that

one in because my cousin lives there." She giggled. "Okay, axe Tomball. Asheville, North Carolina it is. The Great Smoky Mountains, one of the United States top tourist sites. How about it? Not that far away, really. Look." She showed Ellie the phone. "Two or three inches. We can do that!"

"Oh, My God! You are a hoot. Where have YOU been all my life?" Ellie thought about it for just a second. "Asheville, North Carolina is my new home. Yes. It's Asheville! I'm going to Asheville." She got extremely excited.

"Okay, two … how you gonna get there?"

"Oh …" The balloon burst. "I don't know. A bus? A train? A plane?"

"Do you have the money for those?" Sarah asked. "My forty dollars is yours, but might not help with a plane ticket."

"I have plenty to do any of them, but I think I need self-sufficiency. Wouldn't a car be a better investment?"

"Yes, however, investment comes with responsibility, Ellie. Do you have the money to tag it, pay the taxes, insure it, and to maintain it? You are a waitress and do not make that much money. I would be careful."

"I think I can do one year's insurance, and tags and taxes are fine … I can do that. Now, I want to get on the road. Where would I buy a nice, economical car for a reasonable price? Should I buy new or used? I have never driven a used car, nor have I purchased one. I wouldn't know the first thing about it." As she spoke a young man dressed exactly like Sarah entered the room. He nodded to Sarah.

"Hey, Kenton." She caught Ellie's hesitancy. "It's okay. He is relieving me from my shift. It must be six o'clock now. Wow. We've been at this awhile. How about letting me get him squared away and we go find you a car? My uncle owns a dealership and he is usually there until at least seven every night. It's not far."

"I'm in!" Ellie sat exhilarated while she waited for Sarah to close out her shift, paying grave attention to what it was Ellie was going to have to look forward to in her new job as a waitress.

* * *

Casey laid on the bed, exhausted from the effects of the roast beef on his system. In all, thirty-six people had gotten sick. The hospital was gracious and had called in medical staff immediately. With a little bit of medication, he was feeling more normal, at least half human at that point. The middle of the night was never his friend. It was only one thirty-seven and he knew that his mind would envelope him until he gave up and paid attention.

Climbing out of bed, he got his computer, the only connection he had to the real world at this point, his phone a thing of the past. Firing it up, he checked his email, loaded the files his assistant sent and went to work looking through to find the erroneous accounts evidence. He had gotten the file of all the marketing firms and added the ones he missed to his list. In the morning, he would begin to call them. He was done with the conference. It was three days before Christmas and the conference was over. Why had they planned this so close to the holiday he would never know? He figured that his boss had a reason, and he was going to find it out.

Statistics prove that most people think about quitting their job on a regular basis, but Casey thought seriously about it. Why was he here? What was the plan for him? Why had the things in his past happened? The same questions began to plague him. Instead of paying heed, he decided to email his sister and make sure he knew what was expected of him for the holiday.

After the email was done, he nestled into the bed and closed his eyes. The last thing he remembered seeing before drifting off to sleep was his recurring dream of spending time with a certain woman. He so wished he could figure out who she was...

Chapter Six

At nine o'clock that evening, Ellie was on the road, map sitting in the passenger's seat of her brand-new Toyota Rav4. In dealing with Uncle Leonard, Sarah talked him into a $25,000 deal. On the way, Ellie had admitted that she had the cash to put down on the car and that her credit was probably destroyed by Tyler. Her family had no need for credit in the years past, so paying cash and getting a fully loaded, four-wheel drive vehicle for the mountains of Asheville was the ticket to success. While Sarah drove Ellie to the dealership she had researched Asheville. Described as Edgy, artistic and inviting it seemed to be perfect for her new start.

Sarah had left Ellie with a hug and a kiss on the cheek, her phone number and a promise of prayer for her success. It was the first time she felt moved by a person other than Jason, but he was obligated. She let herself think back to the time Tyler nearly raped her in his drunkenness and what it was she had to count on in life. It had been so empty. She had tried all she had and ended up so lonely. Women seemed to shun her due to her looks, her money and her ancient history in Duluth. How she longed for the hours of conversation with her college roommate, long gone. When Ellie found out she was a lesbian, she steered clear due to the sororities' treatment of Rachelle. She hadn't missed her in years. Chelle had left school after the ostracizing. Ellie never got close to another sister in the house, but fondly remembered, Chelle.

Maybe she would make contact somehow. Facebook and Twitter could give her a way to find out if she were around still. Ellie wondered what happened to her.

The mapping was printed out. Eau Claire, WI was the first stop. For the night, Ellie rented a room and made the best of it. Having a hard time sleeping, she tried to do what she could to plan things out. The hotel had free internet service, but she didn't have a computer, so she called down. Luckily, they had a computer in the lobby that they let her use for a small fee. What it taught her was that her skills in an office setting were just as she thought. It had been ten years since she had even remotely cared about touching a computer and she had no knowledge of what everyone else was talking about. She didn't even have a Facebook account. All that she had heard was oblivious to her. But, hope availed; she could learn. Her list now contained purchasing a laptop along with necessities. Sarah said she would need a computer to access job applications, just in case she didn't like waitressing and the wear-and-tear on her feet. With fifty thousand dollars left, she must plan accordingly. That was so little and there was so much she needed. Too bad she couldn't tuck Sarah in her pocket, her new friend, and take her with to Asheville and her new life.

The morning brought about a whole new anxiety. She was anxious to just get there and the drive became boring. The scenery was fine, the weather was fine, but she felt anxiety like that of being in jail the first month. After that, she got used to it, but it never really went away. Maybe she would find a good doctor and get some medication. She had felt extremely depressed.

The miles flowed under the tires of the new silver Rav4. Soon she was ready to call it a day, at almost four o'clock and found her next nightly stay in Indianapolis. It was quite different here. She checked in and found a mall. Her spending limit was $3,000 but when it came down to it, she didn't know how to bargain shop. She was looking at clothing that cost $400-500 for just a blouse. It took going to the food court and eating to let her think. What would a waitress wear? How many outfits would she need? What kind of shoes would be best? She started a new budgeting system and still came up short. She would have to wear everything over and over. This was not something that pleased her, nor did it make her happy to think of doing laundry. She had never done her own laundry. Looking around, face flushed with embarrassment, Ellie began to be afraid. Indianapolis was cold and the weather was turning on her. Snow forecasts lent her worry that she would get stuck with nothing to do. The night was calling for four inches. She hoped that the Rav's 4-wheel-drive would take her out of this state and closer to what she now referred to as 'home'.

Leaving the next day with only two more outfits, Ellie wondered how people did it. She spent over a thousand dollars on just two outfits that were nothing like her natural taste in clothing. She bought a navy and a black pair of slacks and a couple of nice white blouses, two pair of shoes—one she just had to have. The five-inch heels would look fabulous and accentuate her legs, although hidden under the slacks. She had not worked out in seven months, saw no need. It might be rough going. Just walking around the mall made her feet hurt, clad in a pair of two-inch heels. She changed into her black slacks and white shirt and headed to the Rav4 to leave, knowing the snow had fallen and the roads were barely cleared, a warning of patchy ice clearly indicative of the danger.

Within 200 miles, nearing Cincinnati, Oh, and the weather became gruesome. Snow fell so heavily that Ellie couldn't see. Afraid of having an accident, she pulled into the first motel she could find. Realizing that this hotel only cost $84 a night, it seemed Ludacris that she spent $700 both nights before. She winced. This budget thing could get ugly. Inside her room, Ellie tried to rest, feeling the anxiety of the situation on top of driving through the treacherous weather had worn on her last nerve. She headed to the hotel bar for a drink at ten past seven, maybe a bite to eat.

Early the next morning, Ellie woke from a deep sleep with a nightmare. She saw Tyler coming toward her with a gun; the gun she saw on the floor beside him that took his life. His blood ran down his chest as he chased her through the streets of Duluth until she woke trying to scream. The safety of the room brought her out of it within a few moments, but she was left to remember the body on the floor and what she saw the night she came out of their home gym and found him dead.

Showering and dressing, she tried to get rid of the sight in her head. She couldn't shake it. Like when she was in jail, the vivid depiction of his dead, lifeless body made her shake from the inside out. Shaking in the very core of her being, she tried to move forward. It felt like she was walking with cement shoes on her feet.

Medication might be the best option. This was unnerving.

Once packed back in her bags from the mall, she loaded the Rav4 and settled into the driver's seat to leave. The SUV would not start. Something broke inside her and anger surged through her veins. She checked the lights and, of course, she had left them on. The battery must be dead. She exited from the car, the sun shining but bitterly cold. Looking around, she headed for the hotel lobby to get help.

Chapter Seven

Casey walked from the hotel, carrying his bags to leave, finally free. He could have spent his time more usefully being on site, revising management as needed. Deep in thought, he had a plan and knew what he wanted to do, but his boss, Ralph Peters would not give him the opportunity. They seemed to point the finger at him, and the final result was an ultimatum. Casey had 120 days to get finances under control, sales equal to mid-line districts in the nation or he would be fired. He was no one's scapegoat.

Ellie rounded the side of the SUV just in time to look up and see a man walking without awareness, off in another world. Before she could say something, she slipped on ice. Her feet came out from under her and to compensate, she reached for the gentleman to catch her. Not paying attention, it backfired.

Ellie slid right into him, but unable to catch her, she bounced off him like she was part of a pin ball game. Casey tried to hold onto the bag carrying his laptop as the two toppled. It flew to the ground with a shattering sound upon landing.

Instincts took over and he reached for the bag to see if it broke.

Ellie fell back against the truck, causing her leg to twist and she heard it break. Searing pain shot up her leg and seconds later hit her head. She screamed in pain.

Instead of helping her, this jackass was tearing through his computer bag worried about his damned laptop? She hit the ground with a thud and slid three feet and he didn't even notice? She was immediately angered by the horrible person that apparently had no humanity.

Simultaneously to Ellie falling, Casey opened the bag,

opened the computer and looked to see if there was any damage. When he hit the power button, he almost fainted. The entire screen had shattered and the Windows screen was in fragments. "Oh, God!" He couldn't believe what happened. Everything he needed was on this hard drive. "Crap! Crap! Crap! Crap!" First his phone and now this? He heard Ellie scream.

Ellie tried to get up, only to fall back to the ground in intense pain.

Angry, Casey started to chew her out. "Why weren't you watching where you were go …" He realized that she was on the ground for the first time. "Oh, no. Are you okay?" Her beauty knocked him over. Her intense brown eyes glared at him in disgust. "What?" He reached for her hand.

She slapped it away. "Leave me alone. You've done enough damage."

"Damage … my computer is shattered. How am I going to work?" He knew it was insensitive, but how dare she glare at him like that, bone-chilling stare and then the anger.

"Are you kidding me? I think I broke my leg." She tried to get up again, but the ankle was gone too.

When Casey saw her try to use her leg and it folded, he realized she was hurt. His heart sped up, guilt ensued. "Here, let me help you." He didn't wait for an answer, lifting her up off the ground as if she weighed nothing, he pulled her up into his strong arms.

If it wouldn't have been for the fact that he never really let go of her, she would have been sent reeling as she struggled to knock him away from her. She swung at him, but he ducked off easily.

"Whoa, lady! What are you trying to do? I'm just trying to help you." Casey didn't understand. She ran into him, broke his computer and now she's acting like he's the ass? He tightened his grip in defense, pulling her even closer, nuzzled into his chest.

Bursting into tears, more from the situation than the pain,

Ellie gave in. Nothing was ever going to get better. This was her destiny in life, one problem after another, compounding the one before. How was she going to get to Asheville now? She sobbed.

"Hey … I'm sorry. It's okay. Let me take a look at it." He scooped her up in his strong arms, away from him so he could console her as he walked toward the passenger's side of the SUV.

Instinctively, to her mortification, she laid her head on his shoulder and sobbed as he carried her the rest of the way. "Open it up for me?" He asked.

She had dropped the keys when she fell. For some reason, she couldn't convey that to him and kept sobbing.

Casey couldn't figure this one out. He had met women and charmed them silly. Not her. She just kept crying and wouldn't let go of his neck. She had a hold on him. Putting her down consisted of peeling her off his shoulder and then gently leaning her against the truck. "Here, stand on the good leg and let's find those keys." He reached down and felt her pockets, nothing.

Ellie's senses shot off the charts. She reacted intensely with a sexual urge. That feeling had not come for her since she dated in college. Tyler never stimulated her sexually and this man touches her, a complete stranger, and her body reacts? What was wrong with her? She tried frantically to find her voice as she pushed him away … sobbing, "Hey … stop … on … the ground. I dropped them." She pointed, hiccupping like a child through her tears.

"Okay. Let me look." He shot around to the front of the truck, his agility apparent. "Got them." He hit the open button and the truck unlocked. Reaching around her, slightly brushing his hand against her side to reach the door, he opened it and lifted her in.

Again, Ellie's body responded to this stranger. He lifted her into the truck and had her heel off and her ankle in his gentle hands within moments.

"Oh, wow. This doesn't look good, Lady."

"Ellie … my name is Ellie." She almost whispered.

"Casey Waters, Charlotte, North Carolina. Sorry for bumping into you." He smiled.

Intense feelings hit Ellie when he smiled. It was uncanny the reaction she was giving this man. His muscles popped through his light blue oxford, through his winter jacket. She felt them when he lifted her up. Her loins ached for him to touch her, but her intensity scared her. Immediately she felt the need to flee from him.

"Okay, I'm fine. Just leave me alone. I can take it from here." She started to get up and climb out of the truck, only to fall directly on her face.

HE LET HER FALL! He did as she asked and stepped back as she put weight on the ankle and immediately it gave way. Screaming, she went down.

Casey rolled his eyes. The ankle looked sprained, could be broken, but she was insistent on him leaving her alone. Typical to a Princess, she looked the part in her nice outfit, high heels and nice vehicle. She was spoiled and he knew the type. It didn't bother him to let her fall as he raised his hands and stepped away from her.

Her anger radiated in her eyes, brownish-orange and so, so angry. She seethed as she pushed herself up from the parking lot muck from the weather. "You … you … S. O. B!"

"What? You said leave me alone. I just did what you asked, Lady." His cute smile, dimpled cheeks and year-round tan couldn't hurt at this point.

He felt a smidgeon of guilt, so he reached to pick her up again, filthy from falling. However, Ellie was not having it. She started flailing about as he attempted to re-seat her in the truck. "Stop fighting me. You're going to send us both back to the ground." He tried to get a good grip on her, but she refused. So, once he stood her upright, he threw her over his shoulder so he could maneuver the door that had now closed again to the SUV.

Ellie was furious. "DON'T … HELP ME!!! LET ME GO!!!" She was screaming, "LET ME GO!!!"

Two women came out of the hotel just in time to hear the 'help me. Let me go' and rushed to her assistance. Gladys and Eva nearly ran through the newly plowed parking lot, thinking that Casey was accosting Ellie. In their fifties, the women, clad in slacks and sweaters with quilting sayings on them, looked the sight running toward Casey and Ellie, arms flailing about, trying to get there as fast as they could on the unsure foothold of a parking lot.

"We are coming ..." Gladys yelled back.

He was trying to set her back in the SUV without getting any dirtier and not hurting her when Gladys grabbed his hand and yanked, causing him to drop her half-in the SUV and half-out. Ellie slid to the ground again with a thud. Her white shirt was now a nice even brown.

Eva turned immediately on Casey, pushing him back. She let him have it, "There'll be none of that you monster!" She literally pushed him away, trying to brute-force him away from the young lady in need.

"I'm just trying to help her." Casey pleaded with the older woman.

"Sakes alive, you weasel. Get away! Get away! Stranger danger!!! Stranger danger!!!" Eva kept yelling, hoping any man would hear and come to their rescue. Making a huge scene of screaming of which Gladys began in unison. "STRANGER DANGER! STRANGER DANGER!" They continued to scream, when a group of women quilters at the other convention the hotel was holding, on break, walked out to go to lunch and heard them.

It was on!

The mistake Eva and Gladys made was exemplified thousand-fold when these mothers heard the 'stranger danger' and intervention was needed. Within moments, sixteen women had Casey, the assaulter, down on the ground, as muddy as Ellie and were trying to put him under citizen arrest. They incessantly chatted the entire time, one ordering the other to hog-tie him, another suggesting they sit on him. All the while, Casey refused to fight these innocent women. The 911 call had been given and the police were on their way.

Casey was easy-going about it, having to be careful not to fight back or else he might hurt one of these ladies aiding poor, poor Ellie. He wondered why she was letting it go this far when she knew the truth and for one fleeting moment, their eyes met and he knew. It was out of spite. What a bitch! Little did she know this did not bother him one iota. He thought it was funny.

Chapter Eight

The sirens brought everyone back to reality, especially Ellie. She told Gladys it was a mistake and they had just bumped into each other, but the other women were deep in. Casey had someone's knee on his head, three women were sitting on him so he couldn't move and someone had twist-tied his hands behind his back. When Ellie saw this, she burst into laughter. It was only moments before that he had looked deep into her eyes and knew that she could have stopped it all and didn't. It was quite humorous watching him, but she knew he wasn't fighting when he could have taken them all.

To stop the women, Ellie yelled, "Hey … he didn't do anything!" trying to get their attention. "Really. This is all a mistake." It didn't work. Even the women standing between her and him, she couldn't get them to listen to her. She yelled louder, "HEY!!! It's a mistake. He didn't do anything!!!" When that didn't work, Ellie put two fingers in her mouth and whistled the loudest, shrillest whistle she could muster. That brought everyone to a halt, just as the police exited the car and rushed to aid her as well and she realized the police were coming.

For a split-second Ellie lost her mind. Anxiety forced its way into her system and she was no longer in control. She had panic attacks in her jail cell when they shut it every day and had gotten used to them, or so she thought. All the sudden she couldn't breathe. She was panting. Her hands became extended limbs of a tree and she couldn't use them and then it got worse. Her fingers curled from lack of oxygen and she couldn't talk. The words would not come. The police officer was asking her questions and all she could see was a Cincinnati jail cell looking out. She was going back to jail!!!

Ellie fainted.

Casey was pulled up, escorted to the police vehicle and shoved inside. The officer had told him to wait and let them figure out what was going on and he would be back. Eva and Gladys were immediately at Ellie's side, trying to help yet again.

Eva, in near hysterics at this point was screaming, "Get an ambulance! Get an ambulance!"

Within a few moments, Ellie regained consciousness and could talk with hesitancy. She kept telling herself that none of that would happen now. She was not going to jail. She was fine. The ambulance pulled up and she was placed on a gurney. Another nightmare had begun.

Casey could see the fear register in Ellie's eyes from the side of the police car where he now stood. A simple explanation had him free and within ten minutes the police were gone and the quilters apologized profusely. Gladys and Eva had gone to aid Ellie at the hospital and he was left in the parking lot with Ellie's keys in his pocket.

Great! What could he do? His plane was long gone and his computer was in shambles. The conference wasn't supposed to end until the next day, so he had time to do the right thing and he knew what it was. Keys in hand, he opened the SUV, popped the hood and looked at the battery. A quick call for a cab and an hour later he had a new phone, laptop and a set of battery cables for Ellie's SUV. Plugged in and motor running, he had performed retribution for his knocking her down and causing all this commotion. He hadn't been looking and probably walked so close to her vehicle that he did cause the ruckus.

He knew he had done the right thing. He scribbled a note and put it on the window, under the wiper blade and headed back into the hotel lobby, where he told her to catch him for her keys.

Looking forward to seeing her again in some strange way, Ellie monopolized his thoughts. Her eyes blazing, fire and ice, bore into him. When he picked her up, her scent had tantalized him. That soft little mouth, even when wincing in pain, was so kissable.

He had to shake her from his mind to concentrate on setting up his new computer system and downloading the day's memos to deal with. He had purchased an external hard drive connector and the tools to remove his old so that he could load it on the new computer and kept himself busy doing just that.

Three-and-a-half hours later, Gladys, Eva and Ellie, sporting crutches and a pretty pink cast from the knee down, entered the lobby. Casey saw them come in and his heart sunk. He had just made a new plane reservation for early evening and now guilt pangs erased that plan immediately. He would have to drive her to her destination.

Eva spotted him first and came to apologize. "Sir, Eva Cranston." She held out her wrinkled, tiny hand and shook his with gusto. "I'm sorry for mistaking you for an abductor. So sorry."

Gladys chimed in. "Yes. We are so sorry. Thank you for trying to help our little Ellie."

He watched Gladys and Eva say goodbye as if they were

immediate family members. Hugs, kisses, fond wishes and they were gone, leaving Ellie to face him at last.

Ellie swallowed down her irritation and asked, "My keys, please?"

He started to hand them to her and just when she grabbed to snatch them, he pulled them back. "Wait. How are you going to drive? Right leg, gas pedal, and a cast? Bad combination ... pain pills?"

She was furious. Pointing out the obvious sent her off the charts. Her once rosy cheeks from the winter wind now turned profusely red, her eyes narrowed and she started to speak, when he cut her off.

"Casey Waters. It's nice to meet you, Ellie." Her name dripped from his lips. "I would assume you are above arguing about the fact that you can't drive, so there are two options here. One, I buy you a plane ticket to remedy my rudeness and behavior. I am terribly sorry that I wasn't watching where I was going and bumped into you, causing all of this." His hands waved, suggesting her filth, the cast and her demeanor. "I'd like to make it right. Where are you headed?"

She stood in awe. Had he really apologized? He was such an ass and then he apologizes. She had seen it before. He needed to make himself feel better, so now, with her inability to drive, she would take advantage of it. "Ashville, NC."

"No kidding?" I'm headed home to Charlotte." He smiled brilliantly.

Caught completely off-guard with the dimples a mile deep, she caught her breath.

He saw the attraction again. "I'm driving you home." He turned to pack up his things. His back to her, he grinned.

She wanted to argue. But, in reality, she had no other option. The cast was in place for at least four weeks. The ankle was broken in two places, the leg in one and the possibility of torn ligaments remained. They couldn't do much more than set it at this point and she had promised to seek medical attention in Asheville.

Casey was more than amused. He had seen the anger, didn't understand it, but he saw it. She was so obvious. She was attracted to him and he had all the cards. He stood, turned and dangled the keys in front of her, "Any arguments, Tiger?"

It burnt her to the very core when he called her that name. It sent chills down her spine. Her father used to call her than when she argued with him, fights she never won.

Chapter Nine

Ellie maneuvered the crutches and made her way out the door Casey held for her without saying a word. The pain pills had kicked in and she hardly cared that she would be in the vehicle with him, alone, his cologne taunting her for the next six hours.

Settled into the SUV, Ellie was asleep within fifteen minutes, not a word spoken between the two.

By the time they hit Lexington, Casey was aware of Ellie's very fitful sleep. He wasn't sure if he should wake her or not, but listening to her mumble, he knew this woman had secrets he might not want to know. She went back and forth between small sobs, possibly from the pain, to pushing at something to keep it away from her. He kept driving.

He stopped in London, KY and thought of waking her, but she had finally stopped fighting the sleep, so he opted not to. Grabbing two sodas, a microwave burrito for both of them and some bottled water he headed back out to find her still sleeping soundly.

On the road again, he turned the music on and let it play softly in the background. The miles flew under the tires of the RAV and he was actually enjoying the peace of mind, thought process and her perfume, which permeated the truck. He was starting to get a little tired even though it wasn't nine o'clock yet so he drank her soda after finishing his. The caffeine from the soda started to bring him back to life when Ellie started talking in her sleep.

She moved from mumbles to almost yelling.

"I said no! Get off me!!!" she pushed the air again. "I didn't do it, leave me alone!!! Leave me alone." She sat straight up in the seat; the seat belt constraining her. Grabbing at the seat belt, tore at it to free herself.

Casey, caught off guard, swerved to the side of the road, pulling to a stop on the shoulder and tried to help as she screamed, panic evident. He caught one of her hands as she dug at the seat belt, screaming at the top of her lungs now.

"Hey, it's okay. It's just a dream." He realized she still wasn't awake.

"I didn't do it. Leave me alone!!!" she fought his grip. She was a lot stronger than he thought and fought him for all she was worth.

He reached for the second hand as she swung and hit him in the face. Squarely catching his jaw, he took the hit, but felt his teeth knock together and stun him a bit. He caught her arm and gently folded them to her as he fumbled to get the seat belt undone.

"Ellie. Ellie!!! It's okay. It's me ..." She swung a couple more times catching him, but nothing like the square shot the first time.

She woke and quit fighting immediately, turning to his voice. He was so close to her and smelled so good. Drowsy from the pills, exhausted from the dream of being arrested again, fighting the handcuffs and the shackles they put on her, she leaned in and kissed him fully.

The kiss began slowly, her soft lips brushing against his as she reached for his face as if to cradle him softly. She became more intense when he reacted. It was so sudden that, to his surprise, he participated. He ran his hands through her hair, grabbing the back of her head and pulling her to him, fully experiencing her lips, tongue flicking softly over her bottom lip. He kissed her so softly after that, and felt something deep inside his soul. He could give this woman everything. Everything he held back from the others, so desperate to take it from him, he handed over in a simple kiss. Her moan brought him back to reality very quickly.

As quick as it started, it stopped. Nothing abrupt, she finished the kiss with a small peck, leaned to the side, rolling away from him and snuggled into the seat like a child. She began to softly snore, her breathing slow and easy. Rolled up in the fetal position in the seat, she slept angelically.

Stupefied, he sat there trying to figure out what had just happened. The SUV purred gently contrasting his racing senses, on fire. Direct conflicting emotions began at once. That was the best kiss he had ever experienced. She had taken control, taken him to a place he never had been before and his arousal was instantaneous. He wanted to make love to her right this moment. To softly lay her underneath him and let him show her what making love was all about. He wanted to skillfully bring her pleasure and fulfill her needs. What had she just done to him?

He could do nothing more than stare at her, to watch her sleep so sweetly curled up, her feet in the seat. Ten minutes passed and he made no move at all. The nigh came rushing back when a semi buzzed by them, too close, and scared him back to his senses. He was still parked on the shoulder.

Pulling back onto the interstate, Casey could think of nothing more than the fact that she was dangerous to him. He had enough trouble. History could not repeat itself. He could not rescue every troubled woman he ran into. His next relationship, should he ever have one, would be with a healthy woman who could handle his inability to commit. The very thing that kept him sane.

They spent two more hours on the road and arrived on the outskirts of Asheville just before midnight. With no knowledge of where to take her, he had to wake her up. "Ellie ..." He spoke softly, trying not to scare her. "Ellie ..." He brushed her shoulder. With no response, he softly shook her arm only to have her grab his hand, intertwine her fingers in his and pull him arm around her. He pulled over again.

"Ellie!" He was a little more forceful this time as he pulled his hand from hers, finally awakening Sleeping Beauty.

Rousted from the deep sleep, Ellie stretched as much as she could, only to have stabbing pain from her leg. "OUCH!!!!" She grabbed to find the pink cast and returned to the world she hated.

"Oh, God ... "

"Hurt?" He asked.

She nodded. It hurt badly. She didn't even know where she had put the pain pills had she wanted to take another. They had knocked her out and now she realized she was hungry. "Where are we?" She cooed.

"We're here. Asheville. I don't know what your address is." He pulled back onto the highway, safe that she wasn't going to pop him in the jaw again.

The next problem arose. She didn't want him to know she didn't have one. She fought for a good answer and couldn't find one. "I am staying in a hotel until I find one. I start a new job here next week and my things won't be here until the middle of the week."

"Oh, okay ... what hotel?"

Again, she fumbled for reasoning when a Super8 popped

into sight. She pointed. "Right there, easy breezy." She felt huge relief. Then it dawned on her he had no way of getting to Charlotte. "What are you going to do? How will you get home?"

Casey had already made arrangements to have his driver pick him up the next day. "I'm good. I'll grab a room there too and we'll be just fine." He pulled into the hotel.

In the lobby, Ellie got a room and paid cash. When it came his turn, Casey reached into the back pocket of his jeans to get his wallet and it was gone. He felt his front pockets to find nothing. It hit him like a ton of bricks that when he had bought the burritos the guy that had been standing talking to the clerk had bumped into him. "SHIT!"

"What?" Ellie was confused.

"That bastard stole my wallet." He was now the furious one. How could he be so stupid? He never carried vulnerable. "He got my cash and my credit cards. Damn it." He ran his hands through his curly blonde hair.

Ellie rolled her eyes. Either this guy was a complete idiot or bad luck was following them like a black cloud of rain.

"I'll get you a room. It's the least I can do." Ellie turned to the clerk.

"No. How about I sleep out in the SUV. I'm good. A great camper in my younger days, I'll be just fine." He grabbed his computer case and headed for the door.

Had Ellie been able to hobble a little faster, she would have stopped him. Instead, she let him go, watched him walk out the door cursing the day. She picked up her key card and headed out to find her room with instructions from the clerk.

Casey went to the SUV and laid back the passenger's seat. The cold of the December air seemed to leak in all around him. He grabbed his suitcase from the back and redressed, using every shirt he had and putting a pair of khakis on over his jeans. His coat in place, he tried again. It didn't help much, but he wasn't freezing. Instead of sleeping, he thought about that kiss again. Not able to shake it, he let it run through his mind. She was so fitful in sleep. Maybe she had been abused sexually and or someone hurt her? He found his anger rising at the thought. Protective of all women, that's what it was. Nothing to worry about, he would release his mind as he did after his parents died and let his mind wander his place of peace. Only his place of peace was filled with the smell of Ellie that permeated his presence, sitting in her seat. It was such a simple, clean smell and he couldn't shake it, nor did he really want to.

A fitful hour of tossing and turning brought Casey to give up and head for the hotel lobby. He told the clerk what happened and got the okay to use the Wi-Fi until sunrise. Awake, on his computer in the lobby all night long, he was warm. At around six o'clock, he walked out the door and headed for the SUV to grab his things. From the SUV, he watched the sun peek over the mountainside and come to full daylight. It was a beautiful sight.

Ellie watched the SUV from the window as the sun came up over the crest and could see Casey as he watched it. He was a beautiful man and such beauty was the first look she got at

Asheville, NC. She was home. She hobbled from the window to the bed and tried to erase Casey from her memory and the kiss. The kiss that shattered her inner walls made her ache for his touch. Pretending to go back to sleep had been her only option and he hadn't said a word. She was home and soon he would be nothing but a wind that had blown by, just like the seven months in jail.

Chapter Ten

Casey pulled himself out of the car and headed to find Ellie's room with a quick stop at the coffee pot in the lobby to wake him and release the kinks in his back from no sleep and the cold.

Knocking on her door was quite the challenge with two cups of coffee in his hands, but he did it.

Ellie crawled from the bed, grabbed her crutches, which were now causing her bruises on her sides and hobbled to the door to find the aroma of fresh hotel coffee. "Mmmmm, how did you know?"

"Just a hunch. How did you sleep?" He moved to the table where he put the coffee and dug cream and sugar packets out of his coat, along with a stir stick.

"I never went to bed. I just watched out the window. The sunrise was amazing. I've never been here before." She cooed as she blew softly on her coffee before sipping.

"Really? Well, it's a gorgeous little city. Never heard anyone complain about being here." He was sipping at his coffee, black and strong. The stronger the better.

"Do you get here often?" She half wanted him to say yes and then the other half fought to rid self of his ostentatious personality, the leg-breaker, selfish to only see his broken computer.

"I work here. Well, actually, I work on three sites, but Asheville is our biggest production facility. I'm usually here at least once a week." She looked even more beautiful today than she did yesterday. There was something different about her and he noticed it right away. A calmer demeanor; a softness he hadn't seen until the kiss. Oh, the kiss. He wondered if she even knew about the kiss. Surely, he wasn't bringing it up.

"I'm sure you have to get going. Thank you for the coffee."

"You didn't drink much. Not a coffee drinker?" He had gone to all the trouble of bringing it to her.

She looked over her shoulder to the room with the sink and the brewed coffee beside it.

"Oh." He laughed. "I forgot they have them in the room. Oh, well ... my driver should be here to bring me a company car. I'm going to ... head out." He extended his hand as he rose. "It was nice meeting you, Elaine Justice."

She didn't know what she thought about this man, but as she shook his hand she was grateful. Grateful he didn't bring up the fact that she had kissed him as if he were hers ...

After getting her money from the safe under the seat in the SUV, Ellie counted it and began to make her budget. With $46,742 left, she was about to enter the next phase of her life fully. Preparation was the key. She wrote out a budget that left her $10,000 for the bank and would allow her six months of living without worry of having a job. But, she knew herself well enough to know that touching that money would take an act of God. All she had in life, it was going into a safe place and she would only touch what she needed to meet her immediate needs. The quest began with the thought of employment.

She had no idea where she was going, but she called a cab and stood in the lobby ten minutes later waiting for it. Just after eight o'clock in the morning, she was going to experience Asheville, NC.

Hours later, back in the hotel, aching horribly, Ellie figured out enough on her new cell phone to call Sarah. They talked for a good hour, Ellie explained the horror of the broken ankle and Casey Waters. Sarah and she made plans that when Ellie got settled in Sarah would come for a visit. Ellie began immediately to look forward to it.

* * *

In the back of the limo, Casey picked up the past few days papers he requested, not having time to read while he was dealing with the trouble at work and the conference, not to mention the hindrance to his journey, Ellie. He was exhausted.

Lo and behold, front page of the paper … He saw Ellie's picture with the heading, ELAINE JUSTICE ACQUITTED … He read frantically to find answers to the mysterious Ellie. What he got was more confusion. She might have murdered her husband? The story articulated how evidence nearly supported the conclusion that she would be found guilty, but that her brother-in-law's compelling testimony as to the abuse that happened in the marriage was never identified anywhere but in the immediate family. Her parents both deceased and not having any character witnesses, it seemed she lived in isolation: the story of domestic violence, no matter how obscure, swayed the jury. A very long deliberation, 28 hours, they came back with the acquittal and Ellie was free.

His thoughts raced.

* * *

Ellie and Sarah discussed at great length possible employment options with the bum leg. A Godsend, Sarah came up with a couple. The first, a desk job, which, however, would require Ellie to disclose her past, was not an option. She didn't want to go that route. The other option was to bust open this new laptop she bought and search through the help wanted ads and see if there was anything she could do. If not, she would be resolved to taking the route of a desk job and disclosure. Once they hung up, she fired up the computer and fumbled her way through the next two hours finding the Internet most useful. Sarah had encouraged her to make a Facebook page so that they could keep touch and not waste minutes on the cell phone, but talk only on Sundays, Sarah's day off. Ellie made a Facebook page under a different name and found Sarah to friend her.

The help wanted produced two possible jobs: a private chef and a toll booth clerk for the Interstate. Ellie rescinded to disclosing what she might need to, it was her only chance to be self-sufficient. She still had the Prada watch, if she needed to sell something. If not, she knew what time it was and it was time to get out and get busy.

Ellie read the ad again for the private chef and began a cover letter and resume. Sarah thought it would be better to have everything on paper so that she need not explain much to people. If lucky, she might slide through with no explanation. Ellie listed her volunteer work, googled numbers and addresses and felt very confident following the resume guide she found on the web. Until she came to the references section.

She tapped her fingers on the edge of the laptop thinking through everything and analyzing each person she knew. Miles worked. Sarah worked. Trevor would have to work as well. She called him to ask if it were okay to list him as a reference.

The conversation started out timid, but Trevor warmed up

and spoke freely with her in the end. The animosity that he held

was from a place she didn't understand. She had dated him before

Tyler, but had chosen to marry his brother. When she realized how

devastated Trevor was, it was too late. They had never really

spoken of it all, but Trevor had come to her one night. Tyler had

been drunk, things had happened and Trevor knew Tyler was with

someone else, so he came to Ellie. He begged and pleaded with her

to leave Tyler and run away together. Tyler's only friend in life,

Trevor knew exactly what Ty was capable of and knew what he

was doing to Ellie. He had referred to financial devastation, but

Ellie had ignored it, thinking he was the jealous old love interest

and that he was being selfish. The reason he had such a hard time

on the witness stand, was that he ended up telling the truth and

ended up leaving himself open to charges. Whether he had been or

would be formally charged, she did not know and she did not want

to know. Tyler and Trevor had scammed several real estate deals.

In the end, it's probably what cost Ty his life and Trevor his

freedom. Trevor told about the business dealings, the threats on

each of their lives from disgruntled people they had wronged, and

in the end, saved her. When he had visited Ellie in jail, the only thing she could say to him was to beg him to please tell the truth. He did and she would be ever so grateful. She told him that.

Trevor had no news of what was going to happen, but had been asked not to leave the city. Formal charges were in the works. Hoping he would get a lighter sentence, pleading guilty and testifying, he was positive for the most part. He said he was willing to be reference if he was able. They hung up with deadpan goodbyes. His life was over and hers was just starting. She felt guilty for only a moment when she realized he made conscious choices and this was going to be his consequence.

Finished with her resume and the thought of her old life and extreme pain, Ellie took a pain pill and laid down for a nap. A nightmare woke her from the soft slumber, jolting her back to reality once again. She needed to find a home, a place to feel safe and this hotel was not the ticket. Dressing in her best new outfit, she headed out to rent a house. Newspaper in hand, she slid into the taxi and headed for what the internet said was the best neighborhood.

Traveling past all the houses she saw, Ellie knew she couldn't afford to rent anything here. She rescinded to asking the cabbie. "Sir, I'm new to town and I am looking for a nice neighborhood to rent a home. Any ideas?"

The slightly dirty, unkempt cabbie was very responsive. A smile finally reaching his face, he answered her, "I think there are a couple of neighborhoods around. Let's see what we can find. You know this is by the mile, right?"

Ellie pulled out a fifty and handed it to him. "I understand. Let's see the possibilities."

They drove for nearly two hours before passing a little yellow house with a covered porch. It looked safe, the neighborhood was clean and there were several people walking, and a few kids playing in the yard for Christmas break. Only two days away, Christmas wasn't even a thought for Ellie this year.

"Can you pull over?" She grabbed her pen and copied down the phone number as the cabbie pulled the car to a stop.

"That there's a nice one." He pulled out a cigarette from a pack on the dash. "I'm gonna step out the door here and smoke. Why don't you give them a call and see if you can look at 'er?"

Ellie was already dialing. She waited for an answer. "Hello?" The thick southern drawl of the woman on the other side of the line was just like all the others she had heard here in Asheville, thick and southern.

"Yes, Ma'am. This is Elaine Justice. I am interested in your house at 342 … uh, wait, I'm not sure of the street."

The cabbie heard her, "Sunrise …"

"Sunrise Street. I would like to know if you could show it to me sometime today, please?" Ellie was apprehensive. It was a pretty little house with hedges along the front of the porch. It had charm and charisma. She hoped it would be well kept on the inside. This was all so new to her.

"Sunrise, yes. It's a two bedroom, one bath, and rents for $700 a month. First and last and a one year lease. You still wanna see it, Sweetie?"

"Yes, please. I'm sitting in front of it. Nice house." Ellie was not sure how this went.

"I'm about three blocks away. Twila Newbury here, honey. I can be there just as soon as I get Henry out of his Lazy-Boy. Just sit tight, Sweetie." Twila hung up, leaving Ellie excited.

The cabbie climbed back in. "We good?"

"Yes, she's on her way in a few minutes. You don't mind do you, Sir?"

"I'm no sir. My name's Moses." The black man smiled again. "I am being paid, you don't worry at me. Moses at your disposal, Peaches. We are good." He leaned back in the chair and turned on the radio. They both sat and listened until a blue Lexis pulled into the small gravel drive.

Ellie exited the car, grabbing her crutches and hobbling over to the porch where Twila and Henry stood waiting for her.

Twila seemed sweet, "Well, Sugar, look at you. Those must be terribly uncomfortable?" She was genuinely concerned as she held the door open so Ellie could enter the living room of the home.

Immediately she was met with a beautiful selection of wainscoting and color. The living room was a steel gray wainscoting with a peach paint above. The window treatments were lacy and looked like something she would have chosen. Great light came into the room. The hardwood floor was impeccable, newly refinished. Ellie could see the kitchen from where she stood and the appliances weren't the stainless steel high-end that she had at her old home, but they were nice and they were new.

Twila saw that she liked it, "Pretty, isn't it?"

Ellie nodded. "Did you just redo it?"

"Yes. But for all the wrong reasons, we wanted to sell it, but it just isn't the right time." She backed away from Ellie, looked her up and down. "You gonna take care of it like it's your own? I ain't renting to no one who is going to have wild parties, tear it up and leave me in a bind." She liked this young girl.

"I promise. Can I see the bedroom? It is at the top of my price range, but with a little budget adjustment, I can swing it. Who needs to eat, right?" They both laughed.

"She's right in here, to the left is the master and to the right is the other." Twila led her, holding doors so she could view the rest of the house. It was fabulous. It felt like home. When she caught herself misting up, she tried to hide it ... but Twila caught it.

"You okay? What's your name, Sugar? I'm so bad with names at my age ... lucky I know my own." She patted Ellie on the shoulder.

"Ellie Justice ..." She waited for it to hit home, for Twila to recognize her name.

Twila caught it right off. She thought this youngster looked familiar. "I see. Well," She turned and walked away, turning back,

"You coming?"

Ellie nodded and walked behind her, when Twila headed for the kitchen, Ellie headed for the front door. Fumbling with the handle, due to the crutches and her eyes welling with tears, she felt relief when Twila touched the handle.

"Where you going, Sugar?"

"I ... uh ... I understand, Mrs. Newbury." Ellie tried to exit, but Twila put her hand on her shoulder softly and turned her to meet Twila's kind eyes.

"No. Let's get the application filled out. You got money with you?"

Twila headed to the kitchen, expecting Ellie to follow, where a pile of applications lay. Twila grabbed one. "Okay ... my sister, Nita, she got accused of abusing her kids when it was the God awful abusive husband of hers. I ain't gonna say no more. I like you." She looked Ellie in the eye. "You look at me and tell me I was right thinking you didn't do it."

Ellie's courage was constant. "I did not kill my husband. I promise. This has ruined my life and I just want to start over, but no one will let me. The papers, the news, my picture all over the nation as a killer. I didn't do it, Twila, I promise." And, for the first time, Ellie took back her power. "If I would have killed him, I would have been a lot smarter and planned it out and been out of the country well before I got caught." It felt good to say it. She had thought it a thousand times, but no one was interested in anything but the immediate and that was frying her ass in court. Even her attorneys didn't seem to buy into it, but she knew. Ellie knew she could have planned and completed it without getting caught, or at least she could have given it a good try.

Twila burst out laughing. "I do like you, Sugar." She pulled a pen from behind her ear, next to her impeccably dressed gray hair, up in a bun. "Fill this out, best you can and let's get you in here."

Ellie filled out the paper as best she could, listing Miles and Sarah as references. Handing it back to Twila, she felt an uncertain ownership, but it was an ownership. She had a home.

Ellie had finished up with Twila and met Moses back at the cab. Standing outside smoking again, Moses opened the door to her and Ellie felt as if she were back in the day whereby this would have been a stretch limo and she were important. Today she had a home and now it was ready to furnish. Sarah had suggested Ellie skimp on furniture and so she addressed Moses, "Moses, know any second-hand furniture stores? I need to furnish my new home." She smiled as he took charge, put the car in drive and escorted her to the destination.

Although the day was productive, when she struggled back to the hotel room, Moses in tow to collect her things, she was sad. Holding on until he dropped her back off at her new home was hard, but she did it. A couple of times in the cab she had to wipe tears away; it just wasn't the appropriate time. They had picked up another driver, who came in early for his shift so that he could drive Ellie's SUV to her house for her. Following behind, she felt like things were falling into place, and falling was a good word. Tumbling might have even sufficed.

Back at the house, the moving truck had just arrived and

within two hours Ellie had a house full of furniture. The tears had waited and she was ready.

The second-hand store had only a couple of pieces, but the furniture sign across the street, BLOWOUT SALE, proved immensely productive. Ellie went through, the salesclerk behind her marking sold on tickets and placing them on everything Ellie bought, and she scantily filled the house, room by room.

It was almost nine o'clock when Ellie realized that she hadn't eaten all day and there wasn't a stitch of food in the house. She had her cell phone, so she searched the internet, her new best friend, and called for Chinese delivery. Her first meal in her new home was spread out on the coffee table and she sat on the couch in total silence and ate until the dam burst.

The tears fell without control. Ellie laid back on the couch and sobbed. Her mother had been so ill and Ellie cried because she didn't get to say goodbye. Her father, the bastard, had robbed them of so much, and she cried. She cried at the thought of the leg shackles and the handcuffs, the bruises from wearing them for short periods of time; she cried for the fear she faced protecting herself from the true criminal inmates she lived with. She cried for the deep inner sadness at what Tyler did to their finances, to her life. She cried at the memory of walking in and seeing the blood, his lifeless body, the mind-numbing awareness that things had immediately changed. She cried because she missed her life with him. It might not have been perfect, but it was her life for so long.

Ellie fell asleep crying on her new rust colored couch, holding a pillow for dear life and slept until the next morning in a way that she had not slept for what seemed a million years.

Chapter Eleven

Casey pulled up to the apartment complex where he had

the entire top floor, the penthouse. In the elevator, he was

consumed with emotion fragmented and confusing. Could she

have done it? He couldn't stop thinking about her. Shaking his

head, removing it from his brain, he entered his penthouse. The

black marble and crackling fireplace felt good. If he had the

time he would sit in front of the fireplace and listen to music.

The stress of the last couple of weeks could melt away as he

wished, but there was no time. He hopped in the glass shower,

dressed in one of his best suits and headed into the corporate office. He had made up his mind. If they didn't listen to him this time, he was quitting.

The interaction with his boss that day left Casey feeling empty inside. Again, he had fallen for the reconstruction speech and his important role in it. Casey couldn't say no. That was the worst part of his personality. When it came to giving his opinion, he was great, until decision time. That's why he didn't date. That's why he worked this no-end job for the last fourteen years, when all he wanted to do was open his own furniture store. He loved to refinish wood, antiques, pieces that breathed of the history of the owner. He loved to work with his hands, but he had gone into business thinking that he needed the skills to run the business before he opened it. Why all these years had he not broken away and done it? He lay in bed, staring at the cold gray ceiling and wondered.

Half the night, Casey lay in bed, wondering how he could make the move. The money was no object. His parents had been killed with strong financial situation. According to everyone that money was his to be spent as he wished, but he had never touched it. They had a million-dollar policy each and the accidental death clause doubled it. With interest, which he never paid attention to until it was time to sign taxes and give away hundreds of thousands of dollars at the end of tax season; the total was well over four million dollars. He couldn't face the guilt of spending the amount his parents were worth when they died.

There had been a time when he dreamed of meeting a woman and loving her like his Pap's loved his mother. But that was long gone. Casey knew that the feeling of getting close to someone was worth walking away from. He couldn't bare the pain, a weakness he paid attention to.

With the urge to quit, to walk in and quit the next day, so concrete, Casey made the plan to open Waters Furniture Restoration.

Settled in to starting anew, Casey fell asleep with the vivid impression of Ellie's lips on his own. He slept peacefully and woke the next morning, dressed in jeans and a Polo oxford and went to the office.

This time Casey didn't have to wait for his boss to get in the office—he was going to catch him before a game of golf and his normal arrival time of eleven o'clock. Casey was in at six and waited in the foyer for a mere thirty minutes before Ralph Peters entered. Without the need to go to Ralph's office, Casey let it fly. "Ralph … I got to thinking after talking to you yesterday."

"And?" Ralph hit the elevator button and turned to Casey, as he always did, suspecting that Casey was a huge imposition to his important day.

"And, I quit … No notice, no severance, no complaint, no ties. I quit." Casey handed him the keys to the office and walked out the door as Peter's yelled after him, "You'll never work in this town again, Waters! I promise you that."

Casey whispered, "Thank God!"

Ellie felt greatly rested as she stretched out and looked at what she had just accomplished. She looked forward to this day, something she had not done for years. If the cast had not been there, she was sure she would have a definite spring to her step. However, she had to hobble to the bathroom and figure out how to bathe.

Figuring it out, all clean and dressed again, Ellie set out on another quest. She was applying for jobs today. It started with the phone. She called first on the toll booth position and got the information to apply. She dreaded the thought of a winter in the mountain, baring the cold in that little heated booth. Shivering at the thought, she pleaded with the heavens to open the job as the chef. She might not be qualified with education, but she knew she could do this job. Cooking had been her solstice and she was an amazing cook. Her plan was in motion.

Ellie called the number listed in the ad and waited. Three rings later she heard, "Good morning, thank you for calling the Davidson residence. How may I help you?" The soft voice very professional.

"Yes. This is Elaine Justice and I would like information regarding the chef's position, if it's still available?" Ellie hoped and prayed.

"Of course. Let me get Mrs. Davidson for you. One moment please." There was silence for only a moment before a woman came to the phone.

"This is Stacy Davidson. May I help you?" This voice was short and curt. The friendliness of the first woman gave way to cold, abrupt professionalism.

Ellie was startled a bit at it, stumbled over the first words, "I, uh … Mrs. Davidson, I would like to speak to you about the chef's position you have available." Ellie choked it out.

"Oh, great. I have to get someone hired. The applications so far are nothing like what we are looking for." She continued as Ellie thought.

This woman sounded just like Ann MacMurphy in Duluth. Crass, rude, only cared about the society and what they could show the world, when the alcoholic, cheating husband who hit on everyone, Ellie included, was no match for the pill-popping, smart mouthed, bad gossip Ann MacMurphy. Ellie moved into societal mode. She truly knew how to handle this bitch and she needed that job.

"Stacy … I assure you I understand what you need and what you are looking for. I am instinctive on the event you have me preparing for. For example, I understand a fundraiser must be above and beyond for the mere fact that to get people's money, you must kiss their asses, drag that money out of their wallets and stroke their ego while you do it." Ellie continued, knowing nothing, feeling everything. She had nothing to lose and everything to gain. "Stacy, I can make you look so good. The smell coming from your home, the nutritional content for whatever diet you are on at the moment. I'll do your shopping if you like, prepare every meal and snacks. I will take care of you like I take care of me …"

Stacy interrupted, "What time can I meet with you?"

She did it! She stroked the right ego. Ellie almost barked, "Now is fine!"

"I can do that. Come to 1444 Stratford Road. Come in the back entrance and tell Auddie you are here. She's the housekeeping manager. I have had to have her cook and she's just horrible. She's in the kitchen; you'll see the door from the back drive. Thirty minutes?" Stacy was done.

"Yes, Ma'am." Ellie hung up and dialed Moses' cell phone and booked a ride immediately. Thankfully he was not busy and was on his way.

When Ellie opened the door, she saw the snow had fallen and there was a good eight inches on the ground. Christmas Eve and here she was with a white Christmas. Memories flooded of her mother and her shared Christmases, with Daddy in his PJs and her and her mother in their Christmas dresses. The morning of Christmas with the gift exchange and the little nativity scene that her mother held in such high regard. Tyler had stomped it into oblivion on their second Christmas when Ellie wanted to go to her parents instead of his as he told her they were going to do. She shook it off and made her way through the snow until Moses pulled up.

Moses saw Ellie struggling with the crutches, her leg held high to protect the cast. Jumping from the car, his sixty years forgotten, he scooped her up and carried her to the car, crutches in tow. "What choo doin' Miss Ellie?"

"A girl's gotta do what a girl's gotta do. I have a job interview. Can you get me there in the next ten minutes?"

"Where's it at, Girl?"

She told him the address and he seemed to think it possible.

Casey put his coat on the chair next to him at the Small Business Association and sat down in front of Jacob Laster.

His call had gotten the appointment to prepare his business plan.

"Good morning." Casey chimed.

"Good morning, Mr. Waters. I'm glad you could come down. I've prepared a few series of paperwork that will need to be filed. We must get a Federal ID number and register the business. However, you have several choices of how to do that. The first is a corporation, you may do a partnership if there is anyone else involved, or as a sole proprietorship."

"It's all mine, sole proprietorship. Definitely." Casey talked to Jacob for almost two hours and at the end of that time, he had a plan.

Back at the penthouse, Casey worked diligently on his business plan. He did the financials, the executive summary; he planned the marketing for not only selling the finished pieces, but acquiring the pieces to be refurbished. He was feeling human again … but in the back of his mind sat Ellie.

Arriving at Stacy Davidson's house was a real ride. The snow was still falling lightly, but the paved roads were only cleared in spots. Moses nearly gave her a heart attack more than once sliding on the icy surface. Being from Minnesota, she would have been more apt on her own, but she white-knuckled the seat and hunkered down until they were safely on the Davidson's back drive.

Slipping twice, but making it to the door while Moses protests went unheard, Ellie got to the door and knocked.

Auddie, a small woman, maybe thirty, answered the door. Her hair had fallen from the ponytail and she looked frazzled. "Elaine?"

Ellie nodded and Auddie escorted her in. "You have a broken leg? She will not hire you. This kitchen is huge and ... "

Ellie was almost devastated, but instead, she said,

"Look. I need this job. How can I assure you I can do it?"

Auddie looked at her, up and down. "… Well, how are you going to cook with those crutches? It's Christmas Eve and the guests will be here in ten hours! I NEED her to hire you." Her eyes lit up. "I will help you, but if you mess this up and make me miss Christmas again … my kid will hate me."

Ellie immediately liked this girl. "I can do it. I promise."

She whisked Ellie to the kitchen table and hid her crutches in the pantry. "Don't you get up from this table. She won't pay attention and we will make this happen …" as an afterthought, "You can cook, right?" Ellie smiled as she nodded.

"Good, let me get the little … um, Mrs. Davidson. Turn it on, okay?" She hustled from the room, straightening herself in the oven door glass.

Ellie waited ten minutes for them to return. The house had been huge. As they pulled into the gated drive, snow piled on the sides from fresh plowing: she saw the enormity of the home. It was laid out very similar to her own. She wished she would have had time to research the house itself. At this point, she needed to work her way into this job, and whatever it took, she was willing to do it.

Stacy Davidson entered the kitchen wearing a cream-colored sweater, Dolce & Gabana, a black pencil skirt with heels and was jeweled just like the women Ellie hated in Duluth. They had to show their wealth at and from every angle. This woman was not a problem. Ellie had been dealing with the likes of her for years.

"Thank you for having me." Ellie held out her hand as Stacy sat down.

Shaking it professionally, Stacy and her fake boobs sat down with a legal pad and pen. "Let's get started. You are free to cook today if I hire you, right?" Stacy stared her down, sizing her up.

Ellie answered, "Yes, Mrs. Davidson. I am at your disposal."

Stacy started the interview process. "How long have you been preparing meals for others?"

Ellie answered truthfully, "Eleven years. I worked for Hannah Justice, Senator Justice's daughter, in Minnesota when she became ill. I prepared for her and her husband privately and even catered her events socially. I have prepared for as many as a thousand at a time. Some more intimate, some socially acceptable, some just to show off Mrs. Justice's historic home. It was much like yours. Lovely home … built around 1930?"

Stacy stopped writing and looked up. "1928 actually. How did you know?"

"The architecture is like the time in society. It's lovely. The kitchen is perfect to prepare in. Is that a salamander?" Ellie referred to the warming bin above the professional stove and grill.

"I don't know ... I can't cook." She almost winced.

Ellie saw the weakness. She reached for Stacy's hand across the table. "I'm here. I can do this for you. Are you stressing over tonight? Auddie said you have guests coming."

"I do. Thirty guests in ten hours and I don't have a menu, no groceries, nothing." Stacy melted. The professional exterior was gone and she was failing miserably.

Ellie played to it. "What do you need to see of my skill?"

Stacy pulled her hand from Ellie's gently, looked again at the questions she had written. "Where did you go to school?"

The one question Ellie had no answer for was on the table. As Ellie prepared to lie to her, the phone rang.

Stacy pulled her cellphone from her lap and answered. Within seconds she put her hand over the receiver and said, "You're hired. Work with Auddie. I am going to have to put my life in your hands. Auddie knows the details ... we pay $3500 a month and expect you here from ten in the morning until we are done with dinner ... weekends are on call and you will be paid additionally. Yes?" She waited for Ellie.

"Yes. Deal!" Ellie wanted to scream in excitement.

Stacy walked from the room and Auddie entered.

"What did you do to tame the beast? I haven't seen her in this good a mood since ... well, ever. I like you. Ready?" Auddie went to the pantry and got Ellie's crutches and an apron. "No time to go change until we buy groceries. I don't have the uniform in your size. The last cook was huge. You'll have to wear your own clothing. I'm sure she won't notice; she's a bundle of nerves. Things aren't going well." She hustled about the room while Ellie tried to catch up and get to the other side of the huge island separating them.

"Oh, no!" Ellie had forgotten about Moses waiting out in the cold.

"What?" Auddie stopped in her tracks.

"My cab is outside. I need to go pay him and send him on his way." Ellie started hobbling that way, pulling a fifty from her pocket.

Auddie snatched it up and headed out the back door with no coat, only to slip back in a few minutes later. She handed Ellie some change. "I gave him a ten-dollar tip, okay?"

Ellie nodded and followed her to the island where a list of things was scribbled.

Together they planned the meal, made a grocery list which Auddie was more than happy to collect and get out of the kitchen. It turned out she had never really cooked a day in her life and she was ordering things, picking them up and re-plating them when Stacy decided to place her in the chef's position. When she found containers a week ago, she almost fired Auddie. Some smooth talking got her out of it and after Christmas she would get to go back to her old job of managing the cleaning staff of the household. Auddie told her that she had come from a classy hotel and had run the staff. The hours were bad and she couldn't manage with her three kids and husband at home and so she took this job thinking it was better hours, but Stacy was extremely demanding.

Ellie's heart sunk. Auddie was unable to spend Christmas Eve with her kids because Stacy required her to be at work. Several times Auddie would leave the kitchen during the list-making session to make sure that the cleaning staff was sufficiently doing their job. Ellie had an instant rapport with Auddie. It was fun preparing the list and each time Auddie left, Ellie familiarized herself with the kitchen, got utensils she needed and tried to put everything in one location by hopping to and from collecting. It was exhausting, but she had a job!

* * *

The phone rang in Casey's apartment and he ignored it. Busy working on his business plan, he ignored it a second time before his cell phone rang. Seeing it was his sister, he answered. "Hey, Stase."

"Hey, Case. Where are you? We're waiting." She was to the point of anger. He did this every year.

"Stacy, I'm sorry. I forgot. Is it Christmas Eve already?" He really didn't think about the family and all the glory of the holiday he hated so much. Glancing at his phone and realizing what time it was, he had to get going.

"I was hoping you were on your way when you

didn't answer your home phone, but you are home, aren't you?" Stacy was ready to stomp her feet and throw a huge southern bitch fit. "Casey ..."

"I can be there in an hour and a half. Promise. Let me jump in the shower and I'll be there. Promise ... you know you love me, Sis." He smiled at the thought of his sister ranting and raging about his untimeliness. "Promise. I won't miss anything. Tell the kids I'm coming." He hung up and headed for the shower.

Stacy hung the phone up as she entered the kitchen to check and see if things were progressing. It was nearly four o'clock and the girls had been working all day. The meal was planned, as well as Christmas dinner the following day. She actually liked Ellie, who had completely taken control. The smells that emitted from the kitchen were soothing and credible. Stacy's stomach growled as she entered.

"How's it going?" She swiped a finger full of pate

and tasted it. "Oh, my … this is delicious. It's not liver?"

Ellie pushed her hair behind her ear, long and smooth, she had placed it in a ponytail to cook. "I used a four-cheese recipe that I used to prepare. It's much easier and it's good, yes?"

"Yes. What are these?" Stacy began to sample the items that were being prepared to be plated.

"Here, let me go through them all. I'm plating two plates of each. Thirty guests and a bartender, with the sweets, we should have enough for everyone. This is Tapenade cracker bites, very easy to nibble and all prepared foods so I just had to assemble them. Salmon Tarts," She handed one to Stacy.

"Yummy … and I don't like fish." Stacy was thoroughly impressed.

Ellie continued, "Szechwan cold garlic shrimp. Beef Satay with a peanut dipping sauce. Bruschetta and for sweets, forgotten cookies and Mocha shortbread." She stood back waiting for Stacy to sample each.

"Ellie … where have you been all of my life?" She reached into her pocket for her phone and looked to Auddie. "The house is done. Who is serving the party? You two and who else? Who is bartending?"

Auddie's face registered the shock. Before she spoke she looked at Ellie for help. "I, uh …"

Ellie rescued her. "Auddie is serving and I am bartending. We only need one server, no sense in having anyone else miss time with their family and I'll be serving alone tomorrow." Ellie had been walking a bit on her leg and bartending would be only one place. She didn't have to go anywhere. Who couldn't pour a glass of wine or make a scotch on the rocks? At this point, Stacy was unaware that she was in a cast. Every time she had been in the kitchen Ellie had been behind the island working.

With a frown, "Are you sure that is enough? I can grab Rachel. She's still here."

"Oh, it's plenty. You will be surprised at what we can do." Ellie was proud of her work that day.

"If you say so. Ellie, thank you." Stacy was truly grateful.

"It's all because of Auddie. I couldn't have done it without her."

Stacy blew that off and left the room.

"Whew ..." Ellie sighed each time she left. "She's going to see sooner or later ..."

Auddie laughed. "No, she only sees what she wants. Just think of what will happen when she sees how limited you are and how beautifully you performed any way. You will be stuck here forever, she will never let you go."

They both laughed. Ellie was starting to feel the

pain of being on the foot all day and had not had a pain pill at all. She was half tempted to go cut the cast off that night and buy a walking boot so Stacy wouldn't know. If she got away with it without losing her job, she just might do that despite the pesky breaks.

* * *

Casey pulled into Stacy's house at half-past six. The party goers were just beginning to arrive and he knew how much she hated it when he was late. It was hard for her to be kind to him when the first thing he would do was go get his two nieces from their room and play for hours, missing most of the fun. She required him to come to parties well before so that he could play and still adequately attend.

His black suit, impeccable, in place, he headed up the drive. The snow had finally stopped and was beautifully gracing the stoop of the home he grew up in. It always came with a sharp pang, the entry into the house. When Stacy had married, he wanted her to have it and had signed it over to her. She was younger, but he knew that her goal in life had always been to be Mrs. Pascal Davidson, MD's wife. And now she was.

Pascal greeted him at the door with a warm hug, inviting him to the bar for a drink. "Hey, buddy. Glad you could make it. She went to great lengths to let me know I am to yank you right into the party. No playing with the kids until tomorrow morning. Your punishment." Dark hair perfectly in place and deep brown eyes as kind as his words, Pascal was good-hearted and kidded Casey. They walked from the foyer to the formal living room where other guests gathered.

Ellie stood behind the bar, pouring mostly wine and gathering compliments. She had bathed in the guest shower behind the kitchen where Auddie loaned her a uniform and she had gotten a few minutes to rest her aching leg. If it wouldn't have been for fun she was having this would have been an exhausting day. But, given seven months in jail and the horror, she was just fine. A smile lit her face, her eyes following closely behind. She felt like the perspective of the party, from behind the bar, was the best place for her to be. She was comfortable and was enjoying the company of the guests as if she were invited. And then she saw him ...

Pascal escorted Casey to the bar, unbeknownst the confusion.

Ellie wanted to run, to scream, tears stung her eyes. There was nothing to do but pretend she didn't see him. But he headed directly toward her.

Casey saw her and stopped walking. Pascal continued to talk of the girl's Christmas performance he had missed due to the conference, but Casey stood still.

Ellie went for the truth. She tried to beg him with her eyes to not rat her out. How the hell did he get to this party? Why here of all the places in the world he could be on Christmas Eve? She begged as he finally walked forward the last few steps.

"A gin and tonic, Mr. Davidson?" She asked Pascal. Meeting him only from behind the bar, Auddie had filled her in on the beauty of this man and how he handled the terroristic wife. Stacy nearly abused this man, but he doted only on his daughter's and made his wife's life complete. They were likable to Ellie, who didn't mind the hours. Auddie confessed that the only thing she hated was that Stacy paid so much more than anywhere else, but she required dedication. That dedication cost Auddie time with her kids.

"And, Mr. Waters?" Ellie addressed Casey.

"I'll have Evian with a lime, please." He watched her move around and wouldn't have known about the leg had he not seen it himself. She moved gracefully and poured his drink, sliding it across the counter with a smile.

"There you are, Sir."

"Thank you ..." Pascal was already introducing him

to a couple attending that he did not know.

Ellie watched Casey as she continued to pour drinks and watch the guests devour her tasty treats. The party was hugely successful. She watched Stacy. What she did not see was someone who put on airs for society. She was exactly the same neurotic woman she had been around them. It was exhilarating to see her nearly serving her guests and talking about how Ellie was a Godsend. Many of the guests commented to her as she served their drinks that they would be interested in hiring her as well as if she owned a catering service.

As she poured the last drop of whiskey from the bottle, she began to search for another. The plan was to have stocked what she needed under the bar, but this particular bottle had gone so quickly. This gentleman was slinging them down and this bottle emptied, only pouring a partial glass. "Sir, I'm out and going to have to go find another bottle. Or, can I get you another drink?" She was hopeful.

He was starting to slur his words, more than five drinks now had been poured for him. "I can wait …"

Great! Now what? She tried to catch Auddie's attention, but instead, Casey saw her and thought it was him she was beckoning to. He headed that way.

"Hey …" Casey was at least willing to play nice.

"I'm sorry, I was trying to get Auddie's attention. She was standing behind you." Ellie was beginning to panic.

"Where's my drink?" the man slurred at her.

Casey looked at him, wondering what was going on.

It was her job or her pride, so she asked, "I need another bottle of whiskey, but … well, you know my immobility problem." She whispered.

"Oh … uh, okay. Is this what you need?" He grabbed the empty bottle.

She shook her head.

"It's your lucky day. I know just where it is. I'll grab it." He was gone in a second.

"I'll be right with you, sir." Another gent came to her bar and she refreshed his gin and tonic to his delight. He thanked her and was on his way when Pascal headed her direction.

"Sir, may I pour you another?" She smiled.

"I'm good. One is my limit." He looked around. "Did you see Casey? Mr. Waters?"

"I think he ..." Ellie was trying to cover when Casey rounded the corner with not one, but two bottles of the whiskey.

"Here ya go." He slid them on the counter. "Pascal, did you see where Stacy got off to?" Casey steered Pascal away from the bar and on to find his wife.

"What just happened?" Auddie was standing next to Ellie. "Did he fetch for you?"

"He did."

"How do you know Casey Waters?" Auddie was very perceptive.

"I don't ... really."

Auddie was not satisfied. She laid her tray of food on the bar, hands on hips, "I think you owe me an explanation, considering I hold your job in my petite little hands." She smiled.

"Oh, it's such a long story. Who is he?"

"You don't know who he is?" Auddie was completely flabbergasted. "That's your bosses' brother."

"What?" Ellie felt the flush of panic. Her heartrate increased, her breathing became erratic and she felt her fingers stiffening in an instant. "Oh, God ... Auddie."

Within seconds, Casey, from across the way, watching Ellie, saw her go into the panic and recognized it from the previous fainting spell and was on his way to aide her.

"Scoot over, Auddie ..." Casey gently moved Auddie so he could get around the bar. "Put your arm around my shoulder and let's get you to the kitchen. To Auddie he said, "Just cover for her."

He whisked Ellie to the kitchen and once inside sat her down and grabbed a loaf of bread. Dumping the bread onto the counter, he blew in the bag one time, rounding his hands so that she could use it to regain her breathing. "Breathe in and out into the bag."

She did as she was told and began to feel immediately better.

Casey whisked the bag away from her face after four breaths. "Too much will take you the opposite way. You okay?"

"I am. Thank you."

"What's up with the panicking? You are quick to roll that way." He was aware of what a panic attack was like. He had them as a child after his parents died and luckily his friend's mom knew what to do. She had taught him about a paper bag, but that a plastic bag was just as good, if you didn't use it too long.

"I … well ..." Ellie stuttered.

"I read the paper. I know what happened. Had to be hard as hell being in that situation."

She nodded. "I have to get back to work. I don't want to get fired. I really need this job. Our little secret?" She prayed her would cover her and not blow it all by telling his sister.

Stacy walked into the kitchen. "There you are. Pascal said he saw you head this way. What's going on?"

Ellie tried to jump up, but Casey pushed her back down. "Nothing, Sis. She needed a little break. You know you have to give fifteen minute breaks every four hours, right? I told you that before. Stacy …" He scolded. "I told you that. People can only go so long without taking the air out. You push too hard. Here ..." He grabbed a plate ready to serve and handed it to her. "Be a good hostess and serve your guests. I'll get her back out there just as soon as the cramp in her leg stops. I just brought her here to get a better look at things and make sure she could slave away for you the rest of the night." He smiled and it worked. "Now get … go." He shoved her in the direction of the door.

"Are you okay?" Stacy asked Ellie.

"I'm fine, Ma'am. Ready to get back to it. It's going quite well. Everyone looks very pleased."

Stacy smiled, "It is a success. And, thanks only to you."

"And Auddie ..." Ellie chirped.

"Yes. And Auddie. There will be a nice bonus in each of your checks. Thank you." She headed out the door with a smile on her face.

"There you are." Casey said. "How are you doing this with that leg? Good pills?" He raised his brows.

"I haven't had a pain pill all day long." She fired at him.

"Whoa. I was just playing. Don't bite the hand that broke you." He tried again to be funny, but Ellie was a hard sell. "Okay ... I'll leave you alone. You better? Can I help at all?"

"I think you have helped enough ... really."

"Are you ever going to let me apologize?"

She waited, but he didn't say a word. "Can you help me back behind the bar? I can't hardly move at this point and my crutches are out there."

"How have you done it all day? She doesn't know, does she?" Casey half-whispered in her ear as he grabbed her arm and gracefully pulled her up and placed it around his shoulder.

"I hopped."

He instantly had a great deal of respect for this woman he did not know, but that she felt so close to him that it was painful. "I have an idea. How about I drive you and Auddie home and let Stacy handle it the rest of the way? It's almost over and you'll be safe that way. She got you cooking dinner tomorrow too?"

She nodded. The thought of being home sounded so good. It was Christmas Eve. "I have to be back by eight o'clock."

"You should just stay the night here. I'll work it out."

Ellie had no intention of spending the night in her bosses' house, no matter how beautiful it was. No matter how attracted she was to Mr. Casey Waters, the brother of her new boss and absolutely off limits in so many ways. "No. I have a home and I'm going home no matter what time."

"Okay ... I just thought it easier that way. Its cold out and a holiday. I thought you might be spending it alone."

She eyed him. "Don't do me any more favors. Please." At the kitchen door, he stopped.

"We both know where that gets you." He popped the swinging door open to the crowd of people at the party and she hopped the two steps behind the bar and began taking orders from the guests standing in wait.

Casey watched her for the better part of two minutes before Stacy approached him. "I don't want to know, do I?"

"Stase ... I'm not sure what to think of her, but she's not swayed to my charm. Might be a good sign."

"Really?" Stacy found that quite unreal. Her whole life she watched people fall at his feet, both men and women. Especially women fell for him and fell hard. "What, those boyish good looks, intellect and wit got you nowhere with her?"

"As is best. I'll tell you about it later. Looks like you have a diamond in the rough. Look at her deal with these people."

"Some of your favorites. I see her charm and her beauty are quite secondary to that personality."

"It's more than her experience. She's just bred well. She's a keeper. Glad you like her."

Stacy caught it immediately. "I see. I'll enjoy this

story, won't I?"

"Oh, yeah ..."

Chapter Twelve

From the dark hallway to Jules' bedroom, Casey crept. Opening the mahogany door, so as not to creak or wake his sleeping niece, he entered the room and sat in the chair of her small desk to watch her sleep peacefully.

After about five minutes, she felt his presence and stirred. "Unca-Casey! You're here ..."

He slipped to the bed, covering her more and nestling her in deeper. "Yes, Julsie. I'm here. You knew I would be. I'd never miss a Christmas with my girls. Let me go get Angie and I'll be back ..."

"I knew you would make it." She smiled brilliantly.

Casey opened the adjoining door to Angie's room and woke her gently. "Angie-baby ... my Angie-baby. Wakie, wakie ... its Unca-Casey."

She opened her big green eyes and focused on him. Throwing her arms around his neck, he carried her back and got Jules. "Okay ... here we go."

He carried them, sneaking purposefully through the hallway's wooden cage to a door that led upstairs. Climbing the stairs, the girls completely silent, they reached their destination. The attic was clean and cozy, a space led directly to a huge round window that graced the front of the mansion. He set them down, pulling up a chair and they climbed on his lap and they all three began to watch ... to watch for Santa. The roof present below the window.

Within about fifteen minutes both girls were sweetly sleeping in his arms and he text from his phone and waited.

Pascal awaited the text, having sent the guests home an hour earlier. Cookies bitten off, milk gone … When he got the text, he went through the house to a window that led out to the roof and he lifted a sled out the open window into the cold night air. He laid it gently on the roof, in the snow, and gave it a good shove. From beside the window he grabbed a rope with bells attached and started ringing them. "HO! HO! HO! MERRY CHRISTMAS!!!"

Casey woke the girls when the sleigh passed the window. "There he goes!!!" He stood up, nearly dumping them to the window. "There he goes. Did you see him? Didn't you just see him? BYE SANTA!!! GOOD TO SEE YOU!" He yelled through the window.

"I saw him. There he was! Look Unca-Casey!!! THERE HE GOES! See Angie. See him???" Jules face was lit up with the Christmas warmth provided by the men in her life. She pointed to the sky. "See him!!!"

"I don't see him ..." Her face slid down.

"Right there, Sweet pea!" Casey pointed.

From the other side of the wall, Pascal gave one last ring, much lighter than the last ... "ho ... ho ... ho ... Merry Christmas." He said without yelling.

"There he is!" Angie pointed in the sky and for one brief moment, Casey thought he might have seen a gigantic sleigh filled with gifts and a jolly man in a red suit fly by as well.

Ellie walked out the back door and around the corner to the parking lot where Moses was waiting for her in the cab. Just before getting in, she barely escaped the imminent danger of a sleigh flying off the roof and landing just in front of Moses' cab. Looking to the sky, she heard, 'Ho. Ho. Ho. Merry Christmas." As they drove away in the cab, Ellie looked back over her shoulder in time to see Casey and two little figures watching out the ornate circle window at the top of the mansion. Secretly she waved to him. There was no doubt that it was he; his bulky mass in silhouette in the window.

She was exhausted and her leg screamed at her. Without a thought, she pulled the pain-killers out of her purse and took one, laid her head back on the seat rest and slept most of the way home, only to be in the same cab with Moses less than six hours later.

The ride to the mansion was much less enjoyable. Having to prepare an entire day's meal for five sounded easy until Stacy had handed her the menu the night before. Not just a turkey and all the trimming, but pies, puddings, salads and special cider. She was not looking forward to it, but she was looking forward to not spending the holiday behind bars and for that she was thankful.

Casey poured his second cup of coffee from the pot and leaned back against the counter as the back door opened and Ellie appeared with her crutches. His heart raced.

"Oh … I'm sorry. I thought I would be alone." She wiped the crutch rubbers off so that she didn't slip on the marble floor.

"Here, let me help you." He saw how she labored. "Tired from your day yesterday?"

"I can't tell you how tired I truly am." Ellie smiled through the pain. Her underarms were bruised from the crutches, her arms ached from holding herself up and her leg throbbed with a sharp pang every occasionally.

"What do you have to do today?" Casey knew Stacy well and knew that the former cook put much more time into her job than even Casey did his own.

"Here's the list." She smiled through her thoughts of impossibility.

"Not a problem. Do you know how to do any of

this?" He helped her to sit down.

"I do, most of it, anyway. Do you?"

"All my life. These are family recipes. Did she tell you where to find them? We have them written down and laminated so that anyone can do it. I'll help if you like?" His sincerity was charming.

"Don't you have a Christmas morning to attend?" Ellie had heard them talking last night and there was a whole slew of things Stacy had planned for Christmas morning, including cinnamon rolls that were due in an hour.

"I do. My nieces are expecting me, but we all like to cook and I think you are going to have to give up and let someone help you. Auddie is off and it's just you in the kitchen. How are you going to possibly get around like you need to?"

"I'll get it done. Please don't get me fired, Casey."

It was the first time she said his name and it rolled off her tongue, much differently with her northern accent. He liked it.

"Fair enough …" He needed to be away from her. The yearning he felt was very uncomfortable. He had no idea how to cook, but if she had needed help he would have given it to her. He wanted to tell Stacy that she should celebrate with them, not work. She'd been through so much and from his reading, she deserved a break. "So be it."

He gracefully bowed out of the kitchen and headed to the den where the Christmas presents he had brought were placed. He wanted to get them under the tree before Jules and Angie got down stairs.

Left to her own accord, Ellie began getting supplies and preparation done for the food. For some reason, she just couldn't hop at all. Her good leg kept cramping up as she moved around, causing her to stop, catch her breath and then try to continue. The cinnamon rolls were due out in ten minutes and she had barely gotten them in the oven.

She tried again to hop to where she needed to be to make the icing, but fell on the floor, cast thudding against the marble as Jules walked into the kitchen. The little girl ran to her aid. "Hey, lady cooker ... are you okay?" She pushed her beautiful little face into Ellie's for clarity. "You okay?" Eye to eye.

Once Jules saw the cast she was mesmerized. "Is that a pink cast?" She touched it gently. "You gotta boo-boo, cooker?"

"I'm Ellie ... what's your name?" Ellie struggled to get up off the floor.

"I'm Jules. Here ..." She helped Ellie get up and then stood there, demanding in a certain way that was cute as could be. "Are you okay? I'm supposed to check and see if you have some rolls in dem ovens." Hands on hips, she made her point.

Ellie laughed. "I just put them in, Miss Jules. Yes, there are rolls in dem ovens."

"I had a pink cast last summer on this arm." Jules held out her arm to show a large scar from what seemed to be surgery. "Yep, horse-riding accidental situa-shun. I think that's why they gave our ponies away, cuz not cuz of Angie's all-agistism. I think."

"How old are you, Jules?" Ellie was in love. Kids were so amazing, but she was so bad with them. She never quite knew how to approach them, but this little minion seemed like-minded and quite astute.

"Free." She puffed up as if to say, 'old enough'.

"I see. Well, can you tell your mother that the rolls will be out in fifteen minutes? I was having a hard time finding things. Auddie got almost everything out for me yesterday and I'm not familiar yet ..."

Jules stood dazed. "HUH?" She then grabbed the

grocery list note pad and pen sitting on the counter. "I'm posed to get it in writing if it's more an I can remember. Okay ..."

Ellie was amazed. "Seriously?"

"Yes. Seriousness, Ellie. Serious. Cuz I don't like getting in trouble when I can't remember." She shoved her arms to full length with pad in one, pen in the other hand and demanded the note.

Ellie wrote it out and handed it to the small girl.

"I will deliver this right now, Ellie. Thank you." She grinned, "And dem rolls smell goooooodest."

"Thank you. I'll bring them right out when they are done."

"If you keep tawking, I'm gonna need a new note."

"Oh, okay ... well, the first one is enough. You better hurry along and deliver it for me."

Out the door the little minion ran, bouncing like a ball.

Ellie went back to work, iced the rolls and had them nearly ready to go and in the time, she did that had also gotten the salads ready to go and made the snack tray. She was on a roll as long as she could sit on the bar stool she had brought over to the island. As well, she found a long pole with a hook on the end made for grabbing things off higher shelves, but she used it to maneuver the kitchen as much as possible, minimum moving around. She sang Christmas songs as she worked.

The last bit of icing on the rolls, Ellie was pleased that Casey came to check on her. "How are you doing?"

She handed him the rolls. "First course, would you like to take them or will I get in trouble?"

"I got it. They smell wonderful. Is that our recipe?"

"It is. Why?" Ellie was curious.

"They didn't usually turn out like this. These are huge and smell so good. I want to climb inside the middle of one and eat my way out. Tell me, Yankee, where did you learn to cook?"

"Another time. Deliver ... scoot. Please" She shooshed him out the door and continued to work.

With the full meal prepared and on the dining room table, Ellie was so exhausted she could barely move. She had used the waiting cart to deliver the dishes, which made it easier for her to get from room to room, putting enough weight on the leg to hobble instead of hop. It's the first time she regretted not working out more in prison. It would have been a good use of time. She had done yoga and kept her meditation, but she could have lifted weights and gotten buff ... but chose not to mess with the bigger girl's toys.

All done, she needed to call the family to dinner. She debated momentarily on how to do it, but Jules and Angie saved the day. They appeared out of nowhere. Two gorgeous little girls, like night and day. Yet, they had the same demeanor as if they were twins. Jules addressed Ellie very politely, "Angie, this is our cooker, Ellie. She's very nice and has a big pink cast." She couldn't stop her excitement. "Wanna show her your cast?"

"Maybe later? Can you tell your parents dinner is served?"

Angie spoke right up. "This is lunch, Ma'am. Dinner is what you serve at six. This is lunch, at noon."

"Oh, right ... could you tell them that lunch is served?"

"Wait," Jules said, "This is Christmas dinner, not Christmas lunch. Right, Ellie?"

"Well, actually, that is correct as well."

Stacy entered just before the diatribe and had to laugh. She broke in, "So, you've met my girls?"

Ellie straightened with lighting quick reflexes. "Yes, Ma'am. Beautiful children."

"Can I see the cool pink cast?" Stacy eyed Ellie.

Ellie's heart sunk ten feet and hit the floor before bouncing back up and beating so she could speak. "Yes, Ma'am ..." She pulled her leg out from behind the cart. She was busted and she knew it. She would be fired on Christmas day, but at least she knew her limits now. No jobs standing on her feet. "I'm sorry I didn't tell you, but ... well, there really wasn't time and you needed the help."

Stacy yelled the opposite way, "Pascal ... Casey." It wasn't a 'come to dinner' call and almost scared Ellie.

Was she going to be kicked from the home? Escorted out the door by the two big men? She was afraid.

They appeared within seconds. Stacy continued, "She cooked all that food yesterday, served the bar last night and prepared Christmas dinner today with THAT!"

She pointed to the cast.

Pascal was the first to speak. "No kidding? Fresh? There's no walking rubber on the bottom? You aren't supposed to be on it at all, are you?"

Ellie nodded.

He just shook his head as he moved to the table and pulled a chair out. Once the chair was out, he helped her move to it and sit. "Stase, please get another place setting." He helped her scoot to the table.

"What?" Ellie didn't understand.

"You'll be eating with us and sharing the day." Stacy said. "I owe you so much. How could you do that? I mean ..." She walked toward the kitchen as she spoke, "I can't even do it with two good legs. We found a gem." It was completely silent until she returned. "Sit down, everyone. Here, Ellie, let's get you situated. This is beautiful. Smells wonderful!"

"Smells so good." Pascal said.

Jules and Angie seated next to Casey, one on each side and Ellie sat across the table with Stacy and Pascal on opposite ends.

Casey winked at her and she knew he had told on her. She smiled at him and the meal began with a prayer.

"Heavenly Father," Pascal said, eyes closed, offering a hand to Ellie and to Jules, next to him, "Holy is your name. Holy is your blessed name. As we bow our head before your throne, majesty and honor to you alone. Majesty and honor to you alone for the gracious life you have given us. We are blessed to be together this beautiful day of your son's birth. As we bow before your throne, please help us to give you all the love and gratitude you deserve. The gifts we have been given are nothing in comparison to your love and devotion. We look for the day when we are joined with the angels to glorify you. Thank you for this food and for Casey being here to share with us and most importantly, Lord, Holy in your name, thank you for bringing our new friend to us to share our wealth. We owe you everything and need nothing. Amen."

"Amen" came in unison from the other diners and the food was passed.

The meal was pleasant and even to Ellie was the best she had ever had. She answered questions when asked, which were only about whether she liked the food or a compliment to the food. The family spoke of holidays of past and it was genuinely pleasant. Stacy was kind and considerate, a loving mother. The children adored her and were so well-mannered for their ages that it was a testament to the parents. Pascal was easy-going and an absolute gentleman. He spoke of his practice and many patients he wished well for the holiday and then there was Casey.

Casey said nothing unless spoken to as well. The girls idly chatted with him about how fun opening gifts was going to be and about their apparent excitement with their gifts from Santa. They had each gotten a Barbie doll from Santa. Hard to believe that was the only thing they had received, but that's all they talked about. Each had gotten a Barbie with the same color hair as they had.

Casey watched Ellie from under his lashes, while she shoved massive amounts of food down his gullet. It was hard to stop. Not usually a big eater, he couldn't get enough. It was really good. From Turkey, to pies, to yams and Yankee salads nothing like his mother's recipes Stacy had inherited, the food was stunning. As stunning as Ellie. He thought it best to get over his little crush on the woman who could have murdered her husband and just gotten away with it.

They both were aware of each other, but really said nothing in relation to anything other than answered questions. Once the meal was done, the family took it to the kitchen and put it away, refusing to let Ellie even help. The girls escorted her to the living room, a massive room of rich wood and beautifully mastered tapestry. She felt so at home. She hobbled on the crutches to a deep chair that swallowed her in its leather haven. She sunk in and felt she should never leave this moment.

Jules and Angie walked around the gigantic tree with only a few gifts under it and admired ornaments, taking them off the tree and bringing them to her.

Jules brought the first, "This is my first Chrissmuss ornament. You like it?"

"I do, but won't you get in trouble for touching things on the tree?"

They both looked at her like she was crazy and shook their heads. Angie brought her one of a tiny angel nestled between two lovers. "They called me Angela because I was the angel that they were given as a gift from God." She put the ornament back and they each grabbed another.

Jules said, "This is a duck. I like ducks and its mine

cuz it's a duck." She held it out for Ellie to hold.

Apprehensive that they were all going to get in trouble, Ellie could barely touch it and yet she wanted to see them and couldn't really get to the tree. "That's very pretty."

Angie handed her a ball that said Princess. "This is our mommies. We got it for her, because she's Daddies Princess and keeps him in line." They both smiled at the joke.

"Gorgeous." Ellie said. She heard the adults coming back. "You might want to put them back so you don't get in trouble."

They laughed at her. When Stacy and Pascal entered, they ratted her out. "She is afraid you will be mad because we touched the ornaments." Angie said.

Stacy laughed and sat in a matching lounger next to Ellie. "The ornaments are made to admire. We taught the girls how to handle them and they are very careful. We put their favorites where they can reach them and the others we take down for them. I would hate for the tree to fall on one of them."

Angie coughed and Stacy reacted quickly. "Ange … is it time for a treatment?"

The little girl shook her head and Pascal scooped her up and headed up the large staircase just to the other side of the tree to the second floor.

"She's asthmatic and acquired bronchitis, a nasty addition. She's been very sick, thus the quandary with the cook. I didn't have time to interview without leaving her alone and I just didn't want to chance it. She's our baby and I … well, I was afraid."

"It's about priorities." Said Casey as he entered.

"Your family seems to have priorities in the right place. From what I've seen anyway."

"They do, Ellie." He sat down as well. "I saw your confusion as to the gifts the girls got from Santa." He raised his eyebrow over his left eye, a trait Ellie was beginning to find annoying, questioning her.

"No ... I ..."

Stacy helped her out. "It's confusing to many. We don't spend money on this holiday like some do. We celebrate Jesus' birth and the girls are given gifts by Santa, just wee, little gifts, because the bulk of what we do goes to other families. We are extremely blessed and find it unnecessary to show each other in such an overboard fashion. We help others with the funds we might have spent and we share the day together, never to miss one with each other. Right, Case?"

He nodded. "Enough said, where's Pascal at?"

"Breathing treatment. We have waited this long, we can wait another fifteen minutes." Stacy said, turning to

Ellie, "So … care to explain?"

Ellie laughed at her forward question. "Can I say no?"

Stacy was all about it. "Sure, but you and I are going to talk. Soon."

Casey and Ellie both laughed.

Casey saved her, "I'll get the gifts sorted out. Julsie … want to help me?"

The little blonde bombshell jumped up and down. "I already did it, Unca-Casey. See, I put them all together and the names all match."

"Whose is whose?" He asked her to get a dumbfounded look in return.

"I can't read, silly. I just know that what looks the same goes to the same person and you can read. So, I didn't bother by it." Hands on hips, she dared him to oppose her solution.

"Well, all right." Stacy said as Pascal and Angie bounded back down the stairs. "Jules and Casey have the packages sorted out. Girls, you hand them out for us."

They sat back while Casey instructed them who to hand packages to. Each person had one gift from each one in the room, including Ellie, which confused her even more. Casey just looked at her, "Go with it."

"The family tradition," Stacy said, "is youngest to wisest. "Jules is first, then Angie and then … How old are you, Ellie? 25-26?"

Ellie laughed, "36, but thank you."

"Oh, so I'm next and then Pascal, who is 35 and then … when is your birthday?" Stacy was having fun with` it.

"I'm in May."

Stacy said, "So is Case ... what day?"

Ellie answered, "The 24th."

Casey replied, "No way. Me too. Seriously?"

Ellie shook her head. "What time?"

Casey said, "9:29"

"Okay, this is scary. I'm 9:29 too, but in the A.M."
Ellie tilted her head waiting for the answer.

"That's what my birth certificate says too. 9:29
AM."

Pascal laughed, "What are the odds?" and then he
tried to figure it out. "272 million people in just the U.S."

"Oh, God ... not today, Pascal. Please." Stacy
whined.

Everyone was laughing as Casey pulled a quarter
out of his pocket and flipped it in the air. "Heads or tails?"

"Heads always." Ellie said.

The coin landed and the girls rushed over to look. "Heads it is!" Angie said. You go first Aunt Ellie ..."

Everyone looked at her funny, so she reneged on the name, "I mean, Ellie. Sorry, Ma'am."

"It's okay. Honest mistake," Ellie said.

Stacy moved her packages in front of her and hustled the girls to theirs. "Jules, you get to go first. What would you like to open first?"

"Big-to-little, cuz diamonds only come in small packages," She said and began ripping into packages with a gusto easily found on Christmas day for a three-year-old little girl. Each package had a small piece of furniture. "Oh, I love this one, Unca-Casey. I love this one. I never had a Queen chair ..."

Casey corrected her, "Queen Anne chair, Julsie.

High back, arm and upholstered. Open the next one." He seemed more excited than she did.

The next one was another Queen Anne chair to match and so were the rest. Every single package had the same thing, four of them. "Oh, my … matching ones for the den and the living room. I love it." She ran to him and bear hugged him hard, one chair in each hand. "I love it. They are so pretty. Just like the picture I showed you. Just like it. Queen Sand chairs, just like I showed you. See?" She turned them to Angie who was already tearing into her packages to reveal more furniture.

"Doll House stuff. Look, Mommy. He made me a sleigh bed in four pieces, headboard, footsboard, frame and mattress. Aww, I love it, Unca-Casey." She too hugged him lovingly. Each package had revealed a different piece of the furniture, but Ellie could see that the gifts were labeled 'From Mommy', 'From Daddy', 'From Casey' and 'From' the opposite sister.

Stacy was close enough to her that she filled Ellie in, "He made them doll houses when they were each born and every holiday that is what we do is fill the house with furniture. Hopefully it teaches them patience. They get their home a piece at a time."

"They are beautifully crafted. Where do you get them from?" She turned to Casey.

"I make them ..." He looked to Stacy, "Your turn, Stase. Hurry up, I have to go last again this year. I'm always last!"

Stacy carefully opened her first gift from Jules, a heart on a string. She got a similar heart on a string from Angie and from Pascal a diamond heart on a string. From Casey, she got a daily quote book. "Thank you all so much. They are beautiful. Girls, can you hang your hearts on my tree please?"

They scurried to take the hearts to the tree to place

them as ornaments. Ellie noticed there were several hearts on strings and caught what it meant. "How sweet. Their hearts on a string for the year-round thought of a loving holiday?"

"Something like that." Stacy said. "Pascal, you're turn."

Pascal opened his four gifts, all white socks. He let Ellie in, "the only thing I never have enough of. I can never find socks. Every gift I get is white socks, except my birthday ..."

The girls chimed together, "Black socks!"

"That's right. Black socks for good clothes, not work." Pascal looked to Ellie.

"You're turn."

"I really can't believe you ... well, okay. I know you won't accept an argument." She opened the first package, the size of a shoe box. Inside was a full set of kitchen utensils, stainless steel and very nice from Stacy. The second package was much larger, "pots and pans-Cuisinart. "Very nice. I'm going to love using them. Your kitchen is fabulous."

"Oh, Honey … those are for your new kitchen. I have my own."

Ellie nearly choked on her tongue. "I can't take this."

"You can and you will. New house, new digs … that's what we do here. Every employee got presents from us. You just weren't here when we had our co-worker party last weekend. Keep going, it gets better." Stacy said.

"Better?" Ellie thought how? How could it get better? And then she opened the long slender box with the cast scratcher in it. They all laughed.

"I gave you mine, cuz those things itch!!!" Jules

was bubbling. "I went and asked Mommy to get it for you, cuz I am sure that thing is itchy." She shuddered like she remembered.

Ellie tore it down her cast and quickly scratched an itch she had had for the duration. "Oh, God, that feels so good. It does itch … so bad."

They all cracked up, laughter filled the room as they watched her really go at getting that itch taken care of.

The last gift was from Casey. She was afraid to open it. It was small, about the size of a ring box. She opened it and it was a key. She held it up for the others to see and Jules and Angie giggled incessantly. Everyone giggled after that. "What?" Stacy grabbed the key, "Here, I'll show you, since you can't go to it." She disappeared to reappear rather quickly on a bright blue scooter.

"O … M … G" Ellie laughed. "Seriously?"

Casey said, "Well, I did cause you to fall."

The mortification that registered on Ellie's face was highlighted by the bright red cheeks and the mean eyes she threw at him.

"It's okay. I knew about you before you applied. He called me from the hotel right after. Didn't I tell you Casey is my best friend?" She laughed.

"What?" Ellie was without words.

"I knew who you were, but only by name. I didn't know the full story until I called Casey at home to tell him I was interviewing someone."

Casey interjected, "I do all of her background checks for employment."

"So, you knew?"

"I did. Why do you think Auddie was there to help you out so much? Other than she can't cook a lick. When you called, and said you were interested, I ran your name immediately through Casey and he, although about died, filled me in on what he read in the papers. Now, we still don't know what happened and expect full disclosure, if possible, but yeah, I knew." She grinned.

Ellie rolled her eyes. "I can't believe it."

Casey helped her out. "It was unfair of you … the leg. How were you supposed to cook on your own in a new kitchen and that big a kitchen with a bum leg?" He sighed and continued, "… so I told her I owed you."

"I did have to look you in the eye, though." Stacy was being honest. "I didn't want to worry about it. I have children. The more research I did, the more I knew that this was okay. You're second start?"

"My second start, yes." Her eyes welled with tears. "I just can't … I don't know what to say …"

"Well, how about let's let Casey open his gifts and then we can get the kitchen cleaned up and you and I can talk more?" Stacy liked Ellie a lot.

"Okay … yes."

Casey busted through his gifts like he was the three-year-old. The girls each gave him salt water taffy, Stacy gave him a wool scarf and gloves and Pascal gave him a set of tools for woodworking. Casey looked up at him … "How did you know?"

"I have a little friend at the bank. Congratulations, fellow business owner." Stacy beamed at him. "You'll do great."

"Thank you, Pascal. Stacy, girls … I love you so much. Thank you. I love it all. I'm so blessed."

He even smiled at Ellie, "thanks for sharing this day with us. I hope it wasn't too far removed from your normal."

Chapter Fourteen

Stacy and Ellie cleaned up the kitchen, discussed everything from their childhood and honestly became steadfast friends instantly. They had so much in common. The only downfall was that at the end of the day, Ellie was still her employee, even if she didn't feel like it. The weeks to follow were filled with daily meals, working with Stacy and the girls, whom Ellie had grown to truly adore, and making sure kitchen things ran smoothly. The night had ended with a hug to each of them and Ellie departing for the night. She spent Christmas night alone, crying herself to sleep with sheer joy.

Casey had not been back to the house at all. Ellie heard snip-it's of what he might be doing trying to start his new business, but Stacy was rather hush-hush about it all. Ellie looked forward to every day she went to work, but this was the first she had had time off. An entire weekend she would enjoy on her own. Her leg seemed to be healing and on Stacy's advice, Valentine's Day, she went to see Pascal at his office, a general practitioner; he replaced her cast with a walking cast and she could get around much better. The scooter still came in handy around the kitchen so that she was more able to handle the bulk of the hours. She would arrive at the Davidson home at seven and leave around seven that night. Sundays were different, the family did fend for self on that day, so there was always a day off to recover. Even though she loved working for Stacy and the girls, she cherished her time off.

Lounging in her long pajama pants and big sweatshirt with a hood, the house held such comfort. Laying on the couch, she glanced around. The wainscoting was not as noticeable now as she had chosen pieces of art, frugal in cost, but much to her liking. A local artist that reminded her of Matisse graced the largest area above her fireplace, giving the mantel an extra added depth. The colors were deep and rich against the lighter wall. She watched the painting as she wondered what the sunset dropping amid the forest greens, amber and golds brought for the artist or if they created the place from memory rather than sitting watching from afar. She loved to dream of the day she would be able to venture out into the world and see the beauty rather than head toward ambitious goals. For that moment, she held herself in the painting, walking through that forest. In her mind's eye, she saw deer that didn't shy away, a giant moose with antlers the size of the mantle peeking up at her from a drink of water. She walked through to the densest part of the forest, free from fear, free from inhibitions and just listened to her heart.

Reaching inside, she realized that she was lonely. Life had been adequate not having deep or meaningful relationships, but it was sad now. She missed her mother, who would have loved this jaunt in the forest. She missed her father's hearty laughter ringing throughout, forgetting his vivid yelling and anger at life. She missed college and the nights of fun and frivolity. Ellie realized that she could stand to be close to someone, that she could live with love again and that at this very moment, she sat in the best place she had ever been. The living room of a modest two-bedroom home in Ashville, NC ... nothing fancy, nothing luxurious, nothing like what she was used to and it was grand.

Ellie kicked back and wandered to the day she met Sarah. What was Sarah really like? They had talked on the phone enough and she knew how Sarah thought, but what was she like in the morning? What was she like when she was sad? Did she cry as Ellie did on occasion? Did Sarah have young children in her family? Ellie wondered what life was like when Sarah grew up. Drifting off to Stacy and the girls, Ellie realized they were the only family she had. It was a part of her every day, the girls running to her to do their hair, Stacy asking advice on all sorts of things. The ease with which she fit into their lives and yet she had no real role. She was paid to cook ...

The weekend came and went without Ellie leaving the house. She baked a meal and ate off it the entirety. It was not complicated or stressful, but relaxing and easy. Once she thought she would enjoy a date, but had just as easily not felt it necessary to answer the phone that rang three times all weekend. Monday morning coffee was delightful, one of her favorite things as she sat with Stacy talking about the weekend.

Stacy was filled with joy, "He took me to the symphony and then we stopped for a drink. In all the years," her animation was apparent, "he even danced with me." She gazed over her steaming mug, holding it in both hands. "Can you believe that?"

Ellie shook her head as she sipped the liquid into her veins to energize her enough to get to lunch. "Did you enjoy it?"

"I sure did. And the girls, sound asleep when we got home." She looked into her glass. "Ellie …" she hesitated and then thought it best to not bring it up.

After a few moments, Ellie asked, "What, Stacy?"

"Nothing. It's nothing. So, what are we planning for the menu this week? I'm feeling a little fluffy. Can we do some low cal-low fat?"

Ellie took the yellow legal pad and black pen and began writing a menu that suited her needs. When done, she slid it across the table. "Good?"

Stacy read through. "Excellent. I'll have Auddie help you with groceries. She should be done here any minute with getting everyone started ... Do you think you would come to dinner with us, Els?"

Stacy had adopted 'Els' as the nickname she preferred calling Ellie and she liked it.

"I am the cook, Stase. I don't 'come' to dinner with the family."

"I know. But, well, I have honestly thought about firing you ... because I love being friends with you and you won't open up to me." She pouted into her next sip of coffee.

Ellie laughed, but knew that Stacy was serious. She liked

their relationship too and sometimes she really wanted to know what was going on and would have enjoyed hearing about the social season and who was whom and what was what ... but she was the help. "We can still be friends." Her smile lit up the table.

"Are you seeing anyone?" Stacy raised her eyebrows awaiting the answer, sipping as though it were about the menu itself.

"What?"

"You heard me. I said, are you seeing anyone?"

"Good, gracious, no. I barely landed here. I don't know a soul."

Stacy was embarrassed, but she really liked Ellie and she could see the sadness. "Do you have ... other family?"

Ellie wanted to open up to her, even when the question struck the chord of 'don't tell and no one will know' pang in her gut. "I don't. My parents have both passed and I was an only child." She waited to see if it affected Stacy at all and it didn't.

"I want to set you up." She put the mug down and looked Ellie square-on. "I want to know you. I'm so drawn to your silence, being the big chatty Cathy that I am ... but it's more than that. You can trust me. You know that, right?"

"I think I can ... yes." Ellie really wanted to trust someone and Stacy was the best friend a girl could have. All the things she was told by Auddie were true, but underneath the exterior was a quiet, subtle woman of faith and value. "What would you like to know?"

Stacy was ecstatic. She jumped from her chair and left the room as fast as the words slipped out of Ellie's mouth. So, she sat waiting.

Stacy returned, happily bouncing into the room. "It's set. We are going shopping. Just you and I ... Auddie is taking the girls to the park for a picnic being that it is Spring Break and you and I are taking the day off." She slapped her planner closed on the table for effect and clasp her hands in front of her.

Ellie thought about it for only a second. "I'm in. I have wanted to shop but the cast was such a bore and, well, I work too much."

"I agree. Let's shop, grab some lunch at the Basil Beastro and just take a day. Maybe we can stop for a massage. Wouldn't that be heavenly?"

"Oh, I haven't had a good massage in … years. I used to have one twice a week. That does sound amazing."

"Are you okay with walking? Because I'm in for some serious damage." Stacy was up and headed into the other room, expecting Ellie to follow. "C'mon. I have a closet full of things and we are getting dressed to the hilt. I want to boutique shop and I want to feel amazing doing it. Want to raid my closet?"

Ellie's heart leapt. She had been inside Stacy's walk-in closet only once and it was amazing. They seemed close to the same size, even though Stacy was shorter. At the closet adventure,

Stacy chose a cute pair of cotton capris with a glorious colorful blouse. The temperature outside a mere 50 degrees, she felt spring in the air and was tired of the doldrums of the winter weather. She chose sandals with no heel and offered something similar to Ellie. Ellie's outfit was a pair of cotton capris in vivid royal purple and a white tank with purple trim. The white sandals were so comfortable on her one foot, wishing she could use the other. Stacy seemed to read her mind and got on the phone immediately.

"Pascal please ..." She smiled at Ellie. Putting her hand over her phone mouthpiece, "I'm going to ask if it's safe for you to be done with the walking cast. It's been so long ..." Pascal must have answered. "Can Ellie take her foot out of the cast?" She waited. "Okay, thank you, baby. I'll see you late tonight. We are going shopping. Girl's day out." Happy with herself, when she hung up, she was, again, gloriously happy. "He said yes. But ... he said take it with and if you have any problems, put it back on, but you should be healed. You only have about a week and you would have gone the full time. No one ever goes the full time ... right?"

No argument was going to come through Ellie's lips. Ellie

took the cast off and, as she did each night, went into a scratching frenzy. The skin on her leg was ashy and broken, and had a rash in spots from the constraint.

Stacy saw Ellie's leg and winced, "You poor thing. Here, let me get something for that rash and be careful not to scratch too much, breaking the skin can cause infection." She hopped up and entered the master bath, coming back with a huge first aid kit.

"I don't need anything. I keep it very clean." But, before she could argue the point well, Stacy had ointment and applied it very adeptly.

"There you are. Now, no ashy skin peeking out of those cute capris. Let's roll!" She grabbed a bag that matched her outfit and headed out the door.

Ellie followed, able to place full weight on her leg and a new sense of freedom exuding her gait.

* * *

The boutique smelled like lavender in springtime and was brightly lit. The salesclerk handled Stacy and Ellie the moment they entered as if they were royalty. Immediately they were greeted and details were very important.

Hillary spoke the moment the door closed, looking up from placing new garments on the rack in front of her. "Good morning, Mrs. Davidson. How are you today? And, your friend ... lovely to see you in. We have so many new items. This is going to be a fun day!"

Stacy was delighted to show Ellie how fun shopping with her could be. She bounced to Hillary. "Hillary, this is Ellie. We are in need!"

"Say no more ... I'll get your tea." And to Ellie she said, "Would you like coffee, tea or a banana/strawberry smoothie?"

Ellie thought about it a moment. "I'll take a smoothie. That sounds great."

They were seated in a showroom. This was how Ellie had

been used to being treated and her old life didn't feel so far away. The leather couch coddled them as Hillary brought their drinks and they were catered to with scones and bagels.

"Help yourself. The spring collection is amazing. We have incorporated two new designers: Ann Williams and Robert Blanche. I know you are going to love it. Is there a special situation or are we just balancing our new wardrobe for spring?" She stood staunchly awaiting the answer.

Stacy replied, "We are in need of whole new wardrobes."

"Very good." Hillary assessed them both and said, "Mrs. Davidson, still a 4 I see … and Ellie, a 6?" She was proud to view sizes accurately over 95% of the time.

"You are right." Ellie said. Stacy nodded.

"Perfect. Let me get the girls and they will begin ..." She left the room.

Stacy grabbed a scone and her tea and sat back to enjoy the

show. Ellie followed suit with her smoothie.

"This is how it should be ..." Ellie mentioned before she thought about it.

"I knew you lived this life before. You did, didn't you?"

"I did. I grew up wealthy and bred well. My mother would have been impressed with this store. I love it. I almost miss it ..."

"Ellie, you should miss it. You live it once and it never goes away. I can't imagine what it was like to literally walk away from your life." Stacy had read so much about her friend that it made her sad. Spending the last few weeks digging even deeper, she had found that Ellie had really lived quite a decent life and when she got past all the media hype over the murder trial and her former husband's infractions, Ellie's life was impeccable. She saved the best for last ... "I am a Tri-Delt too."

Ellie's entire being lit up. She had loved her sorority sisters and missed that time in her life that it was so easy. She missed the socialization, the parties and the absolute identity of being involved in the sisterhood. "You are?"

"I am. I knew we were sisters from the moment I met you. Do you have any contact?" Stacy sipped the tea, finishing the scone rather quickly.

"No. I left everything. I spent seven months ..." she lowered her voice ...

But before she could speak, Stacy spoke, "I know all about it. Your life is public. I read until my eyes bled at times, trying to find out the secrets you had that you just seem to hold." She was not afraid to lay it on the line and with the surprise she had for Ellie, in the end, it would all be worth it.

"I hate that ..." Ellie was disappointed at the fact that her life was now an open book.

"Don't ... no one around here cares a thing about you or your 'past life' and we are going to take them by storm."

Ellie had no idea what she meant, but at that moment the

show began. Six girls presented the clothing and it was perfection. Ellie could envision herself in every outfit. To her liking and to her taste, every piece was magnificent. So in awe of it all, she barely spoke the entire time, but to say, 'oh, my ...'

Hillary returned when the girls finished four separate outfit showings each for a total of 24 outfits. "So, shall we order?" She handed them each a listing of each piece with a thumbnail picture and the colors available.

Ellie thought about just how much she could afford and decided that two outfits would suffice and the just under $3,000 would be well spent. Each piece was the more formal of the line and she would find something to wear them to. The theatre had caught her eye in a couple of instances and once she had more time with Auddie had discussed possibly going. She marked her choices and then handed it to Hillary. Her colors were rather muted, more of an evening presence and the depth of the clothing would take some new accessories, for which she would save from her rather nice paychecks from Stacy.

Stacy handed her sheet to Hillary as well. "Hill, that was amazing. Thank you for letting me know they had arrived. I'm so pleased." She rose and kissed each of Hillary's cheeks.

"My pleasure, Mrs. Davidson. I'll have these delivered this afternoon." She began to go when Stacy stopped her.

"Hill ..." She turned to Ellie, "What is your address? Did you have it on your sheet?"

Ellie shook her head no. She hadn't thought of delivery. "I won't be there, I'll be at your house."

Stacy spoke to Hillary, "Please deliver everything to her home after seven this evening. Write your address down for her, please."

Ellie did just that and they were out the door, in the black limousine and headed to their next destination.

In the car, Stacy rattled on about the line and how exquisite it truly was and Ellie agreed.

Ellie could not stop commenting, "I'm going to find some place to wear the midnight blue gown. I just absolutely adore it. I will have to get tickets to the theatre ..."

"I'll go with you. Would you like that?"

Ellie was so happy. "I would love it. I just worry about the duality in the relationship. I must be your employee first, Stacy. I can't blur those boundaries ..." Ellie's joy waned momentarily.

"Well," Stacy said, "I really don't want to blur those lines either, so I did something and you are going to argue and then I will win in the end, so let's just say it's already done and if you hate it, we will go our separate ways altogether."

Ellie hated it when Stacy stomped her foot and stood her ground so staunchly. Usually it was about taking breaks and making things impossible for her to work. Sometimes it felt like she was being babied and it did not sit well with Ellie.

"What did you do, Stacy?" Ellie eyed her.

Stacy smiled the biggest smile Ellie had yet seen. "I got you a new job." She turned in the seat to face Ellie. "Don't argue with me."

"You did what?"

"I got you a new job. All that research I did. I had no idea how capable you were and, well, it's a new job and I will not let you out of it."

Ellie started to argue and then her anger got the best of her. "I make my own decisions, Stacy. You can't just get me a new job. I like working for you. I don't want to lose that. The girls, Pascal, you … you are all I have and it's stress-free, easy and I get paid well. I make my own decisions."

Stacy was digging in her bag for the paperwork she had had drawn up by her attorney the week prior. "Here, read this and just decide. I know it sounds like I already did it, but in the blink of an eye, I can rescind and we can continue on as usual, but, Ellie ..." She whined. "I really want you to be as happy about this as I am."

Ellie looked at the legal document for a business partnership. As she read, she realized that this was a business arrangement between the two of them. The business was a party planning company and she was listed as co-owner of Simply Elegant Party Planning, and an equal 50/50 partnership had been established. She looked from the document to Stacy. "I can't."

"Yes, you can."

"But, I can't. I … there is an investment here and I can't …"

"Damn it, Ellie. You are my partner and it's settled. I made arrangement for your part of the initial investment to be taken out of our profit share over the duration of however long it takes to pay it back to the company. It's already done. Please stop … stop and think about what it means. You don't cook for me anymore and you and I can be best friends and I want that. I want to know you … I have never met someone who enthralls me as much as Pascal other than you and I want to share that. The girls are getting old enough to be away from me and I'm bored … so, so bored and I want to play."

"This sounds like work, not play!" Ellie laughed.

"I know. Isn't it fabulous? Think of the parties we can plan and how many social engagements we can make elegant, divine in every way. We have such good taste and work so well together. I want this."

Ellie sat quietly.

"I knew you would love it." Stacy was so proud of her instinct. She had worked night after night for over a month to develop just what it was that she wanted to share with Ellie and how she could help her friend get back into the life that she felt Ellie missed on occasion, even without her saying it. She felt such joy as the pulled up to the next shop, a jewelry store.

"I'm in." Ellie broadcast happily. "I'm in. What the hell." They hugged in the seat of the limo. "Thank you, Stacy. This is going to be so much fun."

"I know … now, I want to get you a gift."

They piled out of the car and into the jewelry store. The diamonds sparkled nearly as much as their eyes as they oooohhhed and awwwed at each of the display cases before the owner came to greet Stacy.

"Mrs. Davidson. How are you today?" Bradley kissed her cheek and extended a hand to Ellie. "And you … how are you today, Ms. Justice?"

"I'm great. Thank you, Sir." Ellie didn't even question that he knew her name. Stacy was on a mission and it was going to be fun to see what she had in store for Ellie.

"I have your pieces … let me get them for you." Bradley excused himself and moved to a counter behind the counter to get the bracelets Stacy had ordered the week before. He came back with two boxes and handed them to each of the ladies. "I hope you like them."

They opened boxes of two bracelets, matching. They each had two charms on them, one Tri-Delta triangle and one document charm. Ellie looked to Stacy.

"Business partners and sisters. The rest we make together ..." She hugged Ellie hard and long. When finished, she pulled her to arm's length. "This is going to be amazing."

Ellie shook her head. She wanted to hug Stacy longer. It felt so good to touch someone in a nurturing manner. Perhaps that is why she loved the girls so much and their endless affection and touch. "I love it."

Bradley helped them both put on the bracelets and the finished their browsing, looking at huge pieces even Stacy couldn't afford. Back to the Limo they went and to find something to eat. Over lunch they talked about the plans for the business and things started to get even more exciting.

"I just want to make sure that we engage every single client in a way as to draw them back in for every event they handle." Stacy finished with a bite of her caramelized onion and tofu sandwich.

"I think that we have opportunities that no one focuses on and that if we focus on them first, not only will be allow private clients to view our abilities, but we take corporations by storm. The corporate world is always looking for event planners for simple gatherings that they can't be bothered with. If we put our special flair on each event, we will pick up private clients. Like … maybe we throw a simple luncheon for meetings, but have a table of our more elegant offerings. It's like a sampling system, but with paying gigs. Ya know?" The ideas were coming a mile a minute and Ellie could hardly contain her enthusiasm. Lunch wasn't even real, but the resonance of her ideas brought a cathartic feeling.

Stacy was just as enthusiastic, "We are really doing it, aren't we?"

"Of course we are … but did you think of replacing me at the house?" Ellie quipped.

"The new girl, Rebecca … she's been your replacement for two weeks. I couldn't bring myself to do it until I was quite sure that you were ready and well, with the cast off and the enthusiasm for our friendship equaling mine, I just decided it was the right time."

"I think we will do well." She held her glass of water up to clink.

Clinking their glasses together, they swore their faith to the partnership. The plans fell into place within an hour and they had a good idea of where they wanted to start their plight to obtain clients. The first was a massive dinner party that night.

Stacy threw out, "Oh, and we have a dinner party tonight. I was hoping you would pick a grand gown and, well, I had the whole line delivered to your house from the boutique."

"You what?"

"I did. I know. I'm bad. But they will all look so cute on you and you did spend some of your own money. So, gifts are gifts and you bought your own work clothes, once again, self-sufficient." She laughed.

"Stacy … you ARE bad … and I like it." She thought of the glorious clothes. "I loved Ann's line. I couldn't have chosen something more my personality if I would have spoken to her myself."

"I love that slack suit, the peach one. It's going to look so good. And, we get to dress casually unless we are attending an event. I don't want to dress up every day. I want the girls to see that beauty comes in so many forms."

Ellie thought about Christmas. "Do you really never buy Christmas presents? I don't get that as giving as you are all the rest of the year."

"My parents were killed on Christmas and, well, Casey and I just started it and Pascal felt compelled to keep it and it's good for the girls." She shrugged her shoulders.

"Well, they are lucky to have you as parents." Ellie took a sip of her water.

"And so is the new baby?" Stacy knew she dropped the

bomb, but didn't anticipate the reaction.

Ellie choked on her water, "... new baby ... you're pregnant?"

Stacy shook her head. "I am. Just a few weeks now, but I knew every time with the girls and I know this time. We would love to have a boy and will keep going until it's not any fun anymore and I love the fun with the girls. Even though Angie is sick, I still love it. I want a huge family and I'm still young. So far, I have gotten my figure back each time ... so, why not?" She beamed. "It's actually why I wanted to start the business now. I've been thinking about it for some time. Auddie can run the house, gave her full reigns and she's excited."

"I wondered why I had barely seen her this last couple of weeks." Ellie said.

"She was training your replacement and I threatened to throttle her if she told you. I know you are close, but not like us, huh?" Stacy needed the reassurance. Auddie and Ellie were close, but it was different. They were work-close and Stacy and Ellie seemed to have so much in common, even their love of music. One day the radio was playing in the kitchen and Stacy caught Ellie dancing around to a jazz piece. Most people didn't listen to jazz and Stacy loved the methodical influence and feeling about the piece that was playing. They had talked 'real' jazz all day long.

"We are close, even do things outside of work. But I'm such a homebody and she has so many kids. She misses them, so we don't do much. You and I ... best friends, so much in common."

Stacy was happy.

Ellie felt her phone zinging in her bag and reached in to pull it out to answer. "Hello?"

It was Auddie. "Stacy made me promise not to call and congratulate you until after 1:00 and its 1:01. I'm so happy for you!"

"She told you?" Ellie eyed Stacy and in good fun stuck her

tongue out. "I am really happy. How do you feel about your new job?"

Auddie was ecstatic on the other end of the phone. "I get weekends off and she's even got plans for me to take vacations so that I can spend time with the kids. She just flipped like a switch last week and I love it. I have felt energy I haven't had in years and the kids, well, the kids and Thomas are freaking out. I can't wait to see you. Shall we go to dinner this weekend and celebrate?"

"I'd like that. I'll talk to you soon. Thanks for calling, Auddie. Now get back to work before we both get fired." They both laughed.

"So, you really are happy about it?" Stacy finished lunch and pushed the plate to the side just a bit so she could lean in.

"I really am. Where is our office? I want a desk. I'll buy my own for home if you want me to work from there. What's the set-up going to be?" Ellie envisioned a very rich interior desk with deep, rich colors and lots of leather. Just like her father's office, she felt a need for the depth of color to exude the charm of the company.

"I made an office in the house." Stacy was consumed with guilt over not letting Ellie have any decisions on the décor or other inside elements, but she had wanted this to be a surprise. Loving the element of surprise as much as she did, Stacy kept going in hope that Ellie would be okay, "I called Casey and ..."

Ellie heard his name and something in her jumped. Literally moving in her chair, she regained to hear the rest of what Stacy was saying.

"... He and I went over furniture. He's there now and ready for us to come view the entire office set-up. I more-or-less left it up to him."

Ellie's heart skipped a beat, for both good and bad. What had he been doing? He had disappeared from the radar for quite some time, a couple of weeks, and Ellie hadn't had to hear about his dating and frivolous escapades that Ellie so looked forward to and then wish she hadn't listened. He had stirred something in her, but most of it was anger. She was glad he got to roam about freely while she nurtured that broken leg for so long. It seemed it would never heal. She wiggled her toes thinking about it.

"Ellie, are you okay?" Stacy watched her reaction and felt horrible for not letting her be more involved, but she had wanted to surprise her friend. She saw the loneliness in her eyes as Ellie would watch the girl's play and when Stacy spoke of Pascal. If only Ellie knew how lovely she was … "Ellie … are you okay?"

"Oh … yeah. I'm good. This is so exciting. Let's go look. I can't wait." Ellie was truly excited.

They called for the check and left chatting about all possibilities. So much excitement and the entire time Ellie thought in the back of her mind how exciting it would be, if she could just play it cool in front of Casey.

At the house, the girls lapped up their arrival with stories of this and that in their day, each holding a hand and chatting incessantly. Angie had a fondness for Ellie that she found endearing and the sickly child was as adorable as ever with a big red bow in her hair to go with her matching shoes. Ellie wondered if she would ever be healed from the horrible sickness and often wondered how Stacy felt each time the attack sent them reeling. Angie was telling her about their lunch when, out of nowhere, the downstairs doorway to the restroom was filled with Casey. So near they almost touched, she could smell his cologne, sending her senses like a rocket off the chart.

Casey didn't see the girls as he exited the restroom, almost bumping into Ellie. Grabbing her arm, so as not to make the same mistake as last time, he caught her. "Whoa ... looks like we bumped into each other again." His eyes lit up at his own humor, but hers dulled instantly. He hated the way he had no effect upon her.

"We sure did." She guided Angie around Casey. "So, what beautiful surprises do you have in store?"

His smile lit his face. "Oh, I can't even explain ... let me show you."

He led them all to the closed door of the new office. Angie was the first to speak, "I want to show them, UncaCasey. Please, please ... pretty please?" Her cuteness factor was undeniably the most adorable thing about her.

"Of course you can. Please," He reached for the handle to unveil his work, "You show them around ..."

Angie stopped, rearranged her whole demeanor to that of a steward on an airplane. "Okay ... we are about to go into heaven on Earth ..." Her pixie-like features as serious as she could get them. "I present to you ... your office." She stood to the side, swooping her hand in as a gesture of guidance. "What do you think?"

Stacy and Ellie entered the room, in awe, of the deepest, richest colors of burgundy, navy and white. The office furniture was rich cherry wood and gleamed articulate lines, accents and woodworking. Stacy moved to what was her desk area and her hand glided over the wood. Ellie was steered by Jules.

Jules said in her three-year-old voice, "This one is yours. See the flower?" She pointed to the white lilies that were in a vase on her desk.

Ellie could not believe the handy-work of the detail in the desk. It had to weigh a thousand pounds, deep and rich cherry. She ran her hands over the intricacies.

Jules said, "Sit down ... we got you a er ... erg, oh I can't remember, UncaCasey." She looked to him for help.

"Ergonomic, sweetie, just say a chair that won't hurt you ..." He took her hand.

"Ellie, what do you think?" Stacy said from her chair, behind her desk.

Ellie sat down, facing Stacy, within ten feet of each other. "I absolutely love it. The detail is amazing. Just amazing ..."

"It's Toscano carved unicorn, a design I saw in Italy and

thought it fit you." He said.

"I love it." She was absolutely speechless. Nothing else in the room mattered, but that desk. She could feel the vibrancy of the wood, the feel of the carving and each handle on a drawer accenting the carving.

Casey gathered the girls by the hand, "Let's let them get settled in." He pointed to a couple of boxes in the corner, "There are the things you had me pick up. I didn't have time to unpack them. I just got the desks moved in and placed. It took a lot longer than we thought. They aren't light."

"Casey, thank you ..." Stacy got up and hugged her brother.

"Yes, thank you ..." Ellie said from her desk. "These are beautiful, absolutely stunning. Thank you."

"No problem. I hope you both like them." He and the girls exited, one in each hand.

Stacy could barely stand the excitement. "Are you

impressed? I sure tried ..."

"Impressed? I'm speechless. If our work is anything close to his, we will be hugely successful." She believed every word of what she said.

"He's amazing. He's always been gifted and when he dropped the dream, I really worried that he would never really get there, ya know?"

Ellie thought of her dream and how she would never get there. If only one day she might have children then her dream would begin, but as it stood, there was no chance of that. She pushed the thought from her mind and settled into her chair, kicking back, feeling completely grounded. Stacy grabbed the boxes and started opening them and adding black leather accessories to the top of her desk.

"I got some other things as well. The printer will be here tomorrow and the other box should be our laptop computers. I thought it would be better to be mobile for presentations." She kept unloading the boxes.

Ellie just sat in the chair reveling in the feeling. She almost felt like putting her feet up and her hands behind her head as she had seen her father do so many times, but she didn't. Instead, she rose and went to help Stacy unpack and distribute the accessories.

Two hours later, they were behind their completely accessorized, gorgeous desks with phones, laptops, letter trays, pen holders, business card holders complete with business cards and staplers. They were ready to roll.

"So," Stacy said, "This is the first day of the rest of our lives ... how goes it so far?"

"Are you kidding? I'm ready to achieve world peace with this set-up. It's fabulous. I am so happy I could pop like a balloon. So, partner, what is our first plan of action?"

They talked for hours over what the marketing plan should look like, what their vision and mission were and brain-stormed successfully to delve into the details that would define their business. After quite some time the closed door opened to Pascal peeking his head in.

"Am I interrupting?" He creeped quietly in the door and planted a soft kiss on his wife's forehead. Taking a seat in one of the plush sitting chairs opposite Stacy's desk, he kicked his feet, bare stocking, up on the desk and put his hands behind his head.

"Get your feet off my desk, Sir ..." Stacy laughed. "Rough day?"

"It was terse, but successful. How is the new business going?"

Stacy looked to Ellie. With great confidence Ellie explained the details of the new marketing campaign that would get them off the ground within months and prosper their position.

When she finished, taking a deep breath, Pascal reached out and offered his hand to her, taking it, he said, "I think this is a much better situation. Let's celebrate!" He looked to both, "Let me take you to dinner at Pierre's."

Pierre's was the nicest restaurant in Ashville and could be considered quite a lofty experience.

Stacy immediately answered, "A reason to get dressed up? We are in!"

Ellie knew that any complaint would be warded off and agreed, "Are you going to dress me again?" Laughing, she stood to be taken to the magnificent closet once again.

"You know I am … let's go." She kissed Pascal as she left, him holding the door for the women. "We need about an hour. Can you get Casey dressed in something more than his flannels?"

"I'll do my best, but my closet isn't as big as yours is."

Stacy replied, "He has a suit in his car, guaranteed. Make him put it on." She grabbed Ellie's hand and out the door they went.

Chapter Fifteen

Pascal placed his hand in the small of Stacy's back to follow the maître de to their reserved seat. Ellie eyed Casey when they stood at the host station and Pascal reported the reservation. She had been left in the dark on this whole situation and wondered how much Casey had been afforded by way of information. As Pascal and Stacy walked away, Casey placed his hand in the small of Ellie's back to lead her as well, but she turned around.

Ellie asked, "Did you know about any of this?"

Casey knew that Ellie felt left out, "I knew that you needed furniture and that Stase needed to keep it a secret, because she thought you wouldn't agree to it. I didn't know about dinner or anything else. Is that what you are asking?"

"Yes." Ellie let him lead her to the table.

Seated very closely on the opposite side of the table to Pascal and Stacy, Casey's knee rubbed against Ellie's midnight blue gown and caused friction that sent her reeling. How could she be this sensitive? She moved slightly, adjusted in her seat so that they were not touching. Even though she had not seen him, it was almost unbearable sitting next to him. His cologne enticed her senses and his voice melted her as he spoke of new ventures and his ultimate success. There were, by far, more orders than he ever thought possible and his work was constant. At times, he worked through the night, forgetting to sleep. Things were great for him. Pascal had a couple of patients that were in dire need and it was disconcerting to have him speak of their passing, but the beauty of the night could not be doused even with that sadness.

Stacy told them of the plans and how she felt such security in her decision. Ellie chimed in at times about the business and felt the same, a feeling of security and warmth. She was so excited to be able to finally work in a career that she loved and with a friend she had grown to love as well.

The night ended with them finishing a bottle of champagne being opened and glasses poured. When Stacy put her hand over the top of the glass, Casey caught it.

"Really?" His eyes lit up, literally sparkled when he asked if she were pregnant.

Stacy nodded as Casey got up from the table and came to hug her, kissing her head at least ten times.

"I'm so happy for you ..." He shook Pascal's hand. "A boy this time for sure ... and if not, another beautiful princess." Casey returned to his chair, placing his hand on Ellie's leg and causing her to barely hold her glass in the air.

"To the beauty of the world and life as it comes ..." Pascal incited the toast.

"Here. Here." They all clinked glasses and sipped in celebration. After a few minutes of baby talk, Casey sat back in his chair, taking Ellie's hand from her leg and holding it.

"I'm so happy for you." Casey said to his sister. "So happy." He squeezed Ellie's hand.

They finished and walked from the restaurant the block to the car, Casey holding Ellie's hand the entire time, guiding her as if they had been together forever. Once at the car, Casey pulled back a moment.

He said, "Is it okay if we catch a car? I would love to make this last longer and I know you have a sitter to return to." He turned to Ellie, "Would that be okay? Would you like to go for drinks or coffee?"

"Sure." Was all that Ellie could choke out. She didn't want the moment to end, not at all and she was glad to continue with him, even though part of her detested his arrogance. Holding her hand felt safe and strong. She felt as if she were losing control and didn't know how she could do without the touch he was offering her. The champagne had made her feel a little light-headed, but in any case, she wanted to keep the feeling just as badly, if not more, than he did.

"Sure. We'll see you tomorrow!" Stacy got into the car and Pascal shut the door, entering from the other side.

"Great evening. Thank you for sharing it with us … and don't do anything I wouldn't do!" He winked at Casey.

Casey nodded and they watched them leave.

"So …" Casey said, "What would you like to do? It's only 7:30 and we have an entire night to frolic and flee from the everyday dullness …"

"Did you just say the word FROLIC?" Ellie laughed.

"I did. Frolic … to flit about without hesitation, no goal in mind." He smiled down at her.

"Webster's definition?"

He grimaced, "Not necessarily … am I close? I know I used it correctly in the sentence." He laughed at that.

"You did … It's just, well, such masculinity to use the word frolic ... you know."

He slapped his hand on his side like a gay man, snapping his hips in place, "Oh, honey ..." Lisp in perfect rendition of a drag queen. "Let me tell you how well I know the word frolic ... fro ... aft ... lick ... lash ... it's all the same to me." He took his hand off his hip and walked away from her with a sashay shante that would legally pass, stopping only to see if she was catching up when he extended his hand. Ellie came to him and handed her hand, once again to the delight of his exquisite skin and touch.

They walked a couple of blocks, talking furniture, business and about Stacy and Pascal before coming to a quaint Irish Pub.

"How about this? Care for a lager?" He opened the door for her to a noisy, rambunctious group of rowdy men drinking from a boot. They walked inside before he whispered in her ear, "These guys are rugby players and most of them married and headed home within the hour. Can you deal with the noise until then? We'll practically have the place to ourselves when they leave ..."

She started to answer when someone noticed Casey and headed right for him, a huge greeting hug and handshake. They guys all slapped him on the back and welcomed him, having been ages since he last visited.

"I know ... I know ... I should come home more often. How are the kids, Michael?" He waited for answers to each of his questions, asking all seven men how their families were before scooting Ellie off to a seat away from the noise. He waved to the bartender who immediately appeared to the table with two dark ales.

Casey asked her, "Do you drink dark beer?"

"How dare you ask a Justice if they can drink a beer, Sir?" Ellie took her beer and clinked it to his mug and drank. She slammed the beer mug on the table, sloshing some out and said, "Justice is English for fair-minded. My great, great, great five-time grandfather was one of the first judges in England. You see, there is this great story here ..."

Casey was enthralled with her words and the way her voice lilted on a keel that was unlike all the southern women he knew. Lost in her words, he mumbled, "Please, do tell ..."

"Well, the Curia Regis, The King's Court, was at first, presided over by the King himself, but that didn't work out too well. See he used to have trial by ordeal, used really until the end of the 12th century. They determined guilt and/or innocence by forcing the accused to pick up a red-hot bar of iron or grab a rock out of a cauldron of boiling water ... something equally painful if they could think of it. The whole system of justice revolved around if they had begun to heal after three days ... then they had God on their side, proving they were innocent."

"How many people were determined 'not guilty'?" Casey asked, genuinely interested.

"I don't believe they recorded it. Sometimes they used water and if they floated they were innocent, but apparently, that did not work, because some men accused of stealing the King's cattle did not sink or something ... anyway. He decided to find a different method and my fair-minded grandfather, who sat in his court as a cook or something, was brought forward to determine their innocence or guilt. His surname was Regis; however, it was changed to Justice and he was then knighted and referred to a Mr. Justice Regis, Knight. The system was restructured by William the II and the Church condemned it in 1216." She shrugged her shoulders almost in embarrassment when she realized just how intently he was listening to her.

"So, let me get this straight … you can drink a beer because your fair-minded grandfather that was once a cook for the King's Court was made the first Judge in England?" He slapped his leg in the dorkiest way, absolutely amusing himself to the fullest. He laughed so hard he could barely catch his breath.

Ellie sat until he was done, unamused, and almost angry at his insolence for her story.

Once he caught his breath and his laughter slowed to controllable, he realized that Ellie was not amused in the slightest. "C'mon, that was funny …"

She didn't budge.

"Seriously, Elle, it was funny ..." He wasn't laughing any longer.

She hated that the way he said 'Elle' was just like the way Stacy said it and it endeared her.

She took a deep breath, "It's not funny. That's my family history." She pouted.

"Oh, my ... not the pout. Please. That's the same look when I dropped you off at the hotel that first night. Please, please don't pout." He said.

"I'm NOT pouting." She pouted.

He laughed again ... "You surely are pouting. The lip goes out and the eyes get really sad ..." Looking into her eyes, he could see the actual pain. "Did someone tease you as a child?" He was very serious.

"My childhood is none of your business, Casey." She was

really getting upset.

"Ellie... I really wasn't trying to hurt you. I was making a joke. I'm sorry. I promise. I didn't mean to hurt your feelings." He handed her a napkin from the table.

She pushed his hand away. "I don't need that. You did hurt my feelings and everyone used to make fun of me. I was too tall and I used too big of words for my age and other kids made fun of me because they couldn't understand me. My mother was my best friend and she played a mean game of tennis, so I was always good at it and for some reason ..."

"For some reason the other kids used it against you. Didn't it make you self-conscious?" Casey knew the feeling.

"Yes, it did."

"I felt that way when my parents died. They were killed ... did Stacy tell you?" He waited for her to answer.

"I knew you had said they were killed at Christmas. How

old were you? Stacy hasn't ever said anything to me." Ellie wanted to know, not only because her best friend seemed to shun the conversation, but because he had brought it up. She was so attracted to him. Hating that about herself, she had to admit as she watched his lips while he spoke, that she was completely attracted to this blond-haired beautiful man. She took her beer and drank the last remaining quarter while he spoke.

"My parents were killed in a car accident when I was six and Stase was just four. We were waiting for them to come home from buying Christmas presents ... why we hate gifts, blah blah blah ... anyway, they were killed by an on-coming driver who was drunk out of his gourd. That's the story."

Ellie reached out and took his hand this time. "I'm sorry, Casey. You were six years old? So much so a baby still."

"Well, I might have been six, but I grew up that day and I've taken care of Stacy every day until she decided to marry Pascal. I let her go then. It was a crazy childhood."

"Were you orphaned? In foster care?"

"No. Actually family fought over us. The two cute little kids … who were going to inherit over two million dollars once they hit eighteen." He sighed remembering the ordeal of the family wanting to raise them.

"That's horrible." Ellie said.

"You can't imagine. Of course, the most powerful family member, my mom's sister, Auntie Doreen, she had the most clout and her husband had a little bit of money, so our poor family failed to be able to fight them long enough. They had the money to pay the lawyers and they got us. Doreen and Uncle Thomas. Two of the most indecent people I care to have known. We stuck together and I grew strong rather quickly and could ward off the throttling I used to get from talking back to Uncle T. He was a bastard. I hated him and he was always picking on Stacy. I would let loose and he would turn attention to me."

"So you would protect her?"

"I had to. She was four years old and they would dress her up and make her pretty to take her and show her off. She hated it. They weren't mean to her, they just treated her like a doll and she was not allowed to speak or vent her frustration without getting it. One time ... oh, you don't need to hear this ... how rude. I'm sorry." He motioned to the bar tender for two more drinks with the wave of a hand.

"I want to hear. Stacy is the best friend I have ever had. I want to know everything about her ..." Ellie was telling the truth.

If only she wanted to know about him ... Casey continued with his story, leaving out the parts of his abuse and how Uncle Tom used to throw him around the room until he was too big and fought back the one time. Fourteen years old and stout, Casey landed a right jab into Uncle Tom's jaw and knocked him clean out. It gave them enough time to run and they did. Casey and Stacy lived on the streets for almost a year before they got caught and could live with their Grandmother Margaret.

"You see, we finally got out of there and could live with

Gramma Maggie. She was wonderful. We were about fifteen and thirteen and Stacy blossomed with Gramma Maggie's help. She really came into herself. Gramma taught her gumption, she called it. She taught Stacy how to stand up for herself and it was on from there." He smiled at the thought.

"So, you were raised by your grandmother? I never knew my grandparents. Just momma and my father."

"No, actually she died six months after we moved in. But, I was sixteen at the time and they let me emancipate and I took care of us ... without the damned money."

Ellie understood completely. "So, you never touched it. You just worked and made do?"

"Exactly. I just worked at the lumber yard to start with. Uncle Tom made me work with him from the time I was ten in the furniture garage he called it. Where he crafted furniture. His lines were bad and his precision sucked, but I would fix them when he wasn't looking and he made a mint off the pieces. I always loved it, even though he always told me I would amount to nothing, I found a true love for it. He worked with my father before, so I was fond of it before and I always knew I was a craftsman, not a furniture maker like him. He never loved a single piece of the work he did. He just followed instructions and they didn't look the same. He went out of business a couple years after we ran away ..." Casey caught his mistake and coughed through the rest of the sentence. "I must have gotten something stuck in my throat. Wow." He took a big swig of his beer, finishing the second and motioning for a third round.

Ellie caught it too. She didn't press the issue, because she knew she could get it all out of Stacy and would. However, the beer was much more stout than domestic and she felt a rush of emotion and a buzzing around the room.

"Are you okay, Ellie?" Casey was up and on his feet within seconds. "Are you okay?"

"I just got a little dizzy. I think I have a buzz." She laughed. She felt so good. And everything in her world had just gotten better, why not celebrate … the last thing she remembered, was that she started to fall and he caught her. Once again, lifted into his strong arms, she was carried away thinking about the kiss in the car that night.

Casey scooped Ellie up in his arms as one of the guys came over to see if everything was okay.

"It's fine, Mo. Just do me a favor and give this number a call and ask them to bring my car. She just had too much to drink. I'm going to run her out for some fresh air." He headed out the door after getting his phone back.

Outside the pub, Casey tried to put Ellie on her feet, but she was completely out, snoring softly inside his shoulder. He gave up and just held her, breathing in her scent and lying his cheek in her hair to steady them while they waited the five minutes that it took his driver to get to the pub. He softly placed her in the car and went to the other side. He was feeling the effects of the beer as well. He hadn't had sleep in almost 48 hours and he was tired. He was so tired he couldn't keep his eyes open, and drifted off to sleep after telling the driver to take them to Stacy and Pascal's.

At the drive, Stacy came running out the door with Angie in her arms. Pascal was right behind her. They were getting in the car, Pascal nearly tossing a crying Jules in the back seat. The driver sped into the space to park and yelled in the back, the three times he tried to wake up Casey had not worked. He jerked the door open and shook Casey awake, waking Ellie beside him.

Ellie couldn't get her bearings, but knew something was wrong. "What's going on?" She saw Stacy and Pascal in the car, Pascal in the back seat with Angie and Jules as they pulled near.

Stacy's had rolled the window down. She was nearly yelling, frantic, "Angie won't respond to the treatment. He wants to admit her this time. It's bad."

Casey was jolted awake. "Let's go!" He nearly shoved Ellie in the front seat and climbed in beside her as they sped off into the night.

Half-way to the hospital, Angie started crying. "I want

UncaCasey ..." she sobbed. Pascal tried to soothe her.

"There, there, baby girl ... look, you can talk again. Let's try not to and just ride to the hospital where they can get a better breathing treatment set up for you. Okay, baby girl?"

Casey turned in the seat, causing both Ellie and Stacy to have to move. "I'm right here, Angel. Right here. We will get that nasty asthma to go away and make you feel better. Okay?" He reached back and held her hand over the seat.

Finally, at the hospital, a team met them at the door with a gurney and a speedy ascent to the room. An hour later they were out of the woods and her color was returning. Ellie was sitting out in the waiting room with Jules, playing a game and trying to help the little girl remain calm, always asking questions she could not answer, when Casey came out.

Jules ran to Casey and jumped into his arms. "Is she okay, UncaCasey?"

"She's much better, sweet pea. Much better. She has the

best doctors and she's going to be fine. Just that nasty asthma and things are starting to turn green. They always seem to be turning green and causing our Angel trouble. But they have a new medicine now and they think it's going to really work much better." He stroked her hair and came to sit next to Ellie in the seat.

"They have it under control?" Ellie asked.

"They do. But they are going to keep her. Her blood oxygen level won't go over 88% and it's not good enough. Pascal has never looked so afraid. He literally cried when they got her in the room. I've never seen it so bad. Angela was purple." He put his hands over Jules ears while he spoke and within a couple of moments she was sound asleep.

Ellie realized how afraid she had been. "That was scary. I didn't know what was going on and Jules kept asking me questions," she spoke quickly, but softly, "and I didn't know how to answer them. She has such knowledge at her age, words I barely knew and she got what was going on. She prayed that IF Angela died that she not be in pain any longer. I nearly lost it." Ellie's lashes immediately wet with tears she had tried to hold back." She couldn't control them any longer. "I was so scared. Is she that sick she could die from asthma?"

Casey could barely resist the temptation to kiss Ellie's red, full lips. "She can. She nearly has more than a couple of times. Asthma restricts the airways and when the inhaler doesn't work or they don't get it fast enough, it gets sketchy. She's okay, Elle. I was just in there. Would you feel better if you got to go see her?"

Ellie shook her head no. She knew she would break down and she didn't want Stacy to see it. Especially now that she was pregnant. Ellie needed to protect her and to keep everything she could as constant as possible. "I'm okay. It was just everything happened so fast. I was asleep and then woke up and everyone was screaming and then the car and the hospital. I hate hospitals." She shuddered at the thought of her mom's dying moments.

"I understand. But, I assure you, everything is okay. I'm going to head back in and make sure they don't need anything else before we leave and then I'll take you home so you can sleep. You look so drained."

Ellie didn't want to go home. She wanted to stay with Jules and Casey. She wanted everyone to be okay and the thought of being alone after racing the poor child to the hospital was terrifying to her. "I want to stay with Jules."

Casey was handing the sleeping child to Ellie when she said the words and his heart ached. She had no children of her own from her marriage, probably for the best, but there had been times when he watched her with the girls and knew she would be yearning for her own at some point. A childless-mother was nothing to bat an eye at. He understood. "I'll take you to the house and tell Stacy you will stay with us." He left the room without looking back and Ellie was glad.

She held Jules close, stroking her hair, whispering it would be okay into the babies' ear. She held on tight to the hope that Angie would be okay and that Stacy never had to go through the pain of losing one of these darling children. Ellie fell asleep rocking gently back-and-forth with Jules.

When Casey returned, he found both his girls sleeping. With a shake of his blond curls, he picked them both up and headed outside where his driver had been waiting. On the way back to Stacy's house, the wind gently blew through the semi-open window, keeping Casey awake and helping him shake the anxiety he felt. The deep breathing patterns weren't working well and he felt as though his world would explode at any second. Until Ellie rustled in the seat beside him, still holding Jules and gathered him into her arms, leaning her head on his shoulder, he had not relaxed. The moment she leaned against him and sighed heavily in her sleep, the new position better than the last, he relaxed. Looking out the window, he could see the stars in the sky and as if on cue, a shooting star. He didn't wish for Angela's health as he usually did, he had prayed that into fruition for the last six hours, but instead, he prayed this woman would fall in love with him as he knew he was in love with her. If she didn't, his heart would never recover. Never had he felt so enchanted by someone who did not seem to realize he existed in any other realm than that of her friend's brother. He knew the odds were against him and it was going to be hell if she ever found out how he felt.

Without waking either of the girls, he laid his head back on the leather of the seat and fell into a light, but restful sleep that lasted all the ten minutes to the house.

Chapter Sixteen

Ellie woke as Casey lifted her out of the car. She said softly, "I'll walk. You take Jules."

Casey grabbed the little girl, holding her close as he closed the door and headed inside the house to her room.

Ellie waited in the kitchen, the coffee maker filled when he returned. "Would you like a cup of coffee? I wanted to make sure some was here if Stase and Pas came home, just in case."

"I'd love a mug."

She poured him a steaming mug of java, black and stout, and handed it to him and sat at the bar with him, facing him.

Neither said anything as they sipped from the mugs. Five

good minutes passed before he spoke. "So, what an evening, huh?"

"Truly. That was crazy." She put the mug down and drew her eyes from his bright red lips, colored with the warmth of the liquid. "Really crazy."

"She'll be okay. She has to be okay. At least it's a state of the art facility and they can do the best job of anyone around." He was speaking more for his own peace of mind.

"I ..." Ellie started to speak when she saw Jules enter the kitchen. "Come here, baby." She reached her arms out and the little girl climbed on her lap. Ellie smoothed her ruffled hair and kissed her forehead. "What's the matter, punkin?"

"I was just thinking in my sleep." Jules snuggled in against Ellie's chest. "I was sad and miss Angie."

"I know you do ..." Stacy kissed the top of her head and held her closer. "We are right here and Momma and Daddy are with Angie. It's okay. How about you try and go back to sleep?

Shall we go back upstairs?"

Jules nodded and Stacy got up from the bar. "I'm going to take her back up. Okay?"

He nodded, "Sure. Do you need help?"

"I want you to sleep with me, Ellie-bear." Jules always called her that for some reason, no one knew why.

"Sure, Sweetie. I'll lay down with you." She shrugged her shoulders at Casey, who completely understood.

"I'll tidy up down here and then I'm going to hit the hay. I'm exhausted. Do you need anything?"

She shook her head no as she passed by him, regretting that the night was over, but glad the night was now complete. Angie was fine and Ellie felt a part of something much bigger than she had ever felt. It felt good. As she passed by, Casey stood.

He couldn't let this opportunity pass or he would regret it forever. Casey stood as she passed, grabbed her lightly and pulled her close enough to kiss her lightly on the lips and then kissed Jules forehead. "I love you …"

As fast as it happened, it was over and he was moving to the sink after grabbing both mugs of coffee to rinse them out. His back to her, she had no choice but to walk, on now wobbly legs, to the stairs and take Jules up to bed. Her lips burned with a fierce intensity. Had he really just kissed her?

After she had left, Casey let out a huge sigh of relief. That kiss, something so simple, so friendly, had shaken him to his very core. What was he going to do about this whole situation? He reeled with thoughts and her vision was imprinted upon his brain in the gown, her hair tousled just the slightest and it kept bringing him back to that first kiss on the road. He lingered much longer than necessary in the kitchen before he went up the stairs to the quest bedroom he always slept in.

For twenty minutes, he lay there staring at the ceiling, seeing nothing more than a movie-like reenactment of the evening. Everything Ellie did he saw in his mind again. The way she laughed, the pout, the endless lilt to her voice that lulled him anywhere but to sleep. In the car, on the sidewalk, in the bar and in the restaurant, he saw her every move repeated as if he were experiencing it again.

Ellie laid Jules in the tiny princess bed and climbed in beside her, the warmth of the little girl so comforting as she began to think of Casey. She hummed softly until Jules fell back asleep and then she herself drifted off to sleep, feeling the kiss upon her lips one last time.

Casey gave up after a period of time and headed to the shower. Cold water just the right temp, he slid out of the clothing and stepped inside to cool off. The beer buzz was gone long ago, but the feeling of being unstable would not leave. His lithe body glided into the shower and as he washed his hair he pictured her next to him, naked, ready to make love. Shaking off the thought, Casey finished the shower and grabbed the robe hanging on the back of the door, sloshing water on the floor walking across to it. He grabbed it and wrapped his wet body inside and headed out to the bed again. Tossing the robe on the chair next to the bed, he grabbed a clean pair of boxers and put them on and then slid in bed and tried to calm enough to fall asleep.

Stacy woke from the bed next to Angie and tucked her hair behind her ear. The child smiled up at her.

"How are you feeling?" Stacy whispered to not wake Pascal, sleeping in the chair next to Angie's bed.

"I'm okay, Mama. I feel better. My lips aren't purple, are they?" She felt her lips as Stacy shook her head no. "They were so cold …"

Stacy snuggled in closer to her baby and laid her head on her chest. "They aren't cold now, punkin. It's going to be okay." She lay like that for quite some time before they were disturbed by the nurse coming in to take Angie's vitals.

Pascal jumped up from the chair as the nurse began. "We need to have a battery of tests run this morning so that we can look at new treatment options. What time is Dr. Worthington coming by for rounds?"

The nurse shook her head; she had no idea. She continued to work on the little girl just as quickly as she could. It was terrible to work on doctor's family members and this was worse than normal, because the little girl had come so close to dying. The nurses drew straws to see who had to come into the room and she had lost.

Pascal continued, "Tell him I would like a full report. I'm going to leave for the hospital in about a half hour." He checked his watch. "Yes, just about a half hour. Can you do that, Nurse?"

She knew when not to piss off the doctor. "Yes. I'll let him know, doctor." She finished up and handed him the vitals she had written on a separate sheet specifically for him. "I thought you would want to keep track." She smiled.

"Thank you, Nurse. I appreciate it." He looked it over and tucked it into his pocket. "It looks good." He turned to his daughter, "It looks really good, Princess. I'll talk to Dr. Worthington later and we will see about calling in some specialists to make sure this doesn't happen again. Okay?" He never felt it necessary to keep things from her. The earlier she learned her illness, the better she could help them manage the symptoms.

Stacy had stood back and watched the nurse as she cautiously maneuvered through the vitals and gave Pascal the sheet of paper. It must be difficult to work with their family, knowing that he was looking so intensely on their performance. It was important for her to ally with the team and always kept quiet so that if they needed to talk to her, she would not be targeted as difficult. Stacy spoke to the nurse, "Thank you so much."

The nurse smiled as she gathered her things and exited the room.

Pascal felt Angie's forehead, brushing her hair to the side. "Princess, we have to find something long term so that this is not so hard on you." He winked at her as his heart finally started to beat again. Feeling as though he were dying inside all night long, he knew it was time to take drastic measures. Without a full team of technology at his hands, it was difficult to feel as though she were safe anywhere other than the hospital. The attack had come on so quickly.

Stacy motioned to Pascal, seeing the seriousness manifest in his facial features. "Can I see you outside before you leave, Darlin'?"

He nodded and they walked from the room.

Stacy was always diplomatic when dealing with Angie's illness, but she was so stressed out she needed to vent it out or it could affect the baby she was carrying. Softly she touched her stomach, "You're scaring me."

"I'm sorry, baby. I didn't mean to. It's okay. She's out of the woods and responding to the treatment, however, we need to feel as though she is safe outside the hospital and I don't feel that way right now."

"What do you mean?" She chilled from head to toe.

"It's okay. I'm thinking long term. I want a different, more aggressive treatment option. She was fine last night and in ten minutes was full-blown. I ... I ..." He struggled for the words to convey his fear.

"I understand. It scared me too. I couldn't get the breathing treatment to work and the emergency inhaler did nothing. It scared me too."

"I'll talk to Worthington and see if we can get a referral. It should be okay and we can see someone today. I'll call them in ..." He had to do what he could. Feeling helpless was not an option he liked in the least.

Stacy trusted her husband and knew that last night was never to happen again. She sighed in relief finally and decided to go with the feeling that hope was in the air. A specialist could help them, hopefully ...

Casey lie awake, staring at the ceiling. Sleep was nowhere nearby. He tossed and turned, tried to get more comfortable. Nothing worked. He never had trouble sleeping. Finally, he gave up and headed for the library. Perhaps some reading would be nice.

Ellie woke like lightning. The dream had been so real. Her fight had caused her to wake up Jules.

Jules lay on the edge of the bed, looking frightened. "What's wrong, Ellie-bear? You were yelling and pushing."

She could see the fear in the child's eyes. First Angie and now this? She grabbed Jules in her arms, sweat seeping through her gown, still dressed from the evening. "I'm so sorry. I had a bad dream. I'm so sorry." She rocked the baby girl.

Jules laid her head against Ellie's chest, "I'm so waked up. But my eyes are so tired." She rubbed her now tear-stained eyes.

"I know. It's okay. I promise. It was just a dream." She felt horrid guilt at the child witnessing her demon.

Stroking her hair, trying to be as relaxed as possible. Finally, she fell back to sleep and for fear of having the dream again, the sweat soaking her new gown and the fact she was not going to get back to sleep, she laid her on the tiny pillow and Ellie slipped from the room.

She wandered back to see if she could find her clothing from dressing for the night. Since she had dressed there, her clothing had to be in the house. She knew that the staff would have taken it to the laundry, never leaving it in Stacy and Pas' room. So that is where she headed.

Once in the laundry, she found her clothing in the washer, it hadn't been switched yet, so she put it in the dryer, luckily it was all light colored and in one load. From there, she went to the bath behind the kitchen and started the shower. She took the gown off and hung it on the back of the door, slightly ajar, so she could hear the dryer. A light load, it shouldn't take much time. The hot water felt good against her skin as she stood under it and let it soothe her aching heart. So much had happened that night and then the dream, so vivid, so real. Her husband had her cornered and she couldn't get away, ending in the jail cell, with her clinging to the bars, screaming to get out. The water made the thoughts run from her mind as she visualized them leaking down the drain. After about fifteen minutes, she washed her hair, conditioned it and took her time, letting the conditioner sit as she used the lavender soap to lather her body. Rinsing and stepping from the shower, she heard the dryer end signal and grabbed the first towel, wrapping it around her head and the second drying off quickly, wrapping it around her body as she moved to the laundry.

Casey read until he fell asleep in the chair, but woke to the sound of someone walking through the house. Light footsteps, he wondered if Ellie was up and moving around. It was nearing six o'clock and he was done with fighting to sleep. He followed the sound of the footsteps.

Once out of the shower and wrapped in the towel, Ellie tiptoed to the laundry. The staff would be coming soon and she wanted to be away from the kitchen area before they arrived. She pulled her things from the dryer and started to dress when Casey entered the kitchen.

He heard her in the laundry and talked from behind the door. "Elle? You in there?"

"I am." She covered her body immediately. "Don't come in. I'm naked!" She said it before she realized it, but it was out.

A fire shot through Casey when he heard her say the word. His brain pictured her perfect body, the body he imagined to be under her gown as she had held her in his arms. He shook it from his mind as quickly as he could. "I'm just putting on some coffee."

"I'll take a mug, if you don't mind?" She was just finishing putting on her slacks and blouse, buttoning it up to the very top before she realized that she didn't want to hide herself from Casey. She wanted him to see her. Three buttons undone, she exited the laundry to find him in the kitchen.

"It smells so good. I need coffee. Slept horribly. Poor

Jules," Ellie said, "She had to suffer my tossing and turning and talking …"

"Bad dreams again?" Casey asked.

"What do you mean, again?" Ellie was intrigued at his question.

"Well … when we were driving down, in the truck. You were dreaming … not good dreams."

"Right. I forgot. That seems like so long ago."

He turned from the countertop with the two mugs of coffee to see her standing, hair wet and curly, hanging just below her shoulders. She looked so innocent, no makeup, and smelled so good. Different, but good.

He took a deep breath as he handed her the mug and held on to his.

Ellie was mesmerized by Casey's eyes, so soft and yet so intensely blue. "I forgot …"

"I didn't forget anything ..." Casey knew if he blurted it out, it would be over with and not on his mind anymore. "Do you remember?"

"Remember what?" She looked directly at his lips and felt the soft fluttery kiss from before and the intensity of the kiss in the SUV on the way to Ashville. "I remember ..." She knew what he was asking.

Before she could think of what the implications of her actions might be, Ellie moved closer to Casey, closed her eyes and waited for him to kiss her. And he did.

Slowly his lips touched hers, softly, fully. It moved to parting his lips to fully beg for her response and he got it. She kissed him with a fervor, a passion from somewhere she didn't recognize. Everything fit together perfectly, just as the first time. His hands in her hair, her hands in his, pulling closer, fighting to know every piece of him. He pulled her off the ground and into his arms and carried her, kissing the entire way, to his room, where he lay her on the bed.

Ellie couldn't fight him, knew they didn't have time and yet, she had to have him. His strong thighs, his arms of steel, even stronger than before because of his making furniture. The way he smelled and the way he consumed her with his hands, such a soft touch that drew fire anywhere he drew.

Ripping off his boxers, revealing his excitement, she helped him undress her until they were both naked and against each other in the bed. Casey made love to her feeling emotions he had never felt before. And Ellie fell hopelessly in love with this strong, yet sensitive man as they fulfilled each other's desire until they were both spent. Lying in each other's arms, for the first time in years, she fell asleep as if she were safe. Nothing could hurt her in his arms and she nestled in, sleeping sweetly.

Casey lay with Ellie's wet hair in his face and he had never been happier except for the birth of each of the girls; the first time he held each of them. This was true joy … and he felt it.

Chapter Seventeen

Auddie saw the coffee on already and was in the middle of managing the kitchen for breakfast when Stacy called. Informing her of the hospital stay, Auddie left the kitchen with instructions and went to check on little Jules.

Up the stairs and through the hall, her heels clicking on the floor, she heard Casey and Ellie in his room. As red as the shirt she wore, Auddie stood for just a moment to figure out what was going on, before scooting down the hall and peeking in to see the sleeping child. She closed the door quietly and headed down the back stairs, avoiding the guest room Casey usually slept in. How dare he bring another woman into the home? Especially when Auddie could tell that Ellie was smitten with him. It was none of her business and she wouldn't fret. She had secretly hoped that Ellie and Casey would get together, from the night of the Christmas party. But, it was a shot in the dark and she knew it.

The rest of the morning Auddie made sure that everything was perfect and left around lunch time after getting Jules ready and headed to the hospital. Not once did Casey emerge from his room. She had wanted to ream him, but it wasn't her place.

Once in the car with clean clothing for Stacy and a few things for Angie, buckled in beside her was Jules, Auddie dialed the phone and waited for Ellie to answer.

Hiding out in Casey's room was more fun than imaginable. By the time they realized where they were, and what was going on, the staff was present. A dilemma for sure. They giggled and laughed, trying not to make noise. Stacy had called and filled them in a couple of times, individually. The first time Casey got the call before Ellie, and Stacy turned right around and called Ellie. The second time she called Ellie first. They took the calls as if they knew nothing and Stacy asked nothing. Not speaking of it was the only option. They would go right back to cuddling and talking about their hopes, dreams and aspirations. Most of Casey's talk was of pieces he was creating and how much he loved doing what he was doing. The orders were coming in and getting to the point that he would be working diligently for the next six months. Each delivery got at least one referral and two pieces of furniture on the average. It was good for business and business was good.

Ellie talked about how much she looked forward to her and Stacy's business. Plans of marketing and value added offerings. She felt light-hearted and carefree, lying naked next to this beautiful man. As he spoke, she watched, enthralled at everything he said when it dawned on her, she had never been in love before. THIS is what her friends had spoken of. THIS is what people died for … and she snuggled up closer to him.

"What?" Casey said as Ellie nuzzled in closer.

"I just want to be as close to you as I can get." She had no shame in her honesty. None.

"I understand." He covered her in his arms and held her close. They remained silent for quite some time before he spoke again, "So ... how the hell are we going to get out of here?"

She laughed. "I was thinking the same thing. It has be, what ... one o'clock or so?"

Casey looked at his phone. It was 1:20. He showed her. They kept their voices low each time they spoke, not wanting to get caught, but not wanting to leave either. The big question finally came from Ellie, "You hungry?"

"Starving."

"Me too." She laughed. Sitting up on her elbow. "What are we going to do? Stacy is staying at the hospital, but the staff sees and they tell Auddie and she blabs to Stacy ..."

He thought about it a moment. "I can go out first, grab us some sandwiches or something. They all know when I eat, I eat a lot … and bring it back up."

"That doesn't solve me leaving this room any time soon. I need to sneak out. You'll have to go see where everyone is and then find a way to get me out of the house without anyone seeing me. They would all assume I was at home."

"Nice plan, Detective … but Stacy knows you stayed here with us. That Auddie has not seen either one of us … not workable."

"Right." Ellie ceded.

"You were supposed to be sleeping here, Auddie and the housekeepers have been in all the rooms at this point, but mine. So … here's what we are going to do." But before Casey had a chance to say, Ellie's phone rang.

"It's Auddie." Ellie grabbed her phone, took a deep

breath and answered. "Hello?"

Auddie broke in very quickly, "Hey ... You are not going to believe the morning here." She barely took a breath before she continued. "I was walking past the guest bedroom and that brut had a ..." She had to watch what she said because of Jules. "Here honey, you can put my music on and use my headphones." She put the earbuds in the child's ears and then continued. "He had a woman in there with him. They were going at it hard too, by the sound of it ..." She continued to rant as Ellie took the phone away, looking to Casey for answers.

He just shook his head. No idea what to do came to him.

Ellie listened more as Auddie spoke.

"It was crazy. Part of me hoped he would fall for you, that his ego would stop and he would let you in. I see the way you look at him and I know that you like him." Ellie turned red at her words.

Casey smiled. He mouthed, "Oh, you liked me ... watched my butt as I walked out of the room?" He stood up and modeled, tightening his butt cheeks for her. And they were very nice, firm buttocks.

She smiled and listened.

"He is horrible. If I would have had more time, I would have bust into that room. I had half a mind to tell Stacy about it ..."

"NO!" Ellie said it before he could stop her. "You can't do that ... Auddie."

"What?" Auddie stopped. "What do you mean, Ellie? Do what?"

"You cannot tell on him, because he's in here with me." Ellie waited for Auddie to catch her breath and for Casey to come out of the aneurism she had just thrown him into. "He and I ... well, I stayed last night. Everything happened so fast.

You must keep it secret. Did you tell anyone else?"

"No, Darlin'. I didn't have time. We were short with you gone and the new girl and … what the hell? Really?" She focused on her driving and made sure that Jules wasn't hearing any of her conversation. Lowering her voice even more, "Are you kidding me?"

"No. Pretty serious. And stuck. We are starving and I can't get out without someone seeing me. I need your help. Where are you?"

"I'm on my way to the hospital. I'll be about an hour altogether. Can you wait that long?"

Casey could hear what was being said and on cue, he crawled up the bed like a panther, pushing Ellie down … "I think we can think of something to do until you get back …" Casey said into the phone and hit the end button.

Auddie was relieved to bring Jules to see Angie and see them together. Angie explained everything that happened and they were like two mature friends discussing events that had happened to someone else.   Their vocabularies were huge and they were much more mature than her own children, who were much older. Stacy looked tired.

"Thank you, Auddie." Stacy said as she moved away from the girls. "I really do appreciate all that you do for us."

"Mrs. Davidson … Stacy … you know I love doing it." Auddie was sincere.

"Thank you." Stacy touched Auddie's arm and took the things she had brought to her. "If you want to scoot on back, I'm good. Jules can stay here with me. Pascal will be off in an hour and we are going to just stay at the hospital until late. I'll bring Jules home and Pas will stay with Angie tonight. I'm brutally tired and, well … the baby." She smiled softly, but worry lines invaded her delicate face.

"Okay. Do you need anything else? I can bring it back on my way home if you like."

"No. I should be fine. I'll shower here in the doctor's lounge when Pas gets back and Jules and I can play a couple games with Angie. She's feeling much better."

Auddie left and when she got to the car she dialed her husband and told him she would be home late. She wanted to make sure that everything went smoothly and someone needed to shut down the house ... or not? She remembered that Casey and Ellie were stuck in his room. She laughed, causing her husband to question her. She ended the call and dialed Ellie's number.

Ellie was deep into the kissing when the phone rang. Nothing in the world could make her want to stop feeling the amazing sensation Casey was causing to course through her veins, her skin afire, her soul open and ready to accept every part of this man. "Wait, baby ..." She breathed. "It might be Stacy."

She rolled from under him and grabbed her phone. "It's Auddie." She pushed the button, "Hello."

Auddie could clearly hear the breathlessness, "Oh, did I

interrupt you?"

"Uh ... no. Not at all."

"You suck at lying, Ellie. Anyway, I'm on my way back. Stacy and Pas are staying at the hospital until late tonight. It's almost three right now. How about I come back and get you out of the room?" Auddie wanted to laugh heartily, but she kept her composure. She liked her friend and hoped that this would end in love. Real love for Ellie.

"Okay ..." Still out of breath, Ellie replied as Casey continued to tickle her skin, running the tips of his soft fingers over her smooth stomach.

"Hi, Auddie." Casey croaked out. "Hurry before we starve to death." He thought he was funny.

"I'll stop and get some take out and run it right up." Auddie hung up as she pulled into a fast food drive through.

Twenty minutes later, Auddie came knocking at the door.

Casey and Ellie had just gotten out of the shower, making love yet another time as quietly as possible. They were newly dressed and ready when she brought in the ribs, slaw and bread. They tore into it, almost before Auddie could get it out of her hand.

"My goodness ... gracious. Hungry?" She wanted so badly to chide them, to rouse some emotion for the something she knew and no one else did. But she held back.

Casey had BBQ sauce on his cheek an inch from his eye, he tore in so fast. Reaching for a napkin, Auddie helping by handing it, she gave in. "Slow down before you accidentally chew off a finger. Geez."

Ellie was more concerned with eating her rib than what they were doing. Little did she care about the situation she had just caused, nor did she think it a problem until Auddie spoke.

"So ... how is this going to play out with your new partnership?"

Both Casey and Ellie stopped mid-bite. They looked at

each other, grinned and took those respective bites.

"Oh, I see. A little odd man out here. That's okay. I get it. However, if I leave this room, you are trapped again until Stacy gets home in about five hours. The staff, they are just toodling around doing their jobs, in and out of the hallway, in and out of the rooms, in and out ..."

"Okay, okay ... what do you think we should do?" Ellie asked, licking her fingers and taking the napkin that Casey was handing her.

Casey spoke up, "It's not a problem. My sister will be happy for us. She wanted us to go to dinner last night. It's actually her idea ... right?" He looked to Ellie for confirmation.

"I dunno." She said, having taken another bite of the most delicious meat she had ever eaten. The fortitude with which she ate amazed her. She was starving. It's as if he had awoken every sense inside her and now it fell to her taste buds. She was ravaged with hunger and this BBQ was hitting the spot. "I don't know ..." She swallowed. "I don't see a problem with us having a relationship ... Stacy wouldn't mind."

Casey choked on is food. The word 'relationship' caught him off guard and the moment he coughed, he knew it was over.

Ellie put her rib down. "I'm sorry. I didn't mean it like that ... I just meant it wasn't a one night stand thing ... you know?" She looked to him for confirmation. The man that had just made love to her for hours on end, he seemed foreign again. He couldn't look her in the eye as he wiped his mouth with yet another napkin.

Casey heard the words come out of her mouth, but he knew better than to speak. A relationship had not entered his mind. They had a good time, but a relationship. He had made a grand mistake.

"I see." Ellie said as she put her food down, grabbed her things and walked from the room.

As she left, she bumped into Ashley, one of the staff member. "Excuse me." Ellie said as she headed straight for the door. Once outside, she got in her Rav and was gone. The tears stung her eyes walking down the stairs, but she did not let them fall. Even in the Rav, she did not let them fall. It wasn't until she was home, in the safety of her own queen bed, with her comfortable covers and her own pillows that the tears fell.

Auddie looked at Casey as if he were a mad man. "Are you serious? You just let her walk out the door?" She turned to follow Ellie.

"Don't." He grabbed her arm gently. "She's really hurt. It will take more than you to get her to be okay. I'll do it." He started to leave the room and then turned around when he heard Ellie bump into Ashley. Ducking for cover was the only option.

Auddie heard it to and whispered, "Go get her, Casey."

He just shook his head no.

Chapter Eighteen

Stacy wandered in the house nearing ten o'clock that night. Everything was closed and the house was quiet. The nursing staff had brought in a roll away cot for Jules to sleep on, after she refused to leave her sister again. Pascal was asleep by eight and Jules was right behind him. Stacy had kissed Angie, wide awake watching television and left for home. Her body ached, her heart was heavy and the baby was fluttering about a little bit. She wouldn't have an easy time sleeping unless the exhaustion was just too much.

She would go back and forth with deep exhaustion, barely

able to speak to Angie, ready to fall asleep, to a hyper mode that made her uncomfortable. It was as if she had too much coffee and had become jittery. Eating a little something was necessary and then she would crawl in a warm tub and relax. That was the plan until she walked into the kitchen from the back door and found Casey at the table.

"Hey." He said. His sister looked terrible. "Everything okay?"

She had kept up with him all day, but lost him somewhere in the afternoon. "It's fine. Are you okay? You look like shit, Case."

"Yeah. I'm fine ... but ..." Casey had prepared all day for this and he was about to deliver his speech to save Ellie face.

"What? What did you do?" She knew the drill. Something happened and she knew Ellie was involved. "What happened? Where's Ellie?"

"Okay ... well, I seduced her last night and it didn't go well." He sort of hid a little of the truth. But he wanted to minimize so that Ellie could still be with Stacy comfortably. He hadn't thought it though.

"What do you mean it didn't go well?" Stacy had enough energy at that point for ten people. Her anxiety was through the roof. She needed her best friend. She needed Ellie. Stomping her foot, standing in front of him, "Casey!!"

"She stormed out of here and well … she was drunk and I took advantage of her, Stacy. She's really upset and won't speak to me. She left this afternoon. I'm so sorry." He looked up at his sister, who was incredibly angry with him. At that moment, he knew that the feelings he had for Ellie were extremely strong, because he would protect her at all expense. Also, he knew that he had jacked everything up when he choked on the word relationship. He had beaten himself up over it all day long. "You need to fix it for her."

"You are damned right I will fix it for her. It's just like high school when all my girlfriends would fall for you and your distance and you would get close and dump them. Casey, how could you?" The tears streamed from her eyes as she left out the same door she had just come.

Casey dropped his head in his hands, picked up the bag he had packed and walked out to his car, awaiting his departure.

Twenty minutes later Stacy had roused Ellie out of bed and was in her living room. Ellie was the polite hostess. "Can I get you something to drink?" She sat on the sofa.

Stacy could see her swollen eyes from crying and her hair looked like whatever happened must have been fun ...

"I'm a mess." Ellie saw her judgement.

"NO, baby ... He's done this before. It's not you. I promise." Stacy was so angry with Casey. Memories of her two best friends and the very same thing happening. She hated what he had done and she was going to fix it. "It's not your fault."

The dam burst and Ellie started to leak alligator tears, which Stacy promptly wipe away. "It's okay." She scooped Ellie into her arms and held her while she cried. "It's okay ..." Stroking

Ellie's hair, Stacy willed it to be okay just like she willed Angie to be okay.

Ten minutes later, Ellie had regrouped and re-engaged. "I'm so sorry. I'm emotional. He's the first one ... since my husband."

"Oh, Elles, I'm so sorry."

"I just didn't expect it ... ya know?" She looked to her friend. Nothing about Stacy at this moment was sisterly to Casey and she was thankful for that. Ellie remembered just how cruel he seemed when he broke her leg. She let her guard down and shouldn't have done so. They were drunk and things got out of hand. Stacy didn't know they slept together and it wasn't something she wanted anyone to know.

"At least you didn't ... ya know ..." Stacy was glad Ellie had not fallen for Casey's wicked charm. So many women had been devastated. "He is a commitment phobe. He just can't do it. You saved yourself by fending him off. Not many women tell him no." She laughed just a little trying to lessen the intensity of the moment.

Little did she know, thought Ellie. His lovemaking was nothing like anything she had ever experienced and, granted, she hadn't been with that many men, but she was no virgin. "Right." She said.

"So, we are okay?" Stacy hoped.

"Are you angry with me?" Ellie asked.

"With you? Oh, heavens no. He a tramp. He's greedy and angry and can't make a commitment. I can barely get him to come for holidays and we have no one else. I am extremely angry at him … you, never. I came over here to make sure you were okay. You are my best friend." Stacy took her gently by the shoulders, turning her so she could hear Stacy better. "You are my best friend and I will have nothing come between us. Nothing. Okay? If he hurts you again, in any way, I'll have Pascal kick his ass. Deal?"

Ellie laughed at that one. Pascal was such a peacekeeper; it was funny. "Deal. How about we forget it happened and go on as we planned?"

Stacy was so relieved, "That would be wonderful. You want to come back to the house tonight? I don't want to stay alone. It's been a really rough day and little baby is fluttering around. I haven't eaten for quite some time and I don't feel very well."

Ellie immediately was concerned for the baby. "Sure. Let me grab some things. Oh, wait … is Casey there?" She couldn't bear to face him.

"No. He would have left. I saw a bag packed when he told me that he tried to seduce you …"

Ellie heard what she said, but it didn't register. She almost wondered what he had said exactly, but things were fine and if today there wasn't a problem, then there wasn't a problem. She loved Stacy like a sister and she had no problem continuing this relationship as they had just thirty-six hours prior. "Let's go. I'm ready."

They headed out the door, each in their own vehicle and drove back to the house where Ellie and Stacy grabbed food, took it to Stacy's room and ate in the bed where they watched an old romantic movie, each of their minds a million miles away. They fell asleep in the big bed and slept well, each finally rested and the sun broke through the darkness the next morning and they began their first day of business together. Ellie filled Auddie in, or at least tried to. However, Auddie was the one who filled her in.

Auddie had told Ellie that Casey blew it all off as nothing but a conquest and when he was done with Auddie, she hated him as much as Ellie was trying to. They vowed to keep it from Stacy and for the rest of the time there, it was a Casey-free-zone. No mention of his name, nor his existence rang through the house for the next month ... until it started.

Stacy was just entering her second trimester, due November 21st. She was bouncy and felt good and Angie had undergone treatments with a new program that really made a difference. They even thought that the child might outgrow the attacks. It started one morning when the girls left for their usual twenty to thirty-minute walk before they started work. Ellie felt fine when they left, but five minutes into the walk, her stomach was a mess. By minute ten, she was throwing up in a trash can in a park, with Stacy standing away from her. The flu wasn't something she wanted.

"Did you eat something bad? If you did, that's better than a virus." She stated as they headed back to the house. "Do you want me to call Auddie to come and get us ..." was barely out of her mouth before Ellie was throwing up in the grass to the right of the path they were walking.

"I don't know what's wrong with me. I felt fine and now ..." She threw up again.

"Oh, Darlin' ... I'm glad you haven't had relations." She laughed. "Sounds just like my morning sickness." Stacy laughed it off as she held Ellie's hair as she continued to throw up. Dialing the phone to have Auddie fetch them, she continued, "We'll get you home so you can rest. Poor baby. Auddie … so glad you answered. Can you come and get us in the park? East side, by the children's play land. Ellie is sicker than a dog. I'll have you drive her home in her truck and then Amanda can get you. She's really sick." She stopped for just a moment as Ellie threw up yet again. "Right. East side. See you in a minute. Might put a bag or something in with you. I'm not sure she will make it without tossing her cookies."

Ellie had started to feel better until Stacy said it reminded her of her morning sickness. It hit her like a ton of bricks. She was late, skipped a month and was due a second month, late. Her breasts had been sore for a month and she had very little appetite. She'd thrown up for over a week, each morning. She knew she was pregnant.

She heaved for another ten minutes and the tears were hard to hold back. She'd always wanted to have a child. Dreaming of caring for her baby and now she was in a pickle. Casey had been nowhere around, even when Stacy had talked about a grand birthday for Ellie and the possibility of maybe she had forgiven

Casey. Ellie's answer was, of course she had. He was drunk and made a mistake. How could she hold it against him for life? The party was planned for Saturday, just two days away. Auddie needed to get to the park immediately. Ellie was in desperate need to go have a pregnancy test.

Auddie showed up as if on cue. Stacy drug Ellie to the car, they piled in and they took Stacy back home. Once alone in the car, Ellie nearly laying in the seat, the tears came.

"What's wrong, Sugar? You have the flu?" Auddie glanced as she was driving.

Ellie shook her head no, trying to non-verbally convey the situation she could not admit.

"Oh SHIT!" Auddie breathed. "You're pregnant?"

"I think so …"

Addie made the next left and headed to a store for a test. Inside, she picked three different kinds and rushed through the checkout line and back to the car. "I bought one of every kind. We'll get to the bottom of this." They rode in silence the rest of the way to the house, but at least Ellie had stopped throwing up.

With the results of all three tests showing positive, Auddie paced the living room floor. Ellie sat on the couch, the sticks laying on paper towels on the coffee table. Twenty minutes of that, and then Auddie's phone rang.

Deep breath, she answered, "Ms. Davidson, she's still throwing up. I hate to leave her here alone."

Stacy was dreading that for two reasons. The first and most important was for Ellie's well-being. The second and more important than even that was that the flu was going around and being pregnant, she didn't want to hurt her child. "Why don't you stay the day with her? I'll cover here."

Auddie's reply was immediate, "Yes, Ma'am. I can do that. Thank you. I'll check in later."

"Thank you, Auddie. You're priceless. Take care of our

girl. If you need anything, juice, medication, anything … just call it in to the store and tell them to put it on my account and deliver it. Okay?"

"Yes, Ma'am. I can do that." Auddie was still blown away. This was not a good situation. She finished talking to Stacy, telling her what there was that needed done and then hung up. She went to the couch with Ellie, now lying on it, hugging a pillow close. "Darlin', we gotta figure out what to do."

"I know." Ellie squeaked.

"What about a fake boyfriend? I'm assuming Casey is the father?" Auddie waits.

Ellie shot her a go to hell look.

"I see. Okay, well, how is that going to go over at the house?"

Ellie took her pillow, covered her head and began to weep again.

"I didn't mean it like that, Darlin'. It's okay." She rushed to Ellie's side, gently pulled the pillow off her head. "It's okay. I promise."

Ellie couldn't fathom the situation. The last couple of hours had completely blown her world. "It's not okay." She sat up and looked at Auddie. "It's anything but okay."

"You gonna keep it?"

She shot Auddie another go to hell look, this time Ellie put in the mean eyes in full force. "That's not an option."

"Then I have a suggestion." Auddie put herself closer to Ellie, and took her hands in her own, "You need another boyfriend. One Stacy had no time to meet. It's a whirlwind situation, your life is your own, never told her kind of thing. Will that work?"

Ellie thought it through. She did keep to herself on each of her weekends off. Any time she had was nothing spoken of, because she literally had no interest in a life outside of work. "It just might work. But, and a big but here, where do I just come up with a boyfriend? Especially one that will take credit for another life?" She felt the tears stream down her face. "I'm sunk."

"No. You aren't. I know men. I know nice men. My husband has some good friends, most of them single. I can find one for you. You never, ever talk about your personal life, so it won't be much other than you disclose. It just might work, Ellie."

"It's going to have to. I refuse to let Casey Waters be the father of my child." The tears stopped. The anger consumed her. More anger at self than at Casey, but she was consumed.

"Okay then … we have, like a day, to figure this out. You aren't going to hide that morning sickness for long and you need to start prenatal care. Have you ever been pregnant before?" Auddie began to think of possibilities. She loved new babies and now they had two on the way. "Actually, Stacy will be extremely happy for you. She loves you like you are one of her own … even made you one of hers with your business. I think it will be okay. She might not like that you have hidden this from her. How about a fake engagement before you reveal the pregnancy? That might be even better … OH!!!" Auddie got even more excited that her plan just might work. "How about you fake it for your birthday … you know. The guy is your date to your birthday party and then he pops the question. It will be amazing. Stacy will love it. She loves that mushy stuff. You in?'

Ellie ceded immediately. It was the only plan and not a bad one. But, before she could agree, a wave of nausea hit her again and she ran to the restroom. Ten minutes later, a full bout of dry heaving, she returned. "I'm in."

Chapter Nineteen

Because they were still vying for business, even though four lavish parties later, Simply Elegant Party Planning still needed customers. Stacy had made a list comparable to a gigantic fundraising opportunity for Casey and Ellie's birthday, combining his business and theirs. It was impeccably done and even though they hired on staff members to do the work, their planning was exceptional. The party started at eight and Ellie's new beau, Landon Albert Francis Rufkin, would be at her side. Landon, who they referred to as Alfie, was a gorgeous man. His long, dark locks of hair enhanced his amazing brown eyes. He was a professional golfer and gay. Meeting every need they had, his closeted gayness even helped the dilemma. Glad to have a child, one he could share parenting with, was a bonus. Auddie had called Alfie that day and they had met for dinner that night. He was not surprised at the request, asked for Facebook pictures and loved that he would now be able to stop the facade he so desperately hated. She was now the light of his life, publicly, and she had even been asked to spend the weekend with him at Palm Springs in a few weeks. Looking forward to that was easy. It was the first she expressed her freedom in this new life. Stacy was more than happy to allow her to invite a guest to her party and the questions had started. Who is he? How long have you known him? How did you meet him? Where did you meet him? And then the big ... pouting largely, why didn't you tell me?

Ellie had answers for all her questions that had been fully fleshed with Alfie. It was all set. He would propose to her at the party, taking away from the emphasis on the birthday immediately so that they could show a relationship that would handle the pregnancy. It was all in motion and she looked stunning in her black dress, cut down to show cleavage and make her feel as sexy as she should when being proposed to. Her hair was done up and her jewelry a gift from Alfie. He had, in two days, set her up with a life you would have never guessed the newness to. As she placed the finishing touches on her appearance, her bell rang.

Opening the door, she met Alfie's dark presence, looking amazing. He was a gorgeous man. "Well, don't you clean up well?" She smiled.

"You, my Northern Belle, are astounding. Look at you!" He took her hand and spun her around. "Just stunning. I like … if I were straight." He laughed his hearty, full laugh that rang through the room. Looking at this amazing woman, he felt sad and yet glad. She offered him an opportunity to stop being a playboy and he loathed the company of women. Spending the day with her earlier had been quite fun. "You're a good catch, Elaine."

She winced at the reference, but they had feigned knowing each other before through the golf circuit her brother-in-law had travelled in his college career. Alfie knew Tyler. That helped a lot, even though it linked her to her old life. It wasn't a pleasant thought, but she needed Stacy to buy in wholly and for Casey to never, ever know she was carrying his child. She had gone to the Ob/Gyn and her due date was December 16th. It wasn't even a month past Stacy's date. The entire plan was in motion and Stacy was excited to finally meet the mystery man she would now marry. They had discussed the options and Alfie suggested an arranged marriage, full financial support of the child and full ownership as to being the baby's father. It was foolproof at this point. Alfie was genuinely a gorgeous and delightful man from what she knew at the time. He had a long-term partner, a professional football player that he wouldn't even disclose the name to her. It would ruin his partner's career if they were found out and this gave him the opportunity to be seen with his partner at times otherwise would not. She was happy to help him in his dilemma and he was happy to help her.

"Shall we go?" Alfie placed his hand at the small of her back, as he had done throughout the day shopping for rings and when they went to purchase her gown for the night. It was like having a best friend to shop with, a companion for his time off. He liked Elaine.

His brilliant smile lit his eyes and turned them an orangish-brown. He was truly handsome. "We shall. Thank you." Ellie was easily provoked to the car.

They laughed the entire way there, silly stories of the golf tour and being gay and how hard it was to not blurt it out at tournaments. Such an evolutionary sport in technology and so far behind social mores. Being gay on the pro circuit was not a great option for Alfie. Arriving at the party, valet service took his Jaguar and they were escorted into the party to an awaiting Stacy.

"Oh my ..." Stacy saw Ellie come in the door, as she spoke to the Mayor and his wife. "Can you excuse me please?" She headed for Ellie.

"We are on ..." Ellie whispered and Alfie placed his hand in the small of her back to lead forward.

"No worries, my love." He referred to her as he would Nathan Sparks, the quarterback of the New Orleans Saints and his lover of over ten years. "No worries." His smile lit his face as

Stacy me them.

"Look at how beautiful you are." Stacy kissed Ellie's cheek and extended her hand. "And you ... Alfie. I have waited long hours to meet you."

He took her hand, shook it lightly and then kissed the outer limit. "It's my pleasure. Elaine has told me so much about you, always talking Stacy this ... Stacy that. It's past time to finally make your acquaintance."

"I agree. Let me introduce you to my husband." Stacy looked to find him in the crowded room. "He's just over here." She led them forward.

Ellie saw him before he saw her and it pained her. Casey was with a blonde. His arm around her in a very possessive stance and he was talking to Pascal. She knew he would be there, but it stung to see him. And then he saw her ...

In mid-sentence, Casey stopped talking, as Stacy, Ellie and Alfie approached. He immediately stuck out his hand, extended to

Alfie. "Casey Waters and my birthday date, Amanda Jenkins."

Alfie shook his hand solidly. "Landon Rufkin. Nice to meet you Casey Waters. And you as well, Ms. Jenkins." He shook Amanda's hand too and then turned to Pascal, awaiting the introduction.

Stacy was quick, "This is my husband, Dr. Pascal Davidson. Pascal, this is Ellie's date, Landon Rufkin, Alfie."

Pascal shook Alfie's hand. "I hear you are quite the opponent this year. I follow a lot and well, we should play sometime if you are up to playing with a real non-threatening entity?" He laughed.

"I'd love to. Your family has proven to take really good care of Elaine and I truly appreciate that. I travel so much, it's hard to be there when she needs someone. I'll call for tee time next week. Let me know when you're free?" Alfie handed Pas his card with his number on it.

"Great. It's a date. I look forward to getting some

pointers." Pas shook his hand again, noticing that Casey was soaking it all in. Stacy had told him what happened and he didn't buy it. He and Casey were close and the look and Casey's face as he tried to pull Amanda even closer, was apparent. Something wasn't right, but what the hell. It was a party and he was going to have a good time. "Let's get you a drink." Pas stole Alfie away and Stacy pulled Ellie with her.

"Let's go mingle … lots of business to be had here tonight and it's your birthday. I can't wait to have you see your gift." Stacy was in the mood to party and with so much to be thankful for, she was going to do it right. "Guess what?" They were out of earshot of anyone.

"What?" Ellie was starting to feel as though everything would be okay.

"It's a boy!" She nearly whispered, but the excitement was barely able to be controlled. "I found out this morning. It's a boy."

"Does Pas know yet?" Ellie was so happy for her she grabbed her in a hug right there in the middle of the room. Tears in her eyes, no new thing right now with her hormones raging, she was so happy for them.

"No … I don't know how to tell him." Stacy looked for Pas across the room and saw him and Alfie laughing as though they were old friends. "Look at them, hitting it off."

"Everyone will love him, Stacy. He's genuinely lovable. You'll see. You have nothing to worry about. How are you going to tell him?" Ellie moved the conversation back to the baby gender.

"I don't know … I thought about delivering a hundred balloons to work, all blue, all saying it's a boy." Stacy had thought about surprising him a thousand ways. She knew he would finally get his dream child, a junior, taking on his name. "He's going to be so excited. He commented this morning, right before I got the call, that this pregnancy was exactly like my other two and it is probably a girl. Not disappointed, not a sign that he was unhappy in any way … he's so grateful. I love that man!" She smiled within.

"I know you do. I should be so lucky." Ellie wished secretly that she could love like that and be loved. But, she would settle for Alfie and his attention, his parenting and his outside relationship.

Stacy was on it, "Do you love Alfie?"

Backtracking, she had to cover or tonight would not work. "I do. Sometimes I wonder if he will love me the same as I love him. Make sense?"

"Oh. It does. You're still new. Give it time. It will deepen and strengthen as you experience life together. Just give it time." Stacy felt for her. She'd watched Ellie live a single existence for so long, it was hard to believe that she was with this gorgeous man. How in the world she kept it a secret, Stacy couldn't figure out? If he were her man ... she'd have shown him off to everyone, as she did Pas. However, her friend was more reserved. "You look so beautiful tonight, Elles. I mean beautiful ... just aglow. He suits you well."

Giving credit to Alfie would change within the next month when Stacy could know that all her mornings running to the restroom with the 'flu' were the reason for her glow. She felt it. Ellie could feel how her skin changed and how her hair was stronger, her nails were stronger. Their walks during the morning would benefit them both and she wanted to take up swimming soon. Birthing in water, as Stacy spoke of, was her goal.

"Let's get a drink." Stacy headed them toward the bar and a group of businessmen from Peoh Companies.

To keep in compliance with her non-drinking, Auddie, who was bartending, knew not to put alcohol in her drink. When Auddie called her earlier, asking about the plan, they made a deal that she would drink vodka 7's all night, minus the vodka. The soda would help her stomach and she could sample the hors de oeuvres. Alfie's arm encircled her waist as he came up behind them.

"Hey, Kitten. How are you doing?" He whispered in her ear intimately and kissed her lightly. "Happy Birthday once again."

Stacy loved how he was treating her friend so far. The look in his eyes when she spoke into her ear and the way he touched her were given her friend approval. She wanted to like Alfie, even though in the remote recess of her mind, she was jealous that Elle had someone she might like more and might want to share more than with Stacy. She sighed deeply.

"Thank you, baby. It's an amazing day." Ellie kissed him again, softly on his sweet lips. How could this man be gay? She couldn't picture him with the big, burly football player she had googled. Nathan was handsome, but a different kind of look altogether. She didn't get it. But, she did get Alfie and what he was trying to do.

"I love you, Kitten." Alfie looked her in the eyes, beautiful and sparkling.

"I love you too." Ellie had practiced with him so that it wasn't uncomfortable.

"Stacy," He turned his attention to her, "when are they opening presents?"

Stacy had planned the whole party out. About 45 minutes of mingling, hors des oeuvres and then gifts and then drinks and music if anyone wanted to dance. "We could do it now, if you like? Special gift?"

"I'd like to think so." Alfie smiled. He reached for his pocket to make sure the ring box was in it. It was and he released the anxiety. His hope was that the newspaper presentation would be met by national exposure and that he was off the hook and no longer required to be a 'playboy' in the tabloids. "I sure hope so."

Ellie just smiled.

"Let's do it." Stacy went to the bar and rang the bell on it. "Can we all get together around the gifts table please? I'd like to give our birthday girl and boy their gifts and then we will have music and dancing."

Everyone made way to the farthest part of the room where there was gift upon gift stacked on the table. The only bad part about having this big a part for a birthday, everyone brought gifts. Casey and Ellie were placed in chairs at opposite ends of the table and Stacy started by dividing the gifts between them according to the card. Ellie had three times as many gifts as Casey, in that most of the party-goers knew her now.

They began opening gifts. Casey received beer steins, shot glasses, ties, socks, a business card holder, a new set of carving tools from Pascal and Stacy, and miscellaneous tokens of affection from the guests. Ellie opened a bracelet, three pair of beautiful silver earrings, a couple necklaces, a business card holder like Casey's, various office supplies in leather with her name embossed, candles, bath products, a silver spoon that said North Carolina and many other wonderful gifts. When done, Stacy handed her the gift from the Davidsons. It was a heart on a string ornament that said Christmas 2014. She dropped a tear on it. "Thank you so much."

Stacy hugged her, "You're family now." Pulling her out to give her the assured look she wanted, "and I have another gift for you just between you and I after the party. Okay?"

"Okay." Ellie felt so special.

"One more …" Alfie walked forward. "Just one more gift."

Ellie was ready. She smiled at him, looking deep into his eyes as though she would have loved him as he walked forward and got on one knee in front of her.

"Elaine …" He pulled the ring out of his pocket on cue and Ellie put her hands to her mouth. "I have loved you from the moment I saw you … I don't have sweet words or meaningful exchange. Just a simple I love you … Will you marry me, please?" He smiled at her.

"Yes! Of course I will." She threw her arms around his neck and kissed him like she kissed Casey Waters the night she got pregnant with his child. "Yes!"

He placed the 1 carat diamond solitaire on her finger and they kissed again as Stacy stood back watching. Inevitably, she knew that this would happen. If not now, then later. But, would Ellie be surprised by the bassinet she was going to give her as a gift later? At least she was not having to worry now that this baby would tear up Casey's life. She knew it would bless her own and true Auntie or not … they were both having babies.

The rest of the night was filled with congratulations, kissing and hugging and good natured tidings for Ellie and Alfie. Even Casey shook his hand and wished them well. He did not, however, speak with Ellie at all. Amanda kept throwing her a dirty look but it was all good. Ellie had the time of her life. Shew as going to be a mommy, and her and Stacy were going to be mommies together. She had dreamed, in the last two days, of breaking things off with Alfie just after little baby was born and them sharing some form of parenting, but her raising the baby on her own. It would be easy … she was sure that Stacy was happy for her and would be happy about the baby, no holds barred.

As the party wound down around eleven o'clock. Pas and

Alfie excused themselves to the den to smoke a cigar. Casey must have left hours before, she had lost track of him earlier. Stacy pulled Ellie into the kitchen. "I have your real gift. The other was from the family. I want you to have the gift from me." She stopped at the kitchen table and took Ellie's hand, looking at the ring. "It's beautiful, Sweetie. He seems like a real good catch and that's a big thing here in the Carolina's. We all gotta have us a good catch. He's a beautiful man. Is he gentle?" Stacy awaited a response.

To be true to her feelings, Ellie pictured Casey making love to her those endless hours. "He's amazing, Stase. Just amazing. Everything about him makes my heart warm, skip a beat or burn with fire … he is a dream." She was sincere. "He is amazing. And I love spending time with him."

"More than with me?" She pouted.

"No. Never … you'll always be my favorite companion. You know that." Ellie supported her to diminish the fear. She knew it well. There were times she wished Stacy could go home with her instead of to her own family, but soon Ellie would be able to do just that: going home to her own family.

"Good, because we need each other. I love you like the sister I never had and I would miss you. I'm kind of jealous. It's a conundrum actually, I'm so happy for you and yet, jealous and yet, so happy again … and, well, here …" Stacy Steered her to a gift behind the kitchen counter … a beautiful white wicker bassinet with a big pink and blue bow on it.

"When are you due?" Stacy asked.

Ellie couldn't move. She was cemented into place. How did she know? When did she know? Did she know? Did Casey tell her? Did she KNOW? Ellie just stared at her and then at the bassinet. "It's beautiful." Tears lit her eyes again.

"When are you due?" Stacy asked softly.

They had discussed postponing her due date for a month to ward off anyone thinking it could possibly be Casey's baby and having a baby four weeks premature could be dealt with. "January

16th." Ellie smiled hugely at her friend as they hugged.

"I can't believe how blessed we both are!" Stacy held Ellie hard. "We are so lucky."

"We truly are, Stase. I'm so happy." Ellie pulled away. "A baby, Stase. I'm having a baby." She was so excited. The first time she could say it with one hundred percent happy conviction. "I'm having a baby."

"We are having a baby. Auntie Stacy and Auntie Elles. I'm so excited. I'm having a boy." She knew it would hit home. Everyone wanted her to have a boy and she was finally having a boy and she could stop. With the fright that she experienced with Angie, it was enough. She wanted to focus on her children and give them everything they deserved. "It's a boy."

"Oh, Stacy!" Ellie was so happy for her. "I'm so happy!" Ellie knew they wanted a boy so they could stop. "This is beautiful. So pretty." She touched the bassinet.

"I know that I love having mine, so the baby can be right

next to my bed. It's wonderful to be able to have them right beside you for the first few months. I thought you would like it, but no one knows you're pregnant." She was glad the secret was out.

"How did you know?" Ellie asked.

"The day in the park. You had been saying for a couple weeks that your breasts hurt and you were expecting your monthly, but you never cramped. Usually you cramp enough that you say something, but nothing for a couple of months."

Ellie almost freaked out that Stacy knew her so well, because she could put the times together. She kept composure the best she could.

"My morning sickness started so quickly. I didn't know until the other day. Being sick like that and then thinking about the night filled with wine and roses six weeks ago … I knew then. I called Alfie and asked him what he thought about children and well, at least he was happy when I told him. I was pretty worried." Ellie lied.

"Is that why he proposed? He is quite the playboy you know?" Stacy was concerned that this was the reason and yet, she wanted it to be real.

"I know. And, he was going to propose tonight anyway. As a matter of fact, he told me this afternoon of his plan right before I told him about the baby. He's very happy and his days of playing are over. He's an honest man from everything I have seen."

"I'm glad you have this, Elles. We are so lucky." They hugged one more time before finding the men in the den.

Stacy opened the door to the den and the smoke was apparent. "Guys, we aren't coming in … but if you want to join us for some cocoa, we'll be in the kitchen. I'm getting a little tired."

Pas snubbed his cigar and handed the ashtray to Alfie. "We'll be right along, Darling. Two minutes."

Chapter Twenty

Three months had passed and school was nearing session. August was hot, even hotter than July had been and being five months pregnant was easier than being six-and-a-half months. Stacy was cranky. The morning of getting the girls ready for school, moving them to a new schedule was proving exhausting to Stacy. There had been no real scares with Angie's asthma, but all the same, it was a full school year for her in Kindergarten. Jules was heading to preschool and the day was beginning with Stacy in tears.

"Are you going to be okay?" Ellie asked across her desk.

"I'm fine. It's just hard the first week or so, is what I hear." Stacy was trying to be a trooper, but she missed her girls already and both at the same time. "I thought it would be easier for Jules to go to preschool, but they are both gone and I'm ... well, I'm ... mad." She sorts of laughed.

"I understand." Ellie said. "One would be bad enough, but both? Geez. What are you mad about?"

"That it was my decision." She laughed heartily this time. "Jules is going to be handful, isn't she?"

They both laughed at the thought. Ellie spoke up with fondness, "I'll never forget the day she met me in the kitchen, with my broken leg. She was so funny. Asked me a question and then needed a note pad and paper in order to relay it correctly. Yes, that little smarty is going to be a handful. And Angie ... I know you are worried, but you put everything in place and she's doing so much better. NO attacks in how long?"

"Over six months. That new med is amazing and her life is so different. She asked me yesterday if she could play soccer. Elles,

I'm so worried the exercise will induce an attack. But, Pas said let her try. So … I will soon be a soccer mom. Jules is going to play as well. It's almost as if they are the same age, Jules is so advanced and Angie is behind due to the sicknesses."

"I agree. They are quite even-steven. But, we have work to do and we should get to it. Saturday is the fundraiser and we need to get confirmation on these three items." Ellie handed Stacy the list.

"I'll do it. Why don't you make these sales calls from the party the other night? Seven requests for services from one birthday party. You are a special little thing, aren't you?" Stacy grabbed her list and handed one back to Ellie across their desks.

That night, Ellie got a call from Alfie. She was exhausted and things had progressed through the pregnancy to the point she was uncomfortable. He had made Nathan aware of their baby, something she had not known that Nathan was in the dark about. The response was not positive.

"What do you mean you can't have a baby?" Ellie was

heartbroken for her child. Now she would grow up without any father, no chance of a father. "You can't do this Alfie. We had a deal."

"I know, Elaine, but he said he would leave me if I marry you now. I can't do it." Alfie was horrified at the predicament.

"There is no way I will argue with you. How about you do this for me? Go out and have a visible affair this week. Make sure it's in the news and plastered everywhere so that I can leave this with no dignity, no reason to contact you again. I'll end the engagement and then Nathan can go about his business not being intimidated by a child. Alfie … you really are stuck in a rut." She was livid, because learning about Alfie on their various engagements with Stacy and Pascal, she had learned that he was with someone married, with a family and he wasn't allowed to have even friends that were gay. He wasn't allowed to do anything but hang out with women that made it okay for them to sneak around. Blatantly placing him in the media as a playboy so that Nathan's wife wouldn't know the difference. "I feel for you."

"I can do that, Elaine. Thank you for understanding." He was truly sad. Looking forward to fathering a child, he was devastated by Nathan's bad attitude and the unfairness of the situation. "I love him, Elaine."

"I know you do. Too bad he loves you the way he does." She hung up the phone.

The next weekend, she saw it in the tabloids, his blatant affair and her name plastered, once again, with bad press. However, it made everyone in Asheville love her even more. They had accepted her and her plight. Stacy made sure of it. She called off the engagement, put the ring in a drawer, she had paid for it and went on with her business as usual. The hardest part was that Stacy figured out quickly that she had no emotions for Alfie. Ellie pretended that he was not attentive and that things had not progressed properly. The only thing Stacy said was she had seen as much and no one needed two bad marriages.

Halloween was a hit. Six parties they planned and hugely successful. Stacy was grouchy like there was no tomorrow, due in two weeks and miserable. She had gained almost 40 pounds and called herself a little fatty all day and night. There was no getting away from her relentless banter.

"I'm so fat. How I ever fit into these jeans before?" She held up a pair of jeans from in one of her desk drawers.

The office was quiet, except for light music that Ellie was playing in headphones attached to her big belly. "I know you aren't doing the jean thing again. Put them up." She scolded. "Put them up."

Stacy did as she was told. "How much have you gained? You're only in your 30th week and you're huge. You're going to gain more than me."

Ellie had to reverse four weeks, so instead of being in week 30, she was in week 34. It was a little hard to keep track of, so she made sure not to ever write anything down and she neglected to use the various journals that Stacy got her, feigning to have one very special journal at home by her nightstand. Stacy had given gift after gift and Ellie was becoming just like her. Whenever she found something she liked, she bought two. She was having a little girl. They had found out early, in a sonogram, but she said she didn't want to know. After six weeks of Stacy demanding to know, she finally told her the truth. Very happy, she had everything from the girls that was girl-fitting, she had already given it all to Ellie. Her house was booming with everything from a gorgeous crib, matching dressers and changing table, all gifts from Stacy, to clothing, bibs, bottles that were pink and yellow and purple, to pacifiers and diapers left over of all sizes, all girl of course, to anything you could think of that you might have left. At one point, Ellie pouted to her that she couldn't buy anything for herself, because Stay kept giving her everything. Stacy's answer ... buy anything you want and give the rest to someone deserving if you don't want it, because that is exactly what she would have done. It was all good.

"How much!" Stacy demanded in her frumpy mood.

"Forty-two pounds." Ellie stated.

"Forty-two pounds. I'm all fat, not baby. You're all baby, like a damned basketball shooting out of your pants all high carrying with my baby girl and I'm low, dragging on the ground stomach, falling over my pants and my arms are fat and my back has fat on it and my legs have cellulite now!!!! Imagine what you will be like in six weeks. I still have two weeks to go." She was near crying as she spoke.

Ellie knew the only thing that would get her out of this mood. "Stacy ... What should I name her? What are you going to name him?"

Stacy immediately shut it all down. "Pascal Isaiah Davidson, Junior."

"No chance of change?" Ellie just knew the drill.

"No chance of change. None." Stacy touched her stomach at exactly the moment Isaiah kicked. "He will play soccer! A kicker for sure. Is baby girl moving a lot? It's probably too early to tell." She reached in her desk drawer and pulled a list out. "Here are some girl's names that I like. You don't favor anything? No family names or anything?"

Ellie shook her head. She just hadn't gotten as far as names. Thinking about it had become a real problem. She would lock up every time she went there. The list Stacy had made was the third. Every time most of the names were the same, which pleased Ellie. Some were family names and she knew it and felt guilty, because the one name she really, really liked, was Stacy and Casey's grandmother's name: Margaret. She had an Aunt Margaret and she always liked the name Maggie. Margaret Katherine, but it was her grandmother's name. If she could just use one or the other. But she really liked them together. Ellie's goal was to find a first name that she could use with Margaret and if she wanted to call her Maggie, then she could.

The list only had six names on it: Blanche, Heather, Harmony, Gisselle, and she hated all of them. The last one, Margaret. It had not appeared on other lists she had made.

Ellie said, "I kind of like Margaret. I had an Aunt Margaret. But I wouldn't know what to put with it. Maybe use it as a middle name? Old school. Ya know?"

Stacy liked that. It was her grandmother's name and she knew that Ellie knew that. "I like it for a middle name. What about first names? None of those are good?"

"Nothing strikes a chord. No." Ellie was already frustrated. She liked her name, Elaine. Her mother had stopped the use of Lainie early on and Ellie had stuck. She could use her nickname or use her proper name on business or professionally. It wasn't childish or, well, she just liked it. What did baby girl look like? Both she and Alfie were dark and if the baby was born with curly blonde locks and light blue eyes, what would she do? It almost made her cry. As a matter of fact, it struck her so hard that she felt a cramp in her abdomen. She should de-stress. Putting the headphones back on the baby bump helped her to feel more secure. She had pumped in French, Italian, classical, jazz and bluegrass music and baby seemed to like it all. Ellie told her stories about her mom and dad, growing up in Duluth and talked to her incessantly at home as though she were already born. Caught in her own thoughts, she missed Stacy talking to her and the cramps were still coming in her stomach. Maybe lunch didn't agree with her? Lord knew that the heartburn felt like a bonfire in her stomach daily.

Stacy asked again, "What letter do you like? Do you have a favorite?"

"Who can have a favorite letter?" Ellie said.

"Well, I liked the letter J and the letter A, because when you write them, they are pretty. The letter E is pretty, you know, in cursive, script. Do you have one you like?"

"I like M's" She said.

"Right … Well, we have Margaret. You can do Mary Margaret, Martha Margaret …"
Ellie broke in, "I'm not naming my child Martha … who calls a little kid Martha?" She thought seriously about it. She really did need a name. "What about Madeline Margaret?"

Stacy said the words, "Madeline Margaret Justice." It sounded good. "I like it. I do."

Ellie said, "I just don't know. I want it to be the best name ever. I wonder what she looks like." She gazed at Stacy as she put her hand on her stomach. She needed some relief. "I have horrible heartburn, it's so bad I'm cramping."

"We should get you some milk. Want me to go grab some?" She was almost out of her seat.

"No. That doesn't sound tempting at all. I can gut it out."

Stacy started riddling off names, "Memphis, Margo, Mathis, Magdeline, Madison, Madonna, Megan, Magnolia ... a big Southern hit, Mahogany, Mayia, Maria, Mable ... What about places: Maine, Michigan, Madrid, Mexico, Maltese, Montana, Monroe, Marietta ..." Stacy was at wits end.

Ellie wasn't feeling so hot.

"You Okay, Elles?" Stacy saw the look of pain on her face.

"I'm fine. Don't forget tomorrow I have an appointment."
Ellie said. Ellie struggled every day not to squeal with delight at
the amount of movement she was experiencing. The baby had
been kind of quiet that day. She tried moving the music again, and
the kid was sitting so low that she didn't know about it. Good
thing she had an appointment in the morning. She could make sure
everything was okay. The difference in time was huge and she
was experiencing so much more than she could share with Stacy.
The past two weeks, she could feel the baby move around as
though she were spinning like a top. She had turned and dropped
and the doctor had been a little concerned about her placement and
early delivery. She tried not to stress, but early delivery could be a
real problem.

"Right ..." Stacy said. Ellie had a glucose tolerance test
weeks early and other things with appointments told Stacy that the
dates were a bit off. She wasn't stupid ... there was something
very fishy about this whole situation, but she loved Ellie and
whatever she said, was good enough for Stacy. Ellie was huge to
only be barley in the third trimester. She looked as far along as

Stacy.

"Have you been having signs of problems?" Stacy couldn't help it. She was in a foul mood and she didn't like it that Ellie wasn't forthright. Knowing the signs of Ellie's honesty, this was not right.

"No. Why? So far, so good. I don't mind being pregnant. The morning sickness was a pain the butt, but I'm enjoying it now. I'm sure that will change when I get to where you are."

"Because I'm grouchy?" Stacy laughed. "That's just me. Most women aren't grouchy like I am."

"Nonsense. You aren't that grouchy, just a little moody. Nothing we can't handle." Ellie took the headphones off her stomach and put them on her own head. "My turn, while I get these calls ready." Shoes already under the desk rather on her swollen feet, Ellie kicked her feet up on her desk to try and relieve the swelling and the endless leg cramps and backache and now the abdominal squeezes. Pregnancy was starting to be a pain in the ass.

They both worked on their own from that point, but Stacy wondered continually if that baby was her brothers. She couldn't help but know that something was very wrong, because Casey never went this long without talking to her and when she told him that Ellie was pregnant, that night at the party, before everyone else knew, the color went out of the man's face. She knew she was right. If it wasn't his child, there was still the fact that they had slept together and neither of them wanted to admit it. She was truly heartbroken, Ellie could have been her sister in every sense of the word if her stupid brother hadn't been such an ass. Oh well … such is life, Stacy thought.

Ellie felt the urge to pee and went to stand up between client calls. Suddenly, she felt as if she wet her pants. Stacy was on the phone when she felt the gushing of fluid. First a trickle and then a gush. Ellie's water broke. All down her chair, she felt the warm liquid leave her vagina. "Stase …"

Stacy was on a call, she held up her hand as she finished

the sentence, "That's right ... $150 per guest and we can work with any number. I can give you a discount if you have more than 50 guests." She held her hand to the mouthpiece. "Yes?"

"My water broke, baby. I need to go to the hospital." She was standing up and gathering her bag when Ellie felt the first contraction and sat back down. "Oh, that hurt."

Stacy was writing what the client was saying. "Yes, sir. 75-80 people. Drop that to $140 per and we have a deal. I can send over the contracts if you like."

"Stase, honey ... we need to go, baby." Ellie was calm, timing between contractions she wrote the time down and looked up again. Stacy was still on the call. "Fax number please?" Stacy still wrote.

Ellie screamed as the next contraction hit and hard. "Stacy!!!!" She doubled over.

"I'll call you back." Stacy hung up the phone. "Your water broke?" She saw that Ellie was soaked. "Is it time? It's too early, Ellie. It's too early ..." She got flustered and couldn't think straight. What was she supposed to do? She couldn't remember a thing. "Ellie? Are you okay?"

Ellie was panting through the contraction. When it finished, she looked at the time. "Stacy, we are in trouble. I'm not five minutes apart and my water broke."

Stacy perked up and fell into mode. She called for an ambulance and stayed by Ellie's side the whole time. Ellie started pushing in the ambulance. The EMT were freaking out.

"Ellie, hold on, we will be there soon. Don't push." He said.

Ellie screamed at him. "I have to push. I have to." And she did.

With every push, the contractions coming every minute or more, she would push. The baby was crowning as they reached the hospital ER entry and they rushed her in. Immediately they sent her up to labor and delivery and right out of the elevator, the EMT giving up, said, "Here one comes, Push Ellie, Push!!!"

They were rolling Ellie down the hall to labor and delivery and had to make a stop, in a water closet. That baby girl shot into the room in a mop closet.

The doctor had no scrubs, had been standing at the nurses' station when he saw her bare down, crowning visible and he ran and got things taken care of.

The EMT yelled, "Doc, she's not going to make it to the room." He shoved the gurney into the open closet as far as he could get it and they backed out to let the doc in.

They rushed baby girl into the incubation room to clean her up and barely got Ellie into the room to deliver the placenta.

All Ellie could say in her sweat-soaked state was "I'm sorry, Stacy. I'm so sorry." She screamed the baby into the world and was wheeled down the hallway to the labor and delivery room.

"Let them get you into the room and get you sewed up and

taken care of. I'll go with our baby girl to get cleaned up and I'll be right back. Okay?" She stroked Ellie's head. "Okay, baby girl?"

Ellie nodded as they started to wheel her away. "Call Alfie please." One last ditched attempt at not claiming that blonde baby that she just birthed, but it was too late, she had hair, it was blonde, a lot of it, and it was curly. She was sunk.

"I sure will, Elles. I'll be right here." Stacy ran with the baby down the hall and watched as they cleaned her up as she scrubbed up so she could hold her. Things moved very quickly. Finally, they were all together in the room. Alfie and Pas had shown up from their golf game and Stacy got to bring the baby in the room and hand her to Ellie, both bawling like babies.

"She's so beautiful, Stase. Look at her." Ellie looked up with large blue eyes, looking like she went for their morning run. "She's gorgeous, Sweetness." Stacy sat on the bed with her, holding her arm around her as Angie, Jules and Pas stood by watching.

"She's beautiful, Ellie." Pas, holding Jules, came to the other side of the bed, but he didn't touch the child.

Angie stood beside Stacy. "Our little princess. What are you going to name her, Elles?" She had asked the magic question.

Stacy tried to help, "I liked Madison Margaret …"

Jules piped in, "I like Addison Margaret too … that's real purdy, Elles."

When the little girl said it, Ellie loved it. "That's it. I like it." She looked at her curly blonde haired child, comfortably lying in her arms, swaddled in the pink blanket.

Stacy was happy, "Madison Margaret, so it is …"

"No." Ellie quietly said.

Stacy got frustrated immediately as she moved her fatness on the bed, so uncomfortable and so jealous that Ellie had her baby in her arms, "No?"

"Addison Margaret Justice ... Addison. I love it." Ellie spoke to the baby. "Hi Addie, ..." The baby moved around for just a moment.

Angie liked that, "She likes it. See, she likes it."

Jules beamed. "Did you let me name her?"

"I did, Kitten. All by yourself." Ellie smiled at her.

Jules kissed Pas, so proud of her little self. "I did it."

Angie was sulking, but just barely when Ellie said, "Is there a name you really like as well, Angie? You can pick a name too, if you like."

"I can?" She looked at her mom. "Really?"

"If Ellie says you can, you can ... be very careful and Ellie can say no. Okay?" Stacy thought Ellie was crazy.

She thought quite some time as they cooed over the 6 lb. 3 oz. baby who was perfect from top to bottom. No one mentioned the fact that a premature baby had entered the world like a Buddha doll, chubby and perfectly formed. But Ellie knew Stacy caught it. She saw it in her eyes as she held the baby, such adoration, her family.

Angie burst out with, "I got it. Masey. Addison Margaret Masey Justice. And you spell it M-A-S-E-Y ... just like Stacy and Casey, so Addie is some part of the family too. Right?" She was so proud of herself.

Ellie just about died. Did she just set herself up for this and how could she tell the child who was now holding her child, christening with her name, no?

Angie cooed to baby Addison, "Addison Margaret Masey Justice ... you sure have a big name for such a little tiny baby girl. You might have to grow into it." She kissed the baby's forehead. "I love you baby Addison."

Jules came up as close as she could to Addison, "I love you too, baby Addison." She kissed the baby's feet through the swaddle.

Stacy was now crying. She took the child back from Angela and said to Addison, "Addison Margaret Masey Justice, we love you so much." And she kissed the baby's forehead, handing her to Pascal.

His first time holding the bundle of joy, he held her with both hands, looking into her face, held very close to his own. "I pray you the will to do good and pray that you are blessed with gifts that help you find meaning in life and true happiness. You are born of talented parents and will go far in this world with the love bestowed upon you, Addison Margaret Masey Justice ... and that love will last forever. This uncle loves you infinitely ..." Ending with a kiss to her forehead, he handed her back to her mother.

"Well, I guess we have it ... Addison. I've never been this happy." She looked at the love in that room and in walked Casey.

Ellie quickly tucked the baby's hair back under the

warming cap and cuddled her closer. She looked to him and saw that he knew too. She didn't know whether to laugh or cry, but she knew he knew.

His smile was genuine. "I heard there was a little minion here who might need a doll house, so I came to ask her what kind she wanted." He walked directly to the bed, where Stacy hugged and kissed him and the girls grabbed each hand and drug him closer to Ellie's bed.

Jules was first, "Unca-Casey, she's so pretty. Her name is Addison Margaret Masey Justice. Isn't that a big, big, big name for such a little tiny weeny baby?"

He caught it instantly, both references to him being the father. "May I hold her?"

Ellie handed her to him immediately. With tears in his eyes, he held his daughter for the first time. She cried in the handing this time, having been so comfortable with mommy. But he cooed a little to her and she settled right down. "Shhhhhh ...

shhhhh … Addison. It's okay." He rocked gently as he walked around the room talking to her where no one could hear. She never made another peep once in his arms.

Stacy grabbed Ellie's hand and squeezed.

The family stayed until ten o'clock that night, kissing Ellie, each one of them and then the baby before they went.

Stacy left with, "You call me if you need anything. Anything at all. Okay?"

She nodded. "I'm fine. I'm a little tired. I'm just going to rest."

"I love you." Stacy squeezed her hand one last time and one last kiss to Addison. "I love you too, baby Addison."

Casey stuck around until they were out of the room. "Can I say goodbye?"

"No …" Ellie said. She was tired of the lie. This was his child and she cheated him out of the pregnancy, she couldn't cheat him out of the child.

"What?" He was hurt.

"You can never say goodbye. She's yours." Ellie handed him the baby. "You already knew that. I can tell."

"Well," he took the baby in his arms again, so comfortably, "trying to hide her blonde curls sure didn't help any." He laughed lightly as he kissed the top of her now sleeping head. "I had my assumption from the beginning and then Alfie came up."

She just nodded. "I tried"

"Epic failure. The dates, the time, he was nowhere around. I made sure. I had him checked out. His boyfriend probably didn't like it much."

"You did?" Ellie let it all sink in. She never would underestimate this family. "You knew the whole time?"

"No. Actually, I just found out. You see, he's very discreet. But, the right people know the right things. You did a pretty good job."

"Are you going to try and take her from me?" Ellie knew that he could.

"Ellie, why would I do that?" He came closer. "I would never take her from her mother. Ever. She needs you. She needs us both."

Ellie was relieved. Her anxiety with him knowing was incredible. "I'm sorry. I didn't know what to do and you didn't want a relationship and well ... I guess you lose. We will have one our whole lives."

Casey felt the sting of her words. There wasn't a day that went by that he did not regret his action that day. But, he knew there was nothing he could say. His love for her would have to suffice in fathering their child. He missed Ellie something horrible. That one day was the best of his life, so easy and yet so passionate and intimate. Almost as intimate as holding his child.

Ellie watched him walking with her. Addison didn't move,

as if she had been in his arms as long as in her womb. They were connected. "Let's just move forward. Can we erase the past?"

Casey matter-of-factly said, "No. There is no erasing the beauty that created her. But, we don't need to talk about it. We will work this out. Let's get the other baby here safely, get you and Addie home and settled and then we will figure it out." He looked up at her, his blue eyes lovingly. "Okay?" "Okay ... Yes."

He handed Addie back to Ellie and they sat and talked for hours about nothing that mattered, giving Addie back and forth, taking turns. Ellie even learned to have her latch on with him in the room, easily having him a part of every feature of the child.

Three weeks later, a week over due, Pascal Isaiah Davidson entered the world and everyone was back at the hospital. This time it was Ellie who got Stacy to the hospital from her house, because she went into labor at three o'clock in the afternoon. The worst time, because they needed to pick up girls at school. Pascal was in appointments he had to leave and Casey didn't get there for the same hour it took him to get to Addison.

Stacy had a much harder time with her labor, six hours, and complained about it regularly while waiting for the baby to be screened. "He's almost as small as Addison. Just 6 pounds and 8 ounces. Look, it's all me!!!"

"Hush it up." Ellie said. "The weight thing is nothing. We'll get it off you fast."

"You hush it up. Look at you almost unable to tell you were pregnant THREE weeks later ..." She shut it up immediately when they handed her Isaiah, dark hair, dark skin and beautiful. "Aww, look at you little boy. Pascal Isaiah Davidson, I love you so much." She kissed his forehead and handed him around for the christening of his name by each family member. When Pascal had finished a beautiful speech, much like his speech to Addison, Stacy reached to hold Addie and he handed Isaiah to Ellie.

"Oh, I'm in love. Pascal Isaiah Davidson, you are one beautiful little boy and so loved. Do you know how lucky you are to be loved by this family? You are so blessed." He squawked at her. "You DO know … good. Because they are the best family to have anywhere." She kissed his forehead.

Casey had just arrived and blew into the room. "He's here?" He walked to where Ellie was holding him, passed right by and kissed his baby girl before taking him into his arms. "Isaiah … what a boy." He kissed his whole face and knelt on the floor so Angie and Jules could be with him. "This your baby?"

They both nodded.

"Two babies now. And two very big girls. He kissed them both."

"Unca-Casey," Angie said, "give him his name."

"Sure, doll. Pascal Isaiah Davidson … welcome to this nutty family. You are very loved and we waited a long time for you to come. Your daddy has some really special plans for you, just like he does for Jules and Angie … they are here to help you get it all taken care of." He kissed Isaiah's forehead to have him

squawk and throw a hissy fit. He rocked the baby back to okay
and then traded him for Addie. Kissing her and coddling her, now
wide awake, she almost seemed like she wanted to smile at him,
just paying every bit of attention to his words as if she understood
him.

Ellie was comfortable with him taking her across the room
and having their little conversations now. He stopped by the house
every day to see her, each day bringing something else for her that
was educational, necessary or good. He doted on his child. They
still had not had the conversation, but as things stood now, it was
fine. They were amicable and seemed to enjoy caring for their
child.

Stacy was in the hospital overnight and then released to
home, where she was met by the whole family, including Addie
and Ellie and Casey. The entire secret was out and everyone but
the girls knew that Addison was Casey's, even Auddie. It wasn't
as hard to recant anything, because Alfie was around such a short
time and not around much when he was around. She had no
contact with him since his break up with her. Stacy was back on

her feet in a jiffy and within a month they were back at work. The holidays had already been booked, planned and all they had to do was oversee. It went without a hitch. They were an amazing team.

The New Year brought new plans. Both Stacy and Ellie worked with the same nanny, so during the day Addison was with Isaiah and they were with Miss Pauline. She was in her forties and took amazing care of the children, notifying each when it was time to breastfeed the children. They worked from the office and pumped when they had appointments. Stacy and Ellie grew closer and closer. Mothering together was amazing.

Addison was easily appeased, a very good baby. Isaiah had his problems. He was colicky and cried a lot. They all took turns trying to get him calmed down, but it was difficult. From the first week, he would scream for hours. Stacy was exhausted; Pauline would get frustrated; the only one who seemed unscathed besides Ellie, who handled it well, singing to the child, was Pascal. He would assume charge of the baby as soon as he got home and hold him for hours. When Isaiah screamed, Jules and Angie disappeared, but Pascal would calmly walk, talk, sing, coo, whatever it took to endure his time with his son and then the day of the fever happened.

Every parent's nightmare, Pascal came home and took the baby from Pauline. He'd had a hard day and was very tired, so tired he couldn't really scream. Pascal washed his hands and took the child, nuzzling him to his chest. "Wait ... Pauline, how long has he been this hot?"

Pauline was exhausted, as she was every day. Addison was easy and got little attention due to Isaiah and his screaming. She was just finishing up changing Addie's diaper when Pascal questioned her. "He wasn't hot an hour ago. I had him calm and gave him a bath. He was fine.

Pascal already had his diaper off and was taking his temp. Climbing immediately past 100 degrees he said, "Get my wife. I'm taking him to the hospital now." He finished taking the temperature, 104 degrees, bundled up the child and headed for the door with his bag.

Pauline had gone to get Stacy, Ellie followed suit to get Addison. If it were catchy, they were going to need to check her too. They all escaped to the ER in a moment.

At the ER, Pascal was furious that they weren't getting in. The child was so weak he wasn't crying and Pascal was throwing a fit when Ellie came to him.

"Pas, let me. Just go sit down for one minute. I'll get us in. Okay?" She tried her damnedest to have him hear her. "You scare them because you're a doctor. Let me try. Please?"

"Okay …" He turned to leave.

Ellie grabbed the nurse and asked her to come aside. "Listen, I know you think just because he's a doctor he's throwing his weight around, but if anything happens to that child, I'll have YOU in a courtroom in less than thirty seconds, about as long as it takes for you to get us in a room. Understand?"

The nurse was shaking her head. "We've been really busy. I'm sorry. There aren't any rooms open. I'm sorry."

"How long before one opens? This is HIS hospital. Can we skip ER and head right to a room? He's a doctor, admitting should be easy and the child has 104-degree temperature. It's not going to go down ..."

"Let me make a call." The nurse scooted to her station, picked up the phone and a moment later they were being led into the ER. The doctor was a friend of Pascal's and told them to find a room, let someone sit in the family waiting room if they were awaiting instructions. "Let's get you in here."

Quickly they were escorted back to a room that was being cleaned as they came in.

"I'm sorry, doctor. This won't take but a minute." She apologized.

"It's okay. Thank you for doing this. Is the doctor on his way?" Pas asked.

"He is coming right down. As soon as I get this to the laundry bin, I'll be back in to do vitals and get him checked in."

She was careful not to touch him after touching the infected materials. "I'll be right back."

Stacy was beside herself and shaking. When Ellie saw it, she started to panic. Addison was still in her infant carrier, so she put her on the floor in a corner, sleeping soundly. To Stacy she said, "Stacy, take my hand. It's going to be okay. It's a fever, we are going to find out what's wrong. Okay? Calm down. Deep breath. Breathe with me. In …. Out …" They took breaths together and she seemed to calm some.

She whispered to Ellie, "It started like this with Angela. I'm terrified he has the same thing … or worse. Or worse, Elles … I know something is wrong with him. I barely want to hold him. He cries so much. I'm a horrible mother." She started to shake again and tears streamed down her face.

"No. You are not a terrible mother. Let's get him assessed and see what they say. Okay? I know it's scary. If it's a virus, then Addison can have it, but we need to get them checked. Okay? Just sit with me and I'll hold you."

Stacy sat down next to Addison, uncovering her a little more so that she could see. Now awake, little Addie was her pleasant self, cooing, playing with her feet and smiling. She was now over 2 months old and she had a bit of personality. Ellie put her arm around Stacy and held her hand until the nurse came back in.

Immediately she triaged the infant, on the table, full and thorough. Pascal and Stacy answered questions and said nothing else. The doctor came in within minutes of the triage and ordered tests, thoroughly assessing the child as well. He left the room and Pascal followed.

Entering the room, Pascal knew Stacy would question him, so he said, "He's ordering tests. He thinks it might have an infection. Due to his crying, he could have an internal infection that they didn't catch and colic is a sign that perhaps something could me amiss. He's running the right tests."

Stacy just shook her head and held the baby close to her chest. He was calm at this point, but he was incredibly hot. She couldn't stand the waiting. They used to do this with Angie, all the time, the waiting, the tests, no answers. She was going crazy. And, she didn't want to cry. She needed to be strong. They waited together, Pascal pacing, Stacy rocking the sleeping, exhausted baby and Ellie watching her healthy baby, praising God for the goodness and begging Him to help this family.

The nurse came back in and drew the babies blood, which caused very little crying. Pascal was furious. He's been crying because he hurts. His pain tolerance is too high. That should have sent him to the moon. He started to do his own assessment. Unwrapping the baby, he did a full assessment, first his core. Pas checked every organ carefully. Nothing. Then he began to move everybody part and joint. When he got to his right shoulder, the baby let out a scream and cried like he did when he was home. Pascal's face lit up. He calmed the baby and did it again. The baby screamed.

"I think it's his rotator …" and ran from the room, leaving Stacy to care for the child.

He came back in with an X-ray tech and they headed for the X-ray machine. Within forty-five minutes, they found that the child had probably dislocated his shoulder in the birth canal and his shoulder was dislocated. They couldn't pop it back in, because it had most likely been torn and now was infected. A battery of pediatricians came in and they called a surgeon and by midnight the child was in surgery.

Sure enough, that is what it was. He had torn a ligament, which had become infected, and the shoulder was not in place. They put it back in, wrapped the baby so it could heal, gave him antibiotics and Ellie and Addison were headed home. Ellie relieved and yet, exhausted. Pas and Stacy stayed at the hospital with Isaiah.

Two days later they were all home again. Casey had stayed with Jules and Angie and life was, once again to resume normalcy.

Isaiah came out of the surgery beautifully and the crying stopped. They had the fever under control and with two check-ups in two weeks, he seemed to be healing fine. He began to thrive and the happiest baby came forth. Tummy time with Addison was filled with laughter. Pauline had quit and Ellie and Stacy interviewed and hired another nanny, this time young and vibrant. Selena was a Hispanic woman who took her job seriously. If they made a note on it, she made it happen. Ellie was extremely happy with Selena and Stacy was ready to make her family.

Casey had to deliver pieces of furniture in Ashville and stopped by the house to see the kids during the day. He was in and out most of the time and it was apparent that he preferred to stop during the day to see his daughter. Having signed the birth certificate, they were in share mode. However, he never asked to take her away from wherever it was that Ellie happened to be. He was happy taking his turn with her in either environment, but preferred when Ellie was working so he could talk to his daughter.

Selena handed the baby to him, freshly changed.

"Hi, baby girl. How's my little Addison?" He cooed to her.

She cooed right back, as if she could speak to her daddy.

"Really? Is that right? Mama kisses you and kisses you and kisses you? I'm sure she gives you kisses for me when I'm not here. Are you having fun with Selena? I like her. She' not mommy, but she sure does take good care of you. I love this dress. It's so cute on you. I'll look for some more like it. Jules is really good at picking out just the right dress and Angie picks the shoes." He sat down with Addison and put her on his knee. She giggled as he bounced her and smiled a smile as big as Texas. Always looking him in the eye, she was enthralled. "Did you like the little rattle I got you? It's one you can put in the freezer and chew on when those teeth come in. Do you have any teeth coming in yet? I read that at three months, they could start. If they hurt, be sure and tell Selena and Mommy and they will get your daddy rattle." He bounced the baby softly, chatting about anything and everything.

From the hallway, Ellie listened. She couldn't see him, but she could hear everything he said. He was amazing and she couldn't stop the fact that she cared for this man. No matter how horrible it was, what he did or said, she couldn't stop dreaming of his touch, the way he kissed her or the way he spoke to their daughter. Madly in love was a bad thing at this point and crying herself to sleep, tired and weepy all the time, it was a bad thing.

"Oh, LORD!" Casey exclaimed. "Did all that just come out of you?" Addison had blown out her diaper and it was leaking in every direction.

Selena saw and grabbed the baby. Casey headed for the door and was out it before Ellie realized what was going on. They met, eye-to-eye, in the hallway where she was eavesdropping.

"Hey …" Casey was startled when he saw her.

Her hands on his chest, Ellie didn't move. It was comfortable until she realized what she was doing. "Hey."

"How long were you here?"

Ellie couldn't answer.

"I need to go change … she blew out a diaper and well, I'm stinky. I'll be right back. Do you think we can talk tonight? You busy?" He was already moving toward the guest room.

"I'm not busy …"

He turned to walk away, "Just give me about twenty minutes. I'll take us all to dinner."

"Okay." She couldn't get anything else out. Literally standing, waiting for ten minutes when Stacy came up.

Stacy was worried to see Ellie standing in the hall, "What are you doing? Is everything okay?"

"Yes. Casey asked if he could take us to dinner to talk."

"Oh. I see." Stacy said.

"What, have you talked to him? What does he want?" Ellie broke down. She pled with Stacy to answer her.

"I don't know. He hasn't said anything to me. He's still mad at me for before. I'm sorry. Just go listen to what he has to say. How bad can it be? He's here all the time and you two get along just fine."

"I'm worried. I can't lose her, Stase. She's my life."

"He's not going to take her, honey. Promise." Stacy put her arm around her friend and led her into the infant room. "How is my baby?" She scooped Isaiah up and held him close. The difference in the baby was phenomenal. He was happy, so happy.

Ellie took Addison, newly dressed and diapered, smelling just fine. "Did you poo-poo on Daddy?" She laughed. "Let's get you ready to leave. We're going to dinner."

"Isn't it funny," Stacy said, "How they just seem to fit into your day and your conversation like they've been here forever?" She kissed Addison on the head. "Hi little princess. You're going to dinner for the first time and look how cute you look."

"She is pretty, isn't she?" Ellie was amazed at her child's looks. The biggest blue eyes and her hair had darkened a little, but it was still blonde and still curly. Her hands were her focal point more so than any toy and she listened very well. Music was something she adored and any time Ellie put it on, they danced until she was exhausted.

"She's gorgeous. Those Water's genes run deep. I'll let you in on a little secret, if you want?" Stacy was going to finally do it. She had to.

"What?" Ellie tucked Addison on her hip and threw the diaper bag over her shoulder, ready to go.

Stacy did the same with Isaiah, minus the diaper bag and headed to her room. "C'mon. I want to show you something."

They went to Stacy's room, whereby she pulled out a photo album from her huge walk-in closet. The one Ellie was starting to miss. "Here … look." She put Isaiah on the bed with plenty of pillows and space for Addison.

Ellie looked through the book; her family album. Pictures of when she was growing up and what must be her mother and father. Mom, had curly blondish-brown hair, much like Casey's and their dad had dark skin and dark hair and eyes.

"Mom and dad ... Addison looks just like my mother. Here." She thumbed through to a baby picture of her mother with their grandmother, Margaret. "This is Gramma Maggie. And here ... if you think momma looks like Addison, look at Gramma Maggie's baby picture."

Ellie looked at the pictures. "They could be twins, Stase."

"I know. It's weird, because I only remember pictures really, but looking at Addison every day reminds me of these pictures. Does she look like anyone in your family?"

Ellie shook her head. "No. She looks just like Casey. I have always been dark on dark, like your father. No one is blonde in our family."

"Does it bother you?"

"No. She's so beautiful. She's perfect. Just like your children. You're right, those Water's genes are strong." Ellie loved the look her daughter bore. It reminded her of the sweet love making that brought her into this world. "I should go. He's probably looking for us and I know we need to figure this all out."

"Right ... well, if you ever want to look or I can have copies made for you. She sure does resemble our side."

They scooped up the kids and headed back out. Casey was waiting for them in the kitchen, playing with the girls, who were cooking with Rachel.

"You ready?" He said to Ellie.

"Sure."

He opened the door for her and then said, "You get her locked in. I'll be there in a second."

Ellie headed out the door and Casey went to Stacy. "Hey, have you spoken to her? What does she know?"

"I promised you I wouldn't and I didn't. I told her I knew nothing. You need to be careful, Casey. She's pretty fragile. I'm not sure what she thinks. She doesn't talk about you at all, other than she's scared to death you are going to try and take Addison.

I'll disown you if you hurt her. I'm serious."

"I know you are. I must do this my way, Stacy. You can't ignore the way you feel and it's how I feel. I don't really care what she thinks. I need to know how she feels. If she hates me, then I'll deal with it. But I want to try before I worry about what comes next." He seemed quite nervous. "I just wanted to know if you told her what I wanted to talk to her about."

"I didn't. She is her own person and she's able to handle herself. You are no match for her strength. I'm telling you, if she says no, then leave her alone. If you make her run away from here, I'll never forgive you. I love her with all my heart and Addison is ours. She needs us. If you scare her, Casey … if you threaten her in any way. I swear." Stacy was getting angry. Her brother was such an ass sometimes. "You're so selfish sometimes."

"I know … I'll work on that." He stormed from the house.

Once seated for dinner at the restaurant, Casey couldn't concentrate on the menu. All he could fathom was her perfume, the way she looked, the sound of her voice and the way she spoke to him about Addison. Every little detail she would relay to him and it made him feel as though he wasn't missing out on anything. That helped some.

"So, what did you want to discuss?" Ellie burst out with.

Casey took a sip of his water. He had rehearsed this and wasn't quite sure he was man enough to do it, but his life hinged upon it. Giving it his best shot without her running out the door was the problem. If he could just get it out of his mouth without making a mistake. "Well, I … well." He took another sip of water. "I … uh. Geez, this shouldn't be this hard. I miss you."

They sat.

Silence is golden only so long and without further response from Casey, he left it up to Ellie. "Miss what?"

Another sip of water and he was ready to try again, "I miss you … miss us." He knew he was not doing well and she didn't understand. All those years he dated women he didn't care about he could talk about anything. A strong point was that he was communicative, but now, he could not speak to her. It was because he cared about her response.

"I don't understand. There has never been an 'us', Casey. What are you trying to say? I can't guess and I'm so scared of what you might want that I want to run away from here and everywhere else and get away."

"No ... no ... that's not it. I think," he gulped really hard, but tried to continue, "I think I am in love with you. I miss you and well, what we had those times we spent like Christmas last year and then well, when we made Addison and Christmas this year ... all of it. I might not have spent much time with you," he kept rambling, hoping she wouldn't leave. "I like the way we are with Addison and how smart and funny you are, not to mention sexy and wow, how good you smell and I ... I suck at this."

She sat in awe, able to say nothing.

"I'm sorry this is so hard for me. I don't want you to run

away. I don't want to take Addison away from you. I don't want

to hurt you and if ever I could take something back, it would be the

choking on the relationship comment. I'm so sorry, Elles. I swear,

I'm so sorry." He took her hands from across the table, but she

pulled them back harshly and quickly like he burnt her. "I'm

sorry."

She sat and thought. Giving herself time by messing with

Addison's dress before turning to him. "What makes you think

you know me well enough to love me?"

He had his chance and he knew it. Suddenly everything

became as easy as it was that day they spent together and the times

they spent that were good, "I love everything about you. You get

so mad at me and, honestly, it's probably a good thing. I like that

about you. I also love the way you are with Addison. She will

never want for anything, you will make sure of that. My thoughts

revert to you a thousand times a day. Music that comes on, I think

of you and wish you could hear the song. Your voice resonates in

my head, especially when I'm carving furniture. And my dreams

... you are so vivid and always kind to me. We don't fight or argue or anything. In my dreams, you didn't break your leg because of me, you didn't hear me choke from my inability at that time," he made sure he stressed his words again, "at that time, to commit. I don't know … if someone tried to hurt you, I would kill them and the thought of Alfie touching you. Wow …" he sat back in the chair. "That made me absolutely crazy."

"So … what you are saying is that if we could erase the past and we didn't have anything to argue or fight about, then you would love me. Well, Casey, we do have things like my broken leg …" and then she heard herself. This man had just proclaimed his love to her and she was going to rip him? No way. It was a waste of time. Instead, she put Addison back in the infant seat and strapped her in.

He watched, knowing it was over. Damn it! He knew she wouldn't listen to him. As he struggled to find something to grab a hold of, to reason with her, he came up empty. If his true feelings didn't work, then he was done. Stacy would hate him and Ellie would run away. It seemed that might be what she did.

"C'mon." She said as she got up to leave.

"What?" He asked.

"Come on, Casey." She held out her hand.

He took it, grabbed the carrier and they walked out of the restaurant. Casey was dazed, confused, but not frustrated. She was holding his hand as if everything were okay. At the car, she fastened in the baby and came to the passenger's side door, where he let her in. Inside the driver's side, he finally spoke.

"Are you okay?"

She thought for a minute and then pretended to be asleep in the seat, her belt across her chest.

"Elles, are you okay? What are you doing?" He was starting to get a little frantic.

She opened one eye, "Casey … rewind and go back to the night in the SUV on the highway."

"The kiss?"

"The kiss … kiss me, Casey." She let him come to her and the kiss was just as amazing. Her mind exploded and her body was nearly on fire. It was this amazing every time.

He kissed her softly, brushing his lips against hers and then it became more passionate. She might feel the same way for him? All he could do was not hurt her. Finally, he had to know. "Elles, all that I said … you said nothing."

Mesmerized by the physical presence he exuded in her world, she was really confused. Questions flew into her head. No answers. "I don't know." She said.

"What don't you know?" He stroked her cheek as he spoke. "You're so beautiful."

"Okay … I have questions." She never moved away from him.

"Shoot."

"Did you break my leg?"

"No. It was an accident and you slipped on the ice. However, I was a brutal beast when I didn't go to you, but to my computer. Of all things … an inanimate object instead of the human being in front of me."

"Why?" She asked.

"Because when I saw you, you were so beautiful and I figured you were just like all the rest."

"What do you mean, Casey?"

"Beautiful women have always tried to own me. I can never be 'owned', ya know? I can never have someone consume me, but I can give myself freely. I've protected myself from loving someone, except for Stacy, Pas and the kids, for thirty-two years and then there you are. I had preconceived notion as to who you were and you are nothing like that. Nothing like those other women."

"Like Amanda?" She finally didn't care if he knew she was jealous.

"Yes, like Amanda … who I paid to come to that party with me. Stacy told me about Alfie. I think she knew you were pregnant and it was mine before that. She called me that day you were puking in the park and made me tell her if we had sex. I lied to her for an hour before she threatened to come to Charlotte and punch me in the throat. I knew as pregnant as she was, hostile and ready to be not pregnant, that she would do it. So, I told her. I didn't know about you. I didn't know you were sick. I didn't know you might be pregnant. Never crossed my mind that you weren't on the pill or something. I just didn't know." He laughed for a moment and kissed her again before saying, "I'm not the brightest bulb in the shop, Ma'am."

"Well, that's surely the truth!" They both laughed. She took his hand in hers, holding it close to her heart. "If you're lying to me to get Addison, I will fight you. Do you understand me? I will fight you to the death."

"I'm not Tyler, Elles."

"I know. Tyler would have hit me that day and it's not fair that you suffer for what another man did to me. I think I feel the same for you, but you're going to have to give me some time. I don't think I understand what you want from me?"

"What do I want … I never thought about it like that? I just needed you to know what it was I felt and how I don't want you to have to fight for Addison, not me. I want us to be a family. My family has you, but I don't. You're always there with them and they love you so much. Stacy has threatened me within an inch of my life if I hurt you. She won't have it."

Ellie laughed. Taking his face in her hands, she looked him squarely, "I won't have it. I'm the mother of your child and I heard those things you said to her and I know that you don't hate me. That you feel something. I knew it this afternoon. I might have known it that night I kissed you on the highway and pretended like I didn't remember and that night we came home from the hospital with Angie … I love what we are together. I've dreamed about you making love to me so much." "Me too, Elles. It comes at night and in the day." He smiled, almost unable to breathe he wanted her so badly.

"Take me home and make love to me again …" She was serious and he knew it.

"I can do that. I would love to do that." He kissed her, grabbing the back of her head, entwining his hand in her hair and pulling her mouth to his roughly, raw with passion.

They drove with her head nestled into his chest. The baby slept soundly, caressed by the lull of the car.

At home, she carefully took Addison out of her infant seat and placed her in her room with the baby monitor on and came back to her bedroom. Casey followed. She turned and walked backwards, curling her finger at him.

They made love not once, but several times, each time better than the last until they were both spent, sweaty and tired. It had been a long couple of days. Drifting off to sleep, Ellie curled in Casey's arms. They slept until the baby woke at three o'clock. Like a zombie, as each time, Ellie got out of bed and went to get the child, who usually slept with her.

"I'll be right back." She went and got the baby, changed her diaper and brought her back to the bed to nurse. "She's hungry. Aren't you, baby girl?"

Addison latched on and ate until she was full, burping between breasts and Casey watched in awe. "That's amazing. I mean, I have seen you do it, but to be here with you, naked and to see her respond … that's amazing."

"She's a good eater and sleeps all but the one feeding during the night. I thought she would be up sooner tonight, because she didn't eat before she fell asleep. You let mommy and daddy have some time, did you?"

He leaned over and kissed Addison's head and then Ellie's. "I love you both."

She almost held her breath, but she knew she had to stop.

He wasn't just the father of her child, but he was the man who she chose to make the child with. She knew she wasn't taking birth control and the thought of a condom never crossed her mind. Maybe he was the one who needed time. She made a conscious decision at that moment to not hold back any longer. He wasn't Tyler, he was nothing like him. Nothing reminded her of Tyler about him. "I love you too, Casey Waters."

"You do?" He was joyous, wanted to jump up and down, but not wake his baby. "You really do?"

"If love is what it feels like to have you always on my mind, to hope that you show up at Stacy's even when I know I'm just going to ignore you if you do. To see you with Jules and Angie and Isaiah and most of all with Addie … to feel you touch me for the last year even though you didn't before. Did you mean for this all to happen today?" She asked.

"What do you mean? Today?" Casey was confused.

"It's March 24th. Did you know that?"

"March 24th? I'm sorry ..." Casey was still confused.

"I'll let you off the hook this once, especially since the date was emblazoned in my mind because it was the day we conceived Addison. Exactly a year ago, Casey. I thought maybe you planned it that way?"

He shook his head. "No. And, that is so weird, we went to dinner that night too and got home after midnight. Just like tonight, everything kind of late and the date ..."

"Men are so ... never mind. Just kiss me again." She leaned over to have him kiss her as she pulled Addison away to burp, asleep again and then took her back to her bedroom. With a kiss and an 'I love you' she returned to Casey, sleeping soundly.

She whispered into his ear ... "You think you'll get away with sleeping tonight? You've got another think coming." She started to run her fingers over his body, paying attention to his muscular pecs, his stomach and then sucking lightly on his nipple.

"Mmmmm ... that's nice. Don't stop." He smiled.

"I knew you weren't sleeping."

"Two can play at that game."

Chapter Twenty-One

Three months later, April showers were making it hard to look forward to spring. The season was wet and although good for foliage, horrible for business. Parties planned outside were moved in quickly and not as prosperous as they would have been outside. Simply Elegant kept plugging away and were still getting new business, so it was okay regarding finances, but the parties just weren't what was expected. Even the three weddings they did were all forced inside and to the disappointment of the bridal party. Each one beautiful, but not as beautiful as it could have been.

They had something different in mind and referrals had dropped.

Casey and Ellie were quite content living their arrangement. Casey was gone for days working in his shop in Charlotte and then came to Ellie's for time with his girls. Stacy was adamant about knowing what was going on, but Ellie kept clammed up about it, afraid to jinx it. Isaiah was thriving and Addison was hitting every milestone early. She was five months old and had said her first word. Of course, it was 'Dada' and he was there to hear it. Casey and Addison had great conversations. She chimed in with garbled gook and he conversed with her as though she were answering every question he asked. Ellie was the happiest she had ever been.

Simply Elegant had the party of the season planned. This fundraiser wasn't just any fundraiser, but to incite the financing of a film. Stacy's high school friend, Bennie Trudeau was shooting a film in Ashville and needed to find investors to the tune of three million dollars. They had a lunch meeting with Bennie that afternoon, so Ellie was careful to dress the part early. She carted Addison off to the nanny and met Stacy, who was already in the office.

Ellie cheerfully bounded into the room, 'This is going to be exciting. However... I thought I would beat you in today and here you are, already working at seven o'clock in the morning. Do you ever sleep?" She put her things on the desk and went to the coffee carafe and poured a mug of steaming hot liquid necessity. Addison still woke in the night and she was, most of the time, exhausted, or so it seemed.

"I just love working and Isaiah woke me early. It's useless to nurse him and then try and go back to sleep. My mental list is already ticking away. So, I came in." Stacy said. She did not add that her ability to sleep of late was insane. For some reason, she had developed some anxiety and it was getting the best of her. Pascal had talked to her about stopping nursing so that she could medicate, but she would hold out a little longer. And she did not mention the pill bottle in her hand that she thought just twenty minutes before of downing and making all the sadness go away.

"Stase ..." Ellie had spoken to her and she hadn't heard.

For several weeks, Ellie noticed that Stacy was preoccupied. "Are you okay?"

"I am fine. But I'm tired." She didn't feel like making nice. She calmly opened the bottle of Pascal's narcotics and took one. Maybe that would help? She put the bottle in her top drawer and paid attention to Ellie.

They had the meeting with Bennie and he was throwing a lot of money their way, plus they had the opportunity to bid the film catering and Ellie liked that. "More and more people are shooting films in this area. I think this could really be a market we can break into and dominate."

"I agree." Stacy said waiting for the narcotic to take the world away. She'd been making it go away for a couple of weeks.

Ellie was excited. "It sounds fun too. Didn't you say that Mitchell Brandt was in this film?"

Mitchell was the foremost film star in the nation and Ellie thought he was the most handsome man in the world, except for

Casey. He was not only going to be in the movie, but they would be catering and see him every meal. A definite bonus to their job.

"It's very exciting. Isn't it?" Stacy picked up the information she had prepared for the meeting and gave Ellie her copy. "Here is what we are up against. I think I understand what they want, but I want to clarify it with them. I made a list, hopefully it's enough."

They made a more detailed list and killed at the meeting. Awarded the contract, they started in two weeks. There were six days of pre-production catering that led into principal photography and they would soon be preparing three meals a day and snacks throughout to fill the catering order.

With merely days left, the workload was immense. Menus, shopping, storage and mobility issues, they ordered equipment and created an ease of workflow with their staff to satisfy the terms of the contract. They would be overseeing it mutually in the beginning, but Ellie would take it after the first week. They had 38 days of filming to contend with and then it would back down to four weeks of post-production and that was nothing in comparison. They just needed to keep a cantina for the executives in the office. It was all ready to go on time and the food truck they purchased was going to help them ease into the work order.

Casey battled to keep his schedule workable unlike before Addison was born. Working kept him from thinking too much and from feeling things he didn't want to feel. Life with Ellie was perfect and he didn't understand where his fears and concerns came from, but he surely had them. Every day he would assume that she was not in this relationship as deeply as he was. His adoration for his two girls consumed his thoughts. They were on his mind continually. Mistakes were made in carving the furniture and two pieces were replaced to get the amount of quality he demanded of self to his consumer.

With the two chairs in tow, he packed up the delivery truck after grabbing the receipts for his client and heading back inside. The pieces looked radiant in the Nancy Culpa's living room and she was extremely satisfied. Her long blonde hair tossed as she expressed her gratitude, Casey knew the signs. He made sure he steered clear of her touching him in any way by keeping the chair in between them.

"I'm just so overjoyed at the workmanship." Nancy cooed as she ran her hands over the finished wood.

Both hand carved, exact matches, he had upholstered the bench seat and the deep rust color accented the style and color of the wood. He ran his hand over the chair arm as he tucked the invoice in his pocket and shook her hand.

"Thank you, Casey. These are truly beautiful. I'm sure you will have new customers when they see what I have." Nancy shook his hand one last time.

"You have my number. Feel free to give it out." He smiled that smile no one could resist.

"I will ... Casey, how about we go for a drink to celebrate?" She eyed him trying to decide if he were the type to play. There wasn't a ring on his finger and she liked what she saw and she always got what she wanted.

"I'm very flattered," Casey was careful not to injure Nancy's feelings. He knew the kind. He knew her well. "I actually have other plans. More deliveries and then home to the family." His smile was genuine.

"If you're sure …" She tried one last-ditched attempt.

"I'm good. Thank you very much for your order and if there's ever anything I can do, let me know." Casey was out the door in moments.

Back in the truck, Casey hesitated before he dialed Ellie's number. He had dated many women and she was the first that did not bother him all day long with incessant texts and calls and he wondered for the millionth time if she was into him as deeply as he was to her? On his way to her house, only twenty minutes away, he waited for her to answer. Usually she was busy and rarely took the call, but she answered and his heart leapt.

Casey couldn't help his excitement at hearing her voice and said as much, "It's nice to hear your voice without the voicemail.

How is your day going?"

Ellie smiled. Her day was crazy and his calls were always a nice distraction, so rare that she wasn't already on a call when he dialed in. "I like hearing your voice too. How did the delivery go? Did she like them?"

"She did. I just got through and I'm going to drop the rejects off at the house. Are you sure that you want them?"

Ellie never understood how insecure Casey could feel with the craftsmanship he exuded in his work. The chairs had minor imperfections and yet he tanked them and started over. "I love them, Darling. I absolutely will be devastated if you don't bring them home. Are you headed there now?"

"Yeah. Last stop and I'm done for the day. Would you like me to come and get Addison?"

"Better yet ... how about I meet you at home and we can make some lunch, make some love when Addie goes down for a nap and I'll take the afternoon off?" She missed Casey. He had been in Charleston for three days and she missed his touch, missed his laughter and she knew Addison missed him too. They were ahead of schedule and menus to grocery list had already been done and the shopping was completed. She had a little time before the grueling hours of production started in two days.

"Sounds great. Meet me there?"

"I'll be about a half hour. Want me to stop and pick up food? I'm famished."

"How about I grab it. BBQ?" Casey knew the way to her heart and it was BBQ. Just like the first day they were together, she would devour the delicate meat and then lick her fingers. He loved her passion, her presence and her soulful expressions. "I'll kick it in gear and meet you at the house. Kiss my baby and tell her Daddy is coming."

"I'll do that, baby. I'll see you in just a few. I love you." Ellie always said she loved Casey, but it was rare that he said it back.

"I love you too ..." Casey said the words he felt and that came so difficultly to his mouth. "I love you too, Elles. See you in about thirty." He hung up the phone and headed for the BBQ pit.

Ellie laid down her phone as Stacy walked into the room. Stress was really getting the best of Stacy and she knew it was time to do something about it.

"El ..." She had recently shortened Ellie's name even more. "I think I need some counseling or something. I'm having a rough time. I'm not sleeping," She continued the list, "Eating, exercising, and well ... I think I might have some severe postpartum depression. My libido is gone. I've lost some weight unintentionally. My baby weight is almost gone and I haven't really tried." Stacy blurted out the details she so badly wanted to hide from the world. Trusting Ellie was easy, and she knew that Ellie cared. "And I've been thinking that ending it all was a good idea ..." Her words trailed off as she saw the immediate spark of concern register in Ellie's eyes.

"Stacy ... why haven't you said anything?" Ellie was now

concerned. Packing up her bag, she continued, "What can we do?"

"Pas wants me to stop nursing and get some medication. Do you regret stopping?"

Ellie thought about it a second, "No. She does very well with the bottle and at four months they are supposed to really have all the antibodies they need. I love the time with her, but Casey does too and I like that he can feed her and have that bonding time. She also bonds with the nanny and you. So, I think it's good for her. Isaiah is really taken to you, that's why it's hard for Nanny to work with him when we are busy. It might not be a bad thing. Even though you pump, she has a hard time getting him to settle in with her. Yesterday, I went in to see Addie and she really doesn't have the bond with him that you do. It might be good for him, darling. I think Pas is right. Let's see about getting you some medication. You aren't really suicidal or anything, are you?"

The words hit Stacy like a brick. She had been thinking that her life was unmanageable for weeks and that things just weren't as appealing to her as they normally were. She didn't want to die, but she wasn't sure she wanted to live. With exception of her children, which caused incredible guilt, she had no reason to be here. Ellie took over the company and Pas was working a thousand hours a week. Her answer was honest in a way, "I don't want to die, but I don't care if I die ..."

Ellie knew that look and had felt the same thing in prison. She threw it on the table in case her friend wasn't being honest with her, "Do you want to live?"

With that, Stacy burst into tears. Usually she could get away with finding a place alone before the accolade of tears drenched her soul. "No ... I'm not sure that I do." She sobbed for two full minutes with Ellie comforting her before she could speak again. "I feel so guilty. The kids need me and I pretend to be busy. Angie is doing great. Jules is even better and Isaiah, well, I know he needs me, but he looks at me with these dead eyes. It's like he knows I failed him with the shoulder and I feel so guilty."

Ellie's heart shattered into little tiny pieces. "I'm sorry, Stacy. I didn't realize ..."

"How could you? You didn't know. I've been thinking it will go away," She sobbed again, "But it doesn't. It never lets up. A black cloud over my head all the time. It's like I walk around in a fog. Sometimes I hear myself laughing or feel myself smiling, but it never reaches inside me. Nothing makes me feel good any more ... even Pas. He tries to touch me and I roll away. I've never done that. Never ..."

"Honey, it's okay. Let's see if we can get you an appointment with a therapist or someone who can get you some medication. I felt this way when I was in jail." Ellie said the words, even though she had never spoken of her time in the jail with Stacy. She had never spoken about it to anyone she realized. "I was insanely depressed. I knew it, but there was nothing I could do about it. I think I was so depressed that it took months of working here before I really got back to normal. There has to be something that can help you."

"Have you felt anything like this with the postpartum?" Stacy felt cheated. She delivered after Ellie, had problems with the baby's shoulder and hitting milestones, the weight and now the depression and Ellie had no problem at all. She was happy all the time and it killed Stacy. Even though it caused her guilt for feeling that way, she was so jealous.

"Not with the pregnancy, no. I did go through complete and utter exhaustion and I got really bitchy. But Casey just took Addie for a couple days and let me sleep the whole weekend, made me breakfast in bed, tucked me in and I snapped right out of it. It doesn't hurt that Addie only gets upon once in the night to nurse and if I leave her in bed with me, it's easy. I sleep right after she's done." Ellie searched Stacy's eyes for answers. "Honey, it's okay. I promise. It will be okay. I'm taking the afternoon off. Would you like to come with me? Casey's meeting me at the house and we can eat some BBQ and then you can nap with Addie and Isaiah, bring him with?

"No. I don't want to take time away. I know you don't get to see him often. I'll call my doctor and get an appointment A.S.A.P. I think meds might help."

"I can stay if you like? We can do something together.

Maybe bake cookies or something, who knows … pick the girls up from school and go the spa? Would you like that?" Ellie wanted to do anything that would help Stacy get through this. She'd read about horror stories where women killed themselves after birthing from PD. She would not have that. Worry took over. She picked up her phone and dialed, when Casey answered, she filled him in. "Casey, honey, Stacy needs me this afternoon. She's got a bad case of the blahs. Can you come and Get Addison and take her for the afternoon and I'll be home as soon as I can get there?"

Casey was disappointed. He'd made special plans, but nothing came between his sister and Ellie. They were kindred and that was nice, because it helped him know that Ellie was okay when he was at home, just an annoyance. "Sure. I'll head that way now." He hung up and took the next right to head to his sister's.

Stacy was now sobbing again, pulling tissue from the box, blowing into it and tossing it into the nearly full trash receptacle. She just couldn't stop; the floodgate had opened; the dam had burst; the tears were in charge.

"There, there ... honey. It's going to be okay. Just let it all out." She put her arm around Stacy and sat close, leaning her to her bosom. "It's going to be okay ..."

Casey arrived at the house, checked on Addison and then scooted to the office where he found Ellie and Stacy. Puffy eyes, a red nose and a scratchy throat, he knew she was in a bad place. Never had he seen his sister cry, with exception to tears of joy and it spooked him a bit.

"Is she okay," He asked.

Ellie nodded. "She's fine. She's been a little depressed, which is perfectly normal after having a baby. Postpartum depression. She's going to take some medication, right, Sweetie?"

Stacy was horrified at the exhibit she was displaying, but she couldn't help the tears or the sadness. She felt very little for the last couple of months and it was starting to become apparent it wasn't going away on its own. After all she had been through in life and the birth of a baby takes her down? She started to tear up again, but by sheer will stopped the new tears. "I'm going to medicate. I can't control it. I've tried positive thoughts, changing my diet, everything. I've stooped to the lowest I've ever been."

Ellie's heart broke to hear Stacy talk about this when she hadn't realized it and they were together nearly every day. "It's not your fault, Stase. Let's just get it under control. Right?" She looked to Casey for support.

"What does Pas say, Sis?"

"He wants me to stop nursing and medicate. I told him about it a couple days ago. I didn't want to stop, but this is bigger than I am. I think he's right."
They both agreed with her.

"What can we do until then? I'm afraid to leave you alone … you are scaring me, Stase." Ellie's honesty was breathtaking.

"I really don't want to be alone. I've contemplated suicide in the last two days …twice. It's scaring me. I care nothing about anyone or anything. Like I said, I don't want to die, but living isn't very appealing either. I thought suicide would mean that I had intense pain, ya know? Pain that would not leave. I have no pain ... I have nothing. No feelings except annoyance. People annoy me. Everyone and everything annoys me. It sounds like such a better idea to go crawl in my bed, pull the covers up over my head and just go to sleep ... forever." Forthright with her family was the only answer and being alone wasn't an option at this point. Stacy could find no reason to go on living.

"Stacy ..." Casey couldn't believe his sister just said that. "What are you talking about? You have three kids to live for and Pas ... what about them?" He was angered by her lethargy. She needed to shake herself loose from the confines of the depression. It couldn't be good for her. His voice raised slightly in his anger, "You need to stop talking like that. You have plenty to live for. Look at this house, our family and our friends ..."

Ellie stepped in, getting up from sitting with Stacy, she grabbed Casey's arm as he finished and steered him out of the room. "Hey ... easy." She knew he didn't understand, but she could not allow him to speak to her in such a way. "She's depressed. It's clinical. There isn't anything she can do about it."

"There sure is. She can get up and stop feeling sorry for herself. I think she's still feeling guilty about not knowing Isaiah was hurt and that's bull." His anger was not subsiding, but fueling. Casey continued, "She's always had it pretty easy. Never had to really work for anything. She's being a big baby."

Ellie felt as though she were propelled back in time to the day Casey didn't worry about the human in front of him, but only the computer that had broken. That she could feel herself back on the ground trying to get his attention. "She's not being a big baby!" With that, she re-entered the room with Stacy, closing the door, shutting him out.

How dare he? She settled back in with Stacy. "Make no mind of him. He doesn't get it."

Stacy could feel Ellie's anger. "It's okay. I don't even understand it. Thanks for staying with me. Pas is on a double at the hospital and I just don't want to be alone." Her eyes welled with tears again and she let them slip down her check.

"Sweetie ..." Ellie snatched a Kleenex out of the box and wiped away her tears, face-to-face, intimately she spoke, "Look at me, Stase. We're going to get through this. Some medication will really help. I can watch the kids and stay with you this weekend. Casey will love the time with Addison. Okay? We're going to be fine. Just fine." She reached out and hugged her friend. They had to be okay. This was all the family she had and it was worth fighting for. "We're going to be just fine."

Casey spent the weekend at Ellie's with Addison. It was a much harder task than when Ellie was there. The nights were filled with Addison missing her mommy and the pumped milk wasn't the same as when Ellie laid the baby in bed with them and nursed. Since Ellie stopped nursing, it was nights that they had hours awake before the baby would go back to sleep and alone with her, she seemed to know that something was different. Three hours later the first night until she fell back asleep and Casey was starting to feel tired. He would get up, trudge to the babies' room and change her diaper. He would then go to the fridge with the crying baby and heat the bottle as Ellie had shown him. By the time he got it between her little lips, she was nearly exhausted from crying, so hungry and so was he. Then the feeding … he would rock her and make sure everything was done just as Ellie had instructed. However, when the baby would fall back to sleep and he would place her back in her bed, he was wide awake. It seemed he got much less sleep and so napping when Addison napped was the plan.

Sunday afternoon, the worst part of the two nights over, he was exhausted. Laundry, meals for himself and making sure the baby had tummy time, good baths, diapers changed, playtime in the playpen and time in the bouncer, he was worn the hell out. How did women do this and work too? A newfound respect was attained for Ellie. Even though she had a nanny at work, she was there every day doing all of this and when he would visit, she did all these things in addition to giving him good attention. No wonder she didn't want to make love as much. She was tired!

Finally, the weekend was over and he was settled in to bed Sunday night when Ellie called for her every four-hour check. The others had been very terse and he knew she was angry.

Apologizing wasn't his strong suit, so he left it to put some time between them.

Ellie called to check on Addison. This was the longest she had been away, but the weekend was filled with watching Isaiah and Jules and Angie, who were absolutely starved for their mother's attention. She steered clear of answers by feigning Stacy had the flu and would run back and forth between keeping the girls busy with projects and Stacy, who had retreated to her room. Finally, everyone was eating dinner and she had a chance to call. "How's Addie?"

Casey missed Ellie and this distance needed to be bridged. "She's good. Missing mommy. Is Pas home yet?"

"He is, but he's been sleeping for the last five hours and will probably sleep all night to be ready to work regular shift tomorrow. I'm really tired. I wish I could sleep in my own bed …" She missed lying with Addison and sleeping in her own home. She'd become so accustomed to her house that it was foreign to be anywhere but home. Missing the baby was starting to depress her as well. Stacy had slept some and wasn't talkative. It was as if Stacy withdrew completely, lost the 'face' of happiness in any way and was very depressed.

"Okay …" Casey was settling in to another night without her, "I miss you."

Ellie heard the words, but didn't feel the emotion behind it. She wasn't in a place to fake anything at this point. "Kiss Addison goodnight and I'll see you in the morning when you bring her over. Early is fine. I'll be up by five o'clock. I miss her horribly."

Casey caught the distance again. "Okay. I'll bring her as soon as she wakes up. Good night."

"Good night, Casey." Ellie hung up. It would be nice if she could talk to Stacy. She had been caught up in the relationship with Casey. It was nice, much different than with Tyler and she knew that he would never abuse her in any way. However, she was completely at a loss of emotion of late. Their lovemaking had been amazing and being held was absolutely what she needed in life after the jail experience. The last month had been different. Casey was working more and seeing them less and it reminded her that things in the beginning were never how they ended up. Would Addison grow up without a daddy? She worried about that.

Auddie peeked in the den and broke her thoughts. "Hey … I'm getting ready to head home. Do you need anything else before I leave?"

Her face was the only bright spot in the weekend. Even the little girls were sullen, always asking about Stacy. "Do you have a moment? I could use a friend." Ellie wanted to get this out. For years, stuffing it down did nothing. Being able to confide in Auddie and Stacy had helped her learn a new way. Auddie was trustworthy.

"Sure, Darlin'. What's up?" Auddie didn't know what was going on, but she knew that it was serious or Ellie would have never left Addison all weekend. "What's wrong?" She took a seat opposite Ellie in a leather chair.

"Well ..." Ellie found it best to blurt, "I am not sure I'm doing the right thing."

"What is the thing you are referring to?"

"Casey ..."

That caught Auddie completely off guard. The business, maybe? Spending so much time working, maybe, but Casey ... They seemed quite happy and Auddie thought them the perfect couple. They spent time together and were fine with time apart. "How so?"

Ellie didn't know if she had words to express what she was thinking, or better, what ran through your mind at nine hundred miles per hour the last seventy-two hours. "He is so selfish. He just doesn't seem to be ... I don't know ... he's just so selfish. Tyler used to be that way. Every time I had something I wanted to do, he would tell me to go do it, only to make me pay. It's hard to explain ... I just, well, it's ... he pissed me off."

"Okay, how did he piss you off? Let's start there." Auddie

was considerably patient, but she was tired and wanted to go home to her family. She'd had to work both Saturday and Sunday because Ellie asked her if she could help. It was fine, but she was tired. The girls were a handful and Ellie seemed to make it worse. She would run back and forth, nearly distraught, trying to appease the girls and then disappear into Stacy's room for endless hours at a time.

"He just has this harsh inability to feel compassion at times. Like when he broke my leg. He never even realized it. I could have died and he would have still checked his computer screen. It isn't even a selfish thing, it's just he doesn't get it. His sister is depressed, postpartum depression and he told her to 'suck it up'." She motioned her quotation marks in the air. Angered and resentful, she didn't know what to do, but all the good times seemed to be slipping in some way. They got so little time together. He would show up after work. She would have dinner ready and then they would play with Addison and go to bed. The lovemaking had dwindled a little. There was just something in him that wasn't right. "It's not right, Auddie. He needs to have compassion to be a father."

Auddie figured most of what was going on had to deal more with Ellie's past rather than the current situation of Casey not have empathy. She'd known him to be one of the best men she'd ever met and playing with Jules and Angie, now Isaiah and his own daughter he doted on, there was nothing to purport these statements. "Ellie ... are you sure that there isn't something else?"

"What do you mean?"

"I mean, well, he's so good with the kids and if you want to find empathy in a person, especially a man, look at how they treat children. He is an amazing father, Ellie. Is something else going on?"

Ellie contemplated before speaking, "I'm not sure. I worry about Stacy and I've worried about Addison all weekend long. I've never spent this time away from her before and I miss her. Emotions are running rampant everywhere and mine are out of control now. You're right. He's a good father. A very good

father and he's amazing with Stacy's kids. I'm just being silly."
She waved it off. Trying to convince herself was a little more
difficult, but not impossible. She was being silly. He doted on not
only Addison, but her as well. There was nothing to complain
about and this was nothing like Tyler … even though Tyler was
just the same in the beginning and then it took a turn for the worse.
"What if it doesn't last, Auddie?"

"That's the million-dollar question. Perhaps you need to
look at it from a logical point of view rather than an emotional one.
You say Stacy is depressed? I'm gathering that's why you were
with us this weekend instead of home?"

Ellie nodded.

"Well, sometimes you just have to take care of things. You
two are an amazing couple. I am jealous of the looks you give
each other, the adoration and passion. This is just a lot of
emotional turmoil. His sister is sick and he might be afraid. They
lost their parents and I would assume losing her would mean
horrible things for him. So, if you look at it logically, maybe he

doesn't want to understand anything; he just wants it to change for the better. Sucking it up is what they did when their parents died. Has he told you the story? Do you understand what hell they went through? One of the girls that works second floor told me the whole story. Her friend went to school with Stacy and knew. It's a devastating story, filled with abuse and abandonment and Casey always took care of her. He would be frightened if something were wrong. I know him to be a good man and there is nothing that he wouldn't fight for in love. Nothing … and he loves you and your daughter. Maybe it's you who needs to ease up and understand. Brothers and sisters are different than other family members."

Ellie felt the fool. She had assumed that he had no feelings when, indeed he did and Auddie was right. He expressed his fear of losing his sister at other times in talks. "You're right. It's just been a long weekend. You go home … you must be tired too. Thank you for working extra. I'll see about some time off real soon. Just let me get her back to normal. Deal?"

"Deal." Auddie rose and they hugged before she left to go

home.

It was not something she was used to, but Ellie liked having multiple people, like a real family, around. It made it so much easier. She drug herself back up the stairs to check on Stacy. Peeking in her room, Stacy was back on the bed, under the covers, her head nearly buried.

Ellie spoke softly in case she was asleep, "Stase …"

"Hey …" she wasn't sleeping, but waiting for Ellie to get back. It made her feel safer to know she was there, but the feelings were blinding her at this point. Dinner with the girls was excruciating. They kept telling her how wonderful it was for her to be feeling better to the point that she wanted to scream at them. Instead, she just ignored their comments and questions. Returning to the bedroom, she grabbed a bottle of pills and got in the bed, but she just didn't have the guts to do it; the guts to die at her own hand. She handed the pills out of the covers and whispered, "I need to go to the hospital, Els."

Lightening-like emotion ripped through Ellie's body and sunk into her brain. "What? Did you take any?" Her heart was racing as she headed for the bed and climbed on it.

Shaking her head, Stacy pulled the covers up higher, closer to removing the world from her view. She couldn't stop the black cloud from enveloping her and she just didn't care, but this little voice in the back of her head, very similar to Angie's sweet and innocent voice, kept saying 'don't do it. Don't do it.' And she knew that it was not an option. "Please ... take me to the hospital. Wake up Pas and call Casey to take the girls. I can't do this anymore." She burst into tears again and pulled the covers up over her head.

Ellie ransacked the bed before she left to get Pas for more pills. She was terrified. Never had she seen someone so depressed and it was making her anxious. Instead of panicking like she did after jail and in jail, she ran to find Pas.

"Pas ... wake up." She touched him gently as to not scare him into a punching blow to her head kind of waking up. "Pascal.

Please. Wake up."

"What ... What? Ellie?" Pas opened his eyes to a very fearing Ellie. "What's wrong?" He was up in a second.

"Stacy says she needs to go to the hospital. It's getting worse. I think she needs to go. She had another bottle of pills in her hand and just gave them to me. I swear, Pas, I only left her alone to call Casey to check on Addison. She could have ... I can't think about it." She was shaking like a limb.

He grabbed her to settle her. "Ellie, you have to pull it together. I'll take her in. Can you stay with the kids?"

She shook her head. "Hurry ... She's scaring me. She cares about nothing. Nothing, Pas. Nothing."

He rushed from the room to their bedroom. Upon entering, he slowed, and calmly climbed in the bed with Stacy. "Baby ... I'm here. Let's get you in to see Doctor Johnson. Okay?" He wrapped his arms around her as she sobbed.

He rocked her until he could get her up to get dressed. She spoke very little, only enough to say, "I'm so tired, Pascal ... I'm just so tired."

"I know, Princess. We're going to let you rest." Up and some sandals on her feet and he escorted her to the car in her night clothes.

Ellie sat in the den, shaking. She hadn't been that afraid in a long time. Just ten minutes and she had gotten another bottle of pills. If she wouldn't have come back at that moment, would it have been too late?

After a fitful night's sleep, checking in with Pas until she finally fell asleep around four o'clock, Ellie got up and showered, dressed and moved to the kitchen to wait for her baby. She needed to hold Addison and take away the pain she now felt. Why hadn't she noticed Stacy's depression? Had it been there for some time and she just missed it in her bliss of new life? The guilt consumed her. Pas had stayed with her at the hospital, where they were keeping her in the psychiatric unit. At least he didn't seem compelled to do something different now. He had asked Ellie what she thought about a privatized situation where Stacy could rest. Having no knowledge of her specific type of depression, she had researched for hours on her phone. There were significant repercussions of it not being treated. She hated the thought of not having Stacy around, but she needed help and she should get it. Giving Pas her okay and thoughts on it, they had chosen a facility upstate and they were on their way.

Ellie had agreed to stay at the house and run things until they could get Stacy back on track. The facility was only forty-five minutes away, but it seemed like she had lost her friend and Ellie felt extremely lonely.

Casey walked in the door with Addison chatting away. When she saw her mother, she grinned from ear-to-ear and babbled even more.

"My baby!!!" Ellie scooped her up and kissed her silly. Both giggling, she held on to Addison for dear life. "I missed you so much. So. So. SOOOOO MUCH!!!" She spun the baby around until she giggled again.

Casey stood and watched. There was something wrong with Ellie, but he waited until she finished before he spoke.

Finally done with her greeting, Ellie tucked Addison on her hip and looked to Casey. "I missed you too." She smiled.

"Is Stacy okay?" He dreaded the question, but simple depression, she would be fine.

"Pas took her to The Villa Pines in Charlotte. I can't stand the thought of her being gone for even a day. I'm so worried about her."

Casey took her face in his hands, looking deeply into her eyes, "Come stay at my house. I've got an office you can use, we can take the girls and the babies ..."

"I can't. We have the film project and it starts tomorrow. I literally can't do it. If we blow this catering, we are done. Foods purchased, everything is ready, I have the truck being delivered this morning and we start preparing tomorrow. I sent Janell down yesterday to set up for the production staff, but principal photography starts tomorrow. I have to be there ... and have no idea if I can do this on my own or not." Ellie was a little intimidated. She knew the plan like the back of her hand, but Stacy and she had always been a good team.

"I'll help you."

If she messed this up, it was possibly a financial devastation. She had to do right by Stacy and stay and work.

"I'll help you, Els. Just tell me what to do and I'll do it. I listen enough to what you say about projects that I think I understand what we need. I'm a good organizer; remember all those years in management? We are a good team. We can do this."

"Oh, Casey ... I don't know." She had no choice but to try it with him. All weekend long she had been more worried about Stacy than business and it had crept up on her. Everything was in motion and the hardest part was to get the truck stocked, menus hung and to make sure the employees they hired were up to speed on the process. She had one day to do it. "Okay … Okay, we can do this."

"We can do this." Casey put his hand up for a high five and Addison reached out and grabbed it. They laughed.

Stacy woke up from a drug induced sleep. Her sedation was necessary when she got to the hospital, because she just couldn't stop crying. The sobbing had started to really feel as though it were painful. The medication list was extensive and Pas and Dr. Johnson had recommended that she enter The Villa Pines. She looked around, knowing she made the trip but remembering little to nothing. It looked like a posh facility. The bed linens were extremely expensive looking and matched the drapes and wallpaper accented the room. It was very nice.

She went to move around and noticed how sore she was. Her energy level was still low, so she didn't have to fight an urge to get out of the bed, but an orderly walked in at that moment.

"Good Morning, Mrs. Davidson. I'm James and I'm here to get you settled in, up and around and ready for breakfast. I've laid out a nice relaxing set of sweats for you to put on after your shower. The shower facility is right there." He pointed. All these rich bitches were always feeling sorry for themselves and coming to The Villa to get away from their horribly fascinating lives. "Up and at 'em, Mrs. Davidson. First step to getting better is getting up and around."

Stacy liked to puke at the amount of nice James was throwing around. He looked one of those men who could smooze you and mean not one word of it.

"What time is it, please?" Stacy rousted to sitting.

"It's after nine o'clock. Breakfast is served from five o'clock to six-thirty, but we saved you a plate. No sense in busting you out of your sleep until you were ready. How about that shower?"

"Okay ... is everything in there?" Stacy moved to standing

now and shuffled that way.

"I'll call Sandra in to help you out." He had opened all the curtains and jotted notes on her chart at the end of the bed.

"I'm fine." Stacy was almost to the shower when Sandra, a large woman in Mini Mouse scrubs came bustling into the room.

Sandra loved her job. Helping get people through mental illness made her feel needed and respected. Kind and generous to her clients, unlike James, who dreaded every day he came to The Villa, Sandra was liked and respected by all. She texted a couple more sends before she scooted Stacy into the restroom. "Hurry up there, sleepyhead. We've got things to do. I'm required to be in the room with you, no sharp objects, suicide watch you know." She text a couple more times, at one point busting out laughing. "That Shonda, she's so funny. So, get a move on, Princess. We have a lot of things to cover today."

Stacy did as she was told and as brusque as Sandra was, she was pleasant and kind and showering wasn't such a bad thing. No sharp objects or anything she could take ... suicide watch? What had she gotten herself in to?

Once showered, hair damp and a Villa sweat suit on, Stacy knew she was locked down, institutionalized. Luckily, nothing mattered yet and so it was nothing but news to her.

The day was filled with schedules, screenings by two doctors, a nurse three times for vitals and a lecture she cared nothing about from Dr. Wendall Fields.

Dr. Fields began his diatribe, "We are dealing with postpartum depression. I have no worries about reaching the psychosis stage. It doesn't sound like you had intent to harm anyone or anything, just a brief stint with suicidal ideology. Are we passed that, Stacy?"

She nodded her head. She just didn't care.

"Good. Your husband cares a great deal for you and you have a beautiful family. He left some pictures for you."

He handed her some snapshots of her family that she held in her lap, tears now rolling down her face at the thought of letting her family down.

"Stacy, what we are going to do is work on some cognitive counselling whereby we talk about things, help you find better ways to cope with these feelings, solve problems and/or set some very realistic goals. I'm going to start you on a therapeutic dose of antidepressants and we are going to see how that works for you. Now, you have two options. There are two antidepressants that I've had extremely good success with. One of them can be used during breast-feeding with little risk of side effects for your child. Which would you like?"

"Whatever you think. You're the doctor." Stacy didn't mean to be flippant, but her face flushed in embarrassment. "I'm sorry. I mean that I'm here to get better. Whatever you think, I trust. My baby isn't here to be breastfed, so it really doesn't matter." She tried to smile at him but that smile never hit her eyes. Dull. She felt dulled.

"I understand," Dr. Fields said. "I truly understand. I also want to do an Estrogen replacement therapy which might help to counteract the drop-in Estrogen. Sometimes it's a rapid drop and partially the reason you are experiencing the feelings you are facing each day. Risk is well worth the therapeutic value of medication. How do you feel about that?"

Stacy thought for a moment before she spoke. "I think that the word therapist, when broken down, stands for THE Rapist. Is there something to that? I really do think that therapy is overrated. My friends listen to me and I've talked to Ellie and she has been there, what makes this different? The medication? How high are the doses and, what is the goal? Oblivion? I don't mind oblivion; the medically induced sleep was very nice. But, I'm not sure that any of this will help, Dr. Fields."

"I see." He said as he sat back in his chair. She was a smart one and her hormone levels were off the chart, out of whack and she couldn't be feeling well at all. He'd seen it several times and often wondered how they would be in two weeks to a month after undergoing therapy and medication to stop the tumultuous vortex they were experiencing. "I think time will tell, Stacy. You don't want to die, you just haven't the energy to fight it any longer … right?"

She looked him in the eye for the first time and saw kindness. "Right. I'm tired."

"I bet you are. I looked at your blood workup and found that you are out of natural balance. Let's see if it's as simple as that. I wouldn't want to delve into things you aren't comfortable with, especially if they aren't bothering you. Pascal filled out the origination sheets and it looks like you are surely a fighter. A life of survival. I think we will get along well. How about we set our goal of starting a light antidepressant, some hormone therapy and I'll meet you tomorrow at eleven o'clock to talk about some things … or we could listen to music? It's up to you."

"Music?" She didn't understand.

"Music is very helpful to establish a mood. Why don't you think of what some of your favorite songs are? Songs you used to enjoy. I imagine enjoying anything these past few months has been difficult, so, when you aren't too tired jot a few down and put them in the box on my door." He stood and extended his hand. "Welcome to The Villa Pines, Mrs. Davidson. Let's get you better and back home."

Stacy stood and shook this kind man's hand. She liked music and she hated talking about her parent's death and her aunt and uncle the molester. No way was she going to talk about those things, but she might like listening to music. Maybe she would just stay here and listen to music and never go home. Never go back to the place that made her so tired. She really was bone tired. Walking seemed like a chore and getting back down the hall seemed like she would be walking through a tunnel that never got her to the destination. She needed to sleep again.

"You keep track of the feelings you have right now the best you can and I'll see you again tomorrow."

She left the room and Sandra entered. "She okay?"

"Watch her. She's pretty far down and those hormone levels a0re extremely low. Put her on suicide watch, level three. I want 24/7 until I see some progress. Her husband described her as an energetic business woman with a sparkle in her eyes, a lightness to her gait and all I see is a woman who could lie down and die. Let's make sure that doesn't happen."

"Yes, Doctor." Sandra said and headed back out the door, down the hall twenty feet to where Stacy seemed to be dragging herself back to her room.

Sandra just walked beside her until they were back in Stacy's room. "Let me get that door for you. They are kind of heavy." Sandra opened the door and escorted Stacy back in. "Those pictures of your family?"

Stacy had forgotten about the pictures in her hand. She handed them to Sandra. "My kids and my husband. My best friend, Ellie, is married to my brother. I really feel bad ..."

"Nope. Can't have that. There's no reason to feel bad,

Stacy. You are sick. You get well and life goes on. Remember that. This is temporary. I'm going to help you unpack and put some things in your closet and drawers there and," She pointed, "over there."

"Okay." Stacy was just tired. "Then can I take a nap?"

"Nope. No napping. We are going to art therapy and then group counselling. We have a new mother's group and I think you will really like the women in it. There's six now." She rattled off names and a little bit about everyone as she unpacked and placed Stacy's things in her room.

Stacy sat on the bed, the pictures now hanging on a little corkboard in her room. She could see her family and they looked as small and far away as they felt. Tears stung her eyes once again.

Thirty-six days of shooting down and two to go and the film catering was going amazingly. Stacy was progressing nicely and Ellie had gotten up each Sunday with the family to see her.

They were headed back in the morning, but a long shoot day was ahead of her. Bennie had been wonderful in helping instrumentally make up for the loss of Stacy working the shoot. Addison was at every location with her and Casey had slipped into his own funk with Stacy gone. Ellie was too busy to do much but work, take care of Addison and go home and fall into bed. Luckily, on cue, Addison started sleeping through the night. She was getting full sleep and waking refreshed and as guilty as she felt for it, she loved this job.

She finished her day and grabbed Addison and was headed out to her car after locking the food trailer when she dropped the keys. Quickly a masculine hand reached out of nowhere as she tried to bend down with all the things she was carrying for the baby and scooped the keys up.

"Here you go. Looks like you've got your hands full." The sweetest, recognizable voice charmed her. Mitchell Grant handed her the keys. His hand lingering longer than necessary. "What a beautiful baby girl. May I?" He reached out and Addison went to him immediately.

He talked to the baby and cooed to her. She was learning more words and to shake her head and she was mesmerized by Mitchell. Saying very little, she mostly listened to him as he spoke to her. Reaching up and touching his cheek, he kissed her hand. "What an adorable little charmer."

Ellie was a little uncomfortable. This man was the most popular actor in this generation and his handsome features made it impossible not to like him. He was charming, well-mannered, compassionate and helpful to all the other film crew and producers. Coming through the line to eat, just like every other crew member, he fit right in. 'One of the boys' as they referred to him. She saw why everyone liked him.

"I was just leaving." Ellie reached her hands out to Addison, who wasn't having it. She was playing with Mitchell's long, curly locks of hair.

"Let me walk you to your car. I miss my nieces and nephews. My kids have been to the set a couple of times as they usually do and we Skype every night. She truly is a beautiful child," He Said to Ellie as she gazed into Addison's eyes. "What's your name, Little Miss?"

"It's Addison." Ellie started walking to the car as he followed closely behind. "Why are you on set so late?"

"Oh, well, they called for a rewrite and I thought I would just stick around until it was done and then run lines with some of the other actors. I stay in a different hotel and it's easier if I just go to them. So ... It beat a room with a bed and the temptation to fall asleep. Once I'm out, I'm done." His laughter rang into the May air.

"I see. Well, here we are." She approached her SUV and opened the door to put Addison in. Mitchell handed the baby to her and she buckled her in the car seat. "Thank you for helping me out."

Addison started to fuss so Ellie handed the baby her cell phone. She quieted immediately and began to play with her mother's phone, hitting redial and dialing Casey's phone number.

The phone rang a few times before Casey answered and said hello a few times before he realized that Addie was playing. He began speaking to her until he heard the adults talking, whereby his voice stopped and his heart began beating rapidly.

Ellie said, "I do really appreciate the help. It's hard carrying all her things from the food truck down the hill to the parking lot. I should use a stroller, but it's just one more thing to have to cart around.

"It's my pleasure. I've wanted to meet you since first day of principal photography. You're a very beautiful woman, Elaine Justice." He used her whole name. Researching her first night in the hotel, he knew he had to get to know her. That outstanding beauty was comparable to his own and two like-people had to unite. "I found it very hard to get you alone … truth … the reason I stayed behind tonight … just so I could kiss you."

Casey was furious as he listened. He slammed the phone shut and shoved it in his pocket. What the hell was going on?

Ellie had been hit on many times in her life, but this didn't feel the same. He wasn't some ogling impersonal man that wanted to have sex with her. She didn't get that vibe from him. What she did get is a man with incredible charm and talent and she was finding it hard to remember that Casey existed, even though she knew better. "I'm sorry, Mr. Grant. I'm seeing someone."

"Seeing someone, huh?" He backed away just as he was going to touch her check and let his hand retreat without connection. "I see. Who is this lucky man you are 'seeing'?"

Ellie felt like she was twelve again, stuttering through, "He's, well … it's Addison's father. My … well, my boyfriend, I guess?" She knew it the moment she said it. The non-committed answer left an opening.

Mitchell closed the gap between them and had his hand on her waist and the other on the back of her neck, slid under her hair in a way that she didn't feel him even touch her. He was smooth and she was in trouble.

"Mr. Grant …" Ellie started to say.

"Mitch … call me, Mitch." His breath touched her lips.

"Mitch … I'm with someone. Addison's father and I are very much in a relationship. I'm sorry to give you the impression that I'm available," She slid his hand from her waist and opened the door and slid into the driver's seat, closing it immediately as she said, "This won't happen."

She started the car and drove away without looking back. Her knees were weak, she was shaking and she could still feel and smell the sweetness of his breath on her lips, which were now on fire. Once she settled down, she dialed Casey's number. Waiting, she got his voicemail and left a message to call her back.

She drove the twenty minutes, back down the mountain to the house and tucked her sleeping baby in bed before she fell on to her own. Not able to sleep, she couldn't get Mitch out of her mind.

Casey sat at the bar waiting for Nancy to show up. Her repeated calls asking for more furniture, but not able to pin her down, she asked to meet him for that drink and she would decide on two rooms filled with his work. After hearing what he heard, he had called and said he would meet her to pin down the order. He couldn't think straight. To any quality craftsman when someone wanted to own their art, you gave them what they wanted. He had driven from Charlotte, every moment seething more and more over the fact that she was with someone else. The late-night calls saying she was just getting home; the endless amount of tired and getting up so early to be on set. What all had happened and how deep did this go? He was so angry.

He waited impatiently until he saw Nancy walk in. A sexy black dress and five-inch-high heels. She looked fabulous and a part of him said make up for the mistake he had made. He knew she wasn't into the relationship as much as he was and his heart ached. Just like last time, he knew that another woman would take that pain away. Nancy was single and ready and he was willing to play tonight.

They had drinks, talked about what furniture Nancy wanted, even returning to her home for him to make sure that what she wanted was well-suited for her home. When she approached him, he was ready and let her lead him to her bedroom. Drinks had flowed freely and she was intoxicated, enough that she stumbled on the way and he caught her, scooping her up and laying her on the bed.

Hanging over her, his lips inches from hers, she passed out on him. Within seconds, long enough for Casey to think about whether he should go through with this, she was snoring softly.

"Well, shit." He sat on the side of the bed. "I guess that's the answer." He tucked her farther on to the bed and left her house, locking up as he went and headed back to Charlotte.

Chapter Twenty-Two

Ellie woke at five o'clock to the alarm, shut it off, checking the baby monitor and went back to sleep. She slept until almost eight o'clock, giving her only an hour to get dressed and out the door with the baby to meet up with Pas and the kids to go see Stacy.

She kept trying to call Casey the entire time, almost as if she were hitting dial, speakerphone, end and redial … no answer.

Once in the van with the children buckled up, Pas asked the question, "Where's Casey? I thought he was coming today?"

"I did too …" was all Ellie could get out.

Pas caught it and his only comment before turning on music and remaining silent the rest of the way was, "Maybe he's meeting us there."

Once at The Villa Pines Stacy was prepared to meet them. She had been recovering quite well and little did they know, today was the day she would be leaving with them. Dr. Fields had done wonders with her depression and she was going stir crazy, ready to get back to work. Daily she checked in with Ellie on the job, but Ellie had so little time to fill her in.

When they arrived and piled in, the girls knowing exactly where they were going and running in to meet their mother just inside the door, Ellie carried Addison and Pas carried Isaiah. The girls were chatting endlessly about their week, each grabbing at their mother, whose eyes had begun to sparkle again. She looked up and winked at Ellie and grabbed Pas and Isaiah at the very same time, holding them all close in a hug. "I missed you so much, Pas." She whispered in his ear, kissing his cheek and then his lips. "I missed you." She turned to Isaiah, "I missed you too little man of mine." She took her baby and held him close.

Ellie noticed the difference immediately and when it was her turn in the hug, she whispered back, "Welcome to the land of the living, Stase."

"I know. Right?" Stacy laughed and said softly, "You get to take me home today. I'm back and ready to work tomorrow."

They both whooped it up as quietly as possible. The girls danced around with them as Stacy chanted, "I get to go home. I get to go home. Look, I feel so much better."

The bags were waiting, she had checked herself out and all that was left was to pack back in the van, which they all did immediately.

Angie was the first to speak inside the vehicle, "That place smelled, Mommy. I'm glad you are coming home. Auddie is getting grouchy."

Jules added, "Yeah. She won't let us do manything ... manything at all."

Stacy turned in the front seat so she could face Ellie. "Fill me in. I can't wait to get into this film. It must have been so much work. I'm so sorry I wasn't able …"

"Quit. It's been very organized and quite fabulous. Long days, but they go so fast, what we are not prepping and cooking, we get to watch what's going on. I have never seen people work so hard and fast to get to a set to see the movie shot. It's so fascinating."

"How is Mitchell Grant?" Her eyes lit up, causing Pas to turn her way.

"Hey now … you're not even all the way home, talking about another man."

They chimed in at the same time, "Mitchell Grant!"

Pas, being the good sport he was, ceded, "Yeah, even I think he's sexy."

They all laughed and then Jules asked, "What's sexy mean?" and they laughed more.

Angie gave it a shot, "It's when big people wear lots of makeup and fake eyelashes and nails. Then they can scratch really hard and that makes them sexy."

Ellie and Stacy looked at each other as Pas said, "She's your daughter."

After the excitement calmed a little Stacy asked where Casey was.

Ellie had no shame to her game, "I have no idea. I'm starting to get worried though. You try and give him a call on Pas' phone. I can't get him."

She made the call. Three rings in and he answered, "Hello?"

Stacy said, "Hey, big brother. Where are you? Everything okay?"

"No. It's not okay. Ask Ellie what happened with 'MITCH' last night and that will fill you in. I hope you're doing okay … I'm not in the mood to talk. I know she's there with you. Call me later when you're alone." He hung up and slammed the phone down on the desk where he sat.

Stacy looked to Ellie, who shrugged. "What?"

"He said ask you about what happened with Mitch last night and that I would know why he's being a whiney baby and not in the mood to talk." Stacy said.

"What?" Ellie was shocked. "Nothing happened with Mitch last night …"

"He seems to be pretty determined that something did." She turned farther in her seat. "Cough it up. What happened?" "Oh my God …" Ellie's face went ashen white. "I gave Addison the phone and she must have dialed daddy." She grabbed her phone and looked through. "Oh my God … she did. Two minutes he was on the phone before I called him when I left. He must have heard it all."

"What? What did he hear?" Stacy was glad to be home,

but this was not sounding good at all. "What did you do, Ellie?"

They forgot the children were in the car. Jules said, "Yeah, Auntie Els, what did you do?"

"I didn't do anything ...:" she wanted to pull Stacy to the top of the van so they could talk without being heard. If he heard Mitch tell her he wanted to kiss her, then no wonder he was angry and not answering. "He heard, well, see, I dropped my keys and Mitch was there, out of nowhere, to pick them up." She motioned with her eyes that it wasn't that simple. "It wasn't me. He stayed around and said some savory things, but I turned him away. I told him I was ... well, committed."

"Then what's Casey throwing a fit about?"

"I don't know, Stase. He had to have only heard part of it. I gave Addie the phone because she was fussing and it was Mitchell Grant. Michael Grant ..." She was blushing. Had she just ruined her relationship with Casey through no fault of her own? "What do I do?"

"Just leave him to me. He's insecure and I bet he's blown it way out of proportion. I'll call him when we get home. Okay?" Stacy asked.

The rest of the ride was solemn at best. The kids were decent, but whiney and no one spoke of the ensuing situation. Ellie was afraid, anxious and building. By the time they pulled back into the Davidson home, it was complete and utter panic. She loved Casey.

Moving to the workroom and pulling out the newest piece of furniture in his work order, Casey sighed in relief. Whenever he could distract his thoughts, find his flow and redeem in himself the qualities that kept him going, life was better. He had spent hours in thought, sitting idly, debating on whether it was going to work out with Ellie. All he knew was that controlling the situation was inexplicitly not going to work. He began carving.

Music played lightly in the background and it just wasn't cutting it. His frustration began when he couldn't figure out the design. Never did he falter in his work, nothing got in to the deep recesses of his creativity. This piece, in particular, a dresser with a matching chest, should be easy, but as he began carving, he saw the likeness of Ellie coming through. It disturbed him and he moved to the stereo and turned it up as high as it would go. He needed to push her from his mind. And that is what he did. By letting the carving continue, he pushed her and Mitchell Grant from his mind. Instead he began viewing his life. It was time to face his demons.

When his parents passed away he was too young to decipher the way of the world, actions of others and how they influence each other as though gears in an engine. Functioning in a world with others added gears and unless they functioned in unison, it brought about nothing less than an engine that did not work. The abuse from his uncle, his aunt watching without helping the innocence of he and Stacy's ages. It angered him. How could someone just sit back and watch used to be a questioned he asked over and over. Finally finding an answer, he realized that she was nothing less than needy. If she did anything she lost the gears function in her own life. Things needed to remain in the pattern she was used to and her husband's behavior, his jealousy and greed inundated her engine, bogged it down. When she died, her last words to Casey had been delivered via a letter.

The letter from his aunt had been burned into his brain. At eighteen, he had read the short and simple letter and finally understood. All it said was that she was too weak to make a statement and she had lived a certain hell over it. She was sorry. From that moment on, Casey realized that his own shortcomings could do the same to another life and he refused. Maybe that's why he could not commit to a woman? Is that why he worried about Ellie? Would she be the woman who could not protect his daughter and he would grow to hate? Would she be able to stand strong and firm as he tried to do? Stacy was his reason to live all these years; protecting Stacy was what was important. When he gave over that responsibility to Pascal, he was lost and never really knew what it was in life he was meant to do until Addie was born. When he saw his daughter that very first time, he knew.

Contrary to what he thought, it was not to protect Addison.

It was to raise Addison in a manner consistent with her being as strong as he was. Raising Addison to be able to handle what came along and always have the desire to do what was right and just. That is what his lot in life was and it became a challenge. How was he raised to always battle, always go for the optimistic approach to any problem and how did he raise her the same?

The carving was moving along, depth and originality. He let himself create as he contemplated life. Why would Ellie reach out to someone else? The only reason was his own shortcoming. Maybe it was time to just lay it on the line? Could he open up and ask her? For the duration of his adulthood, he always had a hard time laying things on the table if emotions were involved. This was going to have to be different, because Addison deserved to be a child that grew up knowing how to communicate. He wanted that for her. If he did his job as a father, he would learn to communicate, to face his fears and to always remember what was important.

The rest of his morning was spent carving with contentment. He had no idea how he would communicate, but for the first time, Casey realized he trusted himself to make good choices and that a commitment was something he believed in. It wasn't what he originally thought. The world was not a horrible place and his world was filled with a presence of love that he only had one responsibility in. He needed to share that love and with every fiber in his being Ellie was the love of his life and he was not prepared to let her go. He wanted to be everything she wanted and wanted to help keep her together. Falling apart was not an option and the way that she looked at him, the way that she touched him, the way that she raised their child ... that was honestly worth giving everything he had. He dropped in prayer, literally fell to his knees and asked for forgiveness. Casey asked that he be allowed to give this a chance and to let his emotion be everything that Ellie needed to keep him from falling apart. This time it was he who needed love and understanding and having it in this capacity was extremely important to the foundation they would build for their daughter ... he prayed.

Ellie landed in the kitchen with Addie in her seat, sound asleep. She had just fed her in the car. Stacy was first in the house, she nearly ran, welcoming the presence of 'home'. Auddie met her with a huge hug and after everything was put away, the kids were given lunch and everyone seemed to breathe that sigh of relief, Stacy approached Ellie.

"Els ... we should talk." Stacy led her to their office. The sanctuary that she missed so much.

Following with Addison in her arms, Ellie managed to make it to the office before she broke down in tears. They fell for the mess she had made of everything, for the fact that she finally had the life she wanted and nothing should get in the way. She had done the right thing and look how it backfired.

"Awwww ... There, there ..." Stacy was heartbroken to see Ellie crying so hard. She took Addison from her arms and put her on the carpet to play with her daddy-rattle. "Here ya go, baby girl ... some tummy time so mommy can get some lovin' from Auntie Stase." She patted the baby on the back and moved to Ellie, hugging her hard. "Let's get you settled and then we are going to talk about this. I can't let this happen. I know I've made awful mistakes with Pascal, but there is something you don't understand about your man … he's a Waters and water runs deep in these veins. We are going to fix this, Els. I can't have you where I was. Nope … no way can you head down that road."

She grabbed the box of Kleenex and handed them to Ellie.

Nothing seemed to stop the flow of tears as she tried to find that place of peace. Her nerves were all over the place. It felt like someone was pulling them like rubber bands and they would snap back, stinging her every time. She couldn't think clearly, all she could do was see the horrible visual images running through her head. Casey with another woman. Casey walking out the door. Addison growing up without a father. Casey hating her for cheating on him when she didn't do anything. The jail and how hard it was to find peace with someone watching your every move. The images prevailed. She broke down again …

Stacy watched, waited and prayed as she sat beside Ellie, holding her while she cried. Maybe she had an affair, everyone knew the charm that Mitchell Grant exuded. If he wanted something, he usually got it. Had he gotten to Ellie? Was her brother the same stubborn brut that walked away from real love every opportunity? She thought things had changed. It was hard when she didn't know both sides of the story, but she needed to stay healthy and that meant taking care of her own needs and those of her children. Everyone else would have to figure out their own living situation. She could not afford to be overwhelmed. He just held Ellie until the tears subsided, watching Addison's beauty as she played on her tummy, cooing, laughing at her own hands and her little blonde curls bobbing to-and-fro with every movement.

Pascal entered as he lightly knocked. "Everything okay?"

Stacy pointed to Addison. "Could you take Addie for me, Sweetie?"

He quickly scooped up his niece and kissed her cheek. "Let's go get you a fresh diaper, Little Lady. Then we can find Jules and Angie and Passie … how about that?" He kissed Stacy on the forehead and left the room.

Stacy stroked Ellie's hair until she finally stopped crying, blowing her nose with finality and taking a deep breath.

"Okay," Ellie said, "I'm okay …" She tried to take a couple of deep breaths and just settle inside her own self. "I didn't do anything. I Promise!" With the words, her anger lit. She dropped a few more tears, realized just how tired she was and remembered that the film project still needed her attention. How would she do it all? She felt completely overwhelmed. "What am I going to do, Stacy? He won't take my calls …"

"Make them anyway." Stacy had always wished that Casey was more approachable. "He will eventually answer. I guess it's just the way we grew up. We never learned how to communicate our feelings, deal with them or even to ask for help when we couldn't. I've learned so much about everything this past month. Ellie, there's a chance he won't be able to tell you what troubles him, but he loves Addie … use her."

"What?"

"Well, I've never let a thing stand between myself and Pascal. We have had our share of miscommunication, spats, downright fights ..."

"Really?" Ellie thought they had the perfect relationship.

"Of course. We've had knockdown, drag out, I wanted to beat his ass fights ..." She laughed thinking how insane they had been. "But, we always go to bed together when possible and we pray together. That always does it for us, but that's because Pascal is such a Godly man. Casey ... not so much. I'm not sure he believes at all anymore. He was so abused and got so tough. If he lets anyone in, they have the potential to hurt him and so he stays away. He's trying with you and he treats you like he used to treat me, as someone he must protect. I say we manipulate him to the point you can at least tell him what happened, face-to-face." She raised an eyebrow.

"I'm in ... make the call."

Pulling back from the carved image in the top piece of the dresser, Casey saw such beauty in his own work. He took the piece off his work bench and leaned it up against the wall for varnishing when a break in the music allowed him to hear his phone. The call was from Stacy, but he didn't get there in time and saw that there were 32 missed calls. Looking at the clock, it was nearing six o'clock in the evening. He'd been working nearly seven hours. Dialing, he waited for Stacy to answer.

"Hello! Where have you been?" Stacy blurted, angry and hurt.

"I was working. What's going on? Is everything okay? Is Addie okay?" His heart skipped a beat waiting to hear. She never called him like this. She left messages. He braced himself.

"No. Addie is running a fever and coughing. Ellie is at work, she got called in and I need you to come help me. Damn it, Casey ... get here."

"I'm on my way. I'll be forty minutes or less. I'm on my way, Stase." Casey hung up, grabbed his jacket and headed out the door at a run. What could possibly be wrong with his child? The scares with Angie and Isaiah were horrible and this was worse. He drove like a bat out of hell, flying down the road with nothing on his mind but prayers that Addie was okay. He couldn't bear to call and ask more, he needed to be there for his baby. He slammed his foot to the floor.

Ellie laid out the dinner, lit the candles, balanced the music and touched up her makeup in the mirror in her hallway. The plan in motion, she was very nervous. Her life was like a jack-in-the-box and she was going to dismantle the pop-up feature to the best of her ability. She called Stacy and told her she was ready. Casey should be nearing town and the plan was to divert him back to Ellie's house to waylay the poor man.

She spritzed perfume into the air and stepped into it so that it wasn't overwhelming. He should be arriving any minute. She paced.

The doorbell rang, to her surprise. Casey had his own key and never rang the bell. She rushed to see who it was, opening to find Grant Mitchell.

"What are you doing here?" She was immediately angry. "You have to leave. Now." She pushed him back, stepping out onto the porch. "Please, leave."

"I'm sorry ... I thought ..."

"Don't think. Leave!" She pushed him nearly off the porch.

"I was just ... I thought that we could talk ... I have an independent feature and I wanted to hire you." Grant was appalled that this woman was so readily willing to push him away. "You look great ... and smell even better." He started to touch her, no one could resist his charm and popularity.

When Ellie tried to back up, she stepped on the doormat with her heel and it sent her reeling into his arms to catch herself ... the moment Casey pulled up and screeched to a halt. The first look he got was of Ellie in Mitchell's arms.

Ellie pushed herself off Mitchell, "I said LEAVE!!!" She started crying, sobbing when she saw the look on Casey's face.

Mitchell turned to see what she was looking at and saw it too. "I'm sorry." He walked from the porch, meeting Casey as he walked down the sidewalk.

Two reporters across the street were snapping pictures as fast as they could. "Can you believe this!!!?"

Casey was so confused. How could Addison be sick and this man be leaving his home? He was so angry that he didn't think when he passed Mitchell without as much as a look. On second thought, he said, "Hey …"

Mitch turned around in time to barely see the fist coming, as it landed straight to his cheek and he was out like a light. Casey turned to see Ellie mortified.

The reporters were now out of the car. The videographer was panning in for a close-up of both Ellie and Casey, standing toe-to-toe on the porch.

"Where's my daughter???" Casey was red with rage.

"Casey ... it's not what you think ..." She turned to follow him into the house. His anger was not conducive to him hearing her at all.

What Casey saw was the love she had prepared for him, her gown for no reason, the candles, the music ... He stopped in mid-flight, turning to Ellie. "Where is my daughter? NOW!" She was close enough to grab and without thinking, he did. He grabbed her bare arms and yanked her to attention. "Where's my daughter?"

"She's with Stacy ..." There was no explaining this situation and he was unable to fathom the mistake. She started bawling.

He let go and rushed from the house, slamming the door. Walking past Mitch, barely coming to, he pretended to hit him again as he walked past making Mitch flinch, remaining on the ground ... for all the world to see.

Casey slid into his car and peeled out to find his sick child.

"How could it have happened just at that time?" Stacy had

just heard, through the sobbing, the story from Ellie. "I'll take care of it. Just get yourself together, splash some water on your face. He's going to be so angry if he knows this was a lie ... Oh, Lord ... we are in trouble."

"I can't do this ... I can't lose him, Stacy. I love him. I love him so much ... why?" Ellie couldn't control the sobs that wracked her entire being. Instead of getting herself together, she got in her car and headed to Stacy's. Wiping tears as she drove, sobbing uncontrollably, she was barely able to drive.

Casey pulled into the parking area and slammed the car in park, running into the house.

Stacy was waiting for him in the kitchen. "Stop!" She nearly screamed it at him as he entered the room. "Stop and listen to me ..."

"What? Where's Addison?" He rushed past her as she grabbed his arm.

He pulled out of the touch. "Where is Addison? What's

wrong with her?"

"I lied to you … she's fine. I promise. This is all a huge misunderstanding." Stacy saw the hurt in her betrayal.

"What are you talking about, Stase? Addison's fine?" He hated nothing more than being lied to. "Where is she?"

Stacy pointed toward the nursery. "She's fine, down for the night." She tried to get him to listen to her. "Please … sit down and let me explain. Please?"

"Explain what? That my … my … Ellie is having an affair with Mitchell Grant? I can't handle this." He ran his hands through his hair. The world was crashing down around him, sucking the air out of his lungs as if he had been hit. "I can't do this …"

"Yes, you can and you are going to listen to me … for once in your life, listen to ME!" Stacy had to pull out the biggest guns she had. This wild-crazed look was not unfamiliar to her. It was the same look when he grabbed her and pulled her out of their uncle's abuse, when he hid them out for a year on the streets of Charlotte and when he ran from the world that was such a horrible place. "Casey, you have to hear me. I swear ... please, listen to me." She tried to hug him as he stood in the room, ragged and raging. "Listen to me, please ..."

He tried to gather his senses, but all he could do was feel. There were a multitude of emotions running through his veins. "I can't ... I can't ... it's all lies. You just want to protect Ellie ..." When he said her name, he crumbled. Falling to his knees, he knew he was in love and had believed in that love. This was going to kill him. "I can't ... I can't ..."

"You can." Stacy dropped beside him, trying to put her arms around him in comfort.

He pushed her away. "You lied to me?" Looking her in the eye to see her nod yes brought him to tears. "I trusted you..."

"I know ... that's why I did it. Please, just let me explain." She knelt in front of him and began to try and explain. "I did it because she needed you to hear her. I don't know what happened at her house, but Mitchell showed up and she told him to leave. She doesn't have anything with him. I promise you that. I promise." She took his face in her hands. "I Promise. She's torn up over you ... she loves YOU! Casey ... she loves you."

"No ... no ... I saw him and he was holding her. She was in his arms and she was dressed and the house had candles lit ... a romantic ...Oh, God!"

"NO! It was all for you. I planned it with her. I don't know what happened, but it was for you, Casey. She was going to tell you how much she loves you and how much you mean to her and lay it all out there for you. She's never been loved like you love her. She doesn't know what to do." She prompted him to look at her. "She loves you, baby ... she is totally and completely in love with you. She needs you ... she needs you to hear her ... let her talk to you. Please. Let her talk to you ..."

Ellie entered to room in time to hear him say, "I can't ... I can't do it, Stacy. I saw her in his arms. She's lying to you."

He glanced up to see her turn and walk out. Stacy turned to see her as well. She scrambled up and headed out the door, running after her. "Stop! Els, stop ... he didn't mean it."

Ellie got back in the SUV and tried to pull out, but Stacy was in front of the vehicle. "You'll have to kill me to get out of this drive ..."

Ellie was tired. She was frustrated, hurt, couldn't stop crying and did not want to kill her best friend. She laid her head on the steering wheel and let the tears come. Sobs wracked her tiny frame and she let it all come. The hurt and destruction for her mother dying such a horrible death, Tyler and all his abuse, finding him dead, missing Sarah, losing her home, everything that had been taken from her ... and then the thought hit her ... this gave him ammunition to take Addison from her. The panic came.

Stacy saw her give up and lay on the steering wheel, but she couldn't get her to open the door. "Ellie!!!! Open the door. Let me in. Please???"

Ellie looked up as she let Stacy pound on the window. The panic was roaring. She couldn't breathe; her heart was pounding out of her chest, so hard it hurt; her fingers began to curl as she gasped for air. The last thing she remembered was watching Stacy pound on the window, frantic as she passed out.

With her foot on the brake, having been ready to leave, the SUV started moving when she passed out.

"CASEYYYYY!!!!!" Stacy screamed, trying to stop the SUV with her own willpower as it began moving forward. "CASEYYYYYYYYY!!!!" She screamed. Holding on to what she could, she pounded on the window. "Ellie!!! ELLIE!!!! WAKE UP< ELLIE!!!!!!" She continued to pound.

Casey could hear Stacy from inside, but he didn't care. About the fourth time she screamed, he caught the frantic tense and headed for the door. They were heading down the drive, Stacy holding on to the SUV like Fred Flintstone using his feet to try and stop it. He hit the pavement at a dead run. They were headed for the gate and traffic and he didn't understand what was going on.

Stacy pounded for her life and could not wake up Ellie. "ELLIE!!!!! WAKE UP!!!! ELLIE!!!!!!!!!"

It was Sunday night; the traffic was heavy. Cars came and went, but the gate was open and when Stacy saw that they were headed for either traffic or the gate post, a huge brick column, and Ellie didn't have a seatbelt on-TROUBLE! She was slumped over the steering wheel … Stacy panicked as well.

Casey caught up with them and saw what was going on. "Let go, Stacy!!!!!" He shoved her out of the way, knocking her to the ground. "ELLIE!!!!!!!!!!!!!!!" He climbed up on top of the SUV in one movement and began one of two kicks to the windshield, the second on shattering it.

They were nearing the traffic, twenty feet away. He kicked out all the window he could and slid inside the vehicle, as they entered the road with two cars coming. The sound of screeching tires, horns honking … he grabbed her and shielded her the best he could and awaited the collision.

Chapter Twenty-Three

A miracle, no one hit the SUV. The first car swerved and landed within feet of hitting either them or the column for the gate. The second car slammed on their brakes, called 911 and ran to assist. Within a few minutes, Ellie came back to in Casey's arms.

She was completely at a loss as to what was happening. Stacy ran to the vehicle, trying to open the door, she wanted in. She needed in.

"Ellie!!! Are you okay?" Finally getting the door unlocked and open, Stacy was frantic as well. "Ellie ..."

Sirens wailed.

Within the hour, they had it all taken care of. The police were aware of what happened. Ellie refused to go with the ambulance. Casey would not leave her side and Stacy was directly on the other. At one point Ellie thought … 'this is the life.'

To be this loved and to have the support of this family, she had to save the situation. "Casey, I need you to let me explain."

"I don't need it. I don't care if you love him … I just need you in my life." He couldn't hear anything. Still in shock, he just wanted to hear she was okay. "Are you okay?"

"I'm fine. I might need a Xanax, but I'm fine. This panic thing really does get me." She tried to laugh, the love registering in his eyes. "I Love YOU!" She kissed him fully on the lips. "I've never been able to believe in any love other than that of my mother and I'm telling you … I know what love is now. I love YOU … I love Addison and Stacy, and Pascal and the kids … I love you all. I would never put that in jeopardy."

"What about Mitch?" He wanted to believe her.

"He showed up at the house … I have no idea. I told him to leave and I pushed him, caught my heel on the mat and fell into him. I'm sorry … I swear."

She looked at him with an intensity he had never seen. If this wasn't love …

Two months later, the ceremony was perfect. On the back lawn of the Davidson Estate, no frills, just friends and family. Casey and Ellie said their vows in front of each other and God. Simple and to the point, they wrote them together and expressed them as promises to God:

Together they turned to their friends and family, held hands and said:

"To share our love, a true gift from God, we ask that you help us to make each other first and only second to God, always respect each other, to stay faithful, to never flirt with another and to make time for each other and you … Please help us share our

love and to dedicate our lives to each other in a way that is healthy and true. We promise to do our best and when we need help, to ask for it. We ask to be blessed in this love for infinity."

The applause was followed by the preacher saying, "You may now kiss your bride ..." and Casey did.

"I now present to you Mr. and Mrs. Casey Waters and their beautiful daughter, Addison ..." The preacher said as they turned to walk the aisle to their new life together.

The Beginning ...